Praise for *The Son of Good Fortune*

A Recommended Book from *USA Today* • *Chicago Tribune*
Book Riot • Refinery29 • *Minneapolis Star Tribune* • *Publishers Weekly*
Baltimore Outloud • *Omnivoracious* • Lambda Literary
Goodreads • Literary Hub • *The Millions*

"Lysley Tenorio's funny and poignant debut novel, *The Son of Good Fortune*, couldn't come at a better time. . . . Tenorio skillfully wrings high comedy from his characters' boxed-in lives in a country that doesn't know what to do with them. . . . Timely."

—*San Francisco Chronicle*

"In this perceptive and sensitive novel, Lysley Tenorio views the troubled American dream through the eyes of Excel, an undocumented immigrant literally born in the air between the Philippines and the United States. The result, in *The Son of Good Fortune*, is a nuanced and subtle account of that most basic American dynamic: the melancholic and sometimes devastating fluctuation between promise and failure, happiness and its opposite."

—Viet Thanh Nguyen, author of *The Sympathizer*

"Mordant and moving. . . . Written with great empathy and sly humor. . . . This is a wonderful achievement."

—*Publishers Weekly* (starred review)

"Full of heart, wisdom, and humor, *The Son of Good Fortune* is an unforgettable novel of mothers and sons, secrets and truth, and what it means to belong, told through the story of one undocumented Filipino family."

—Lisa Ko, author of *The Leavers*

"When you don't belong ~~~~~ where exactly do you belong? Lysley Tenorio's engaging and co~~~~~ identity asks this question with compa~~~~~ *is Star Tribune*

"I have a new favorite nov~~~~~ s in underpinning every moment of fla~~~~~ e ever-forlorn question of identity. *The Son of Good Fortune* is a held study of the glamorous allure of the American dream and the eternal ache of its exclusion. This novel is like a stone skipped across the Pacific, all the way to Manila. Visualize it, that series of rings lingering on the ocean's surface, expanding, intersecting, and intermingling to form a chain that anchors these characters, connects them, and after years of binding them, sets them free."

—Adam Johnson, author of *The Orphan Master's Son*

"*The Son of Good Fortune* is a reminder that many experiences comprise the definition of what makes a person American. . . . Tenorio skillfully sketches out what an all-American boy like Excel experiences in his in-betweenness. . . . A damning yet clear-eyed acknowledgment that for many, the American dream is merely survival."

—Salon

"Tenorio, himself a Filipino immigrant, accurately and compassionately portrays the immigrant experience. . . . Despite its universality, *The Son of Good Fortune* doesn't lack for originality. . . . The story finds a witty voice and sets a unique tone. Despite the drudgery and harshness of immigrant life, Tenorio explores the humanity in the tribulations and creates characters who are as lovable as they are real. With his debut novel, Tenorio excavates joy from the immigrant experience."

—BookPage

"Sharp and compassionate. . . . Tenorio is a gifted, expressive writer about the Filipino American diaspora. . . . A powerful story about what it takes to uncover a sense of oneself when you've been forced to keep it under wraps."

—USA Today

"A bewitching and highly approachable novel on what it's like to be an undocumented American. . . . With his sensitive and subdued style of writing, Tenorio has crafted a novel that speaks to the experience of the undocumented, as well as to what we all must hide in order to survive."

—San Diego Union-Tribune

"Filled with the kind of absurdities that accompany the most difficult truths, Lysley Tenorio's brilliant, witty novel about the love of a mother and son, the immigrant experience in America, and the surreality of our current reality is bold, ambitious, and unforgettable."

—Refinery29

"A fierce, revelatory literary experience. . . . Tenorio has written a resonant story about what one family is willing to do to 'protect the child.' It's seamlessly interwoven with cogent explorations of hybrid identity, racism, immigration history, shifting familial bonds, parental sacrifice, socioeconomic disparity, and even alternative social models. . . . Tenorio humanizes the lives imperiled by shifting immigration policies."

—Christian Science Monitor

"This story is bursting with heart and wisdom, humor and hope. Tenorio's gifts as a writer are on display in this expertly constructed, gorgeously written tale of a family haunted by past mistakes, struggling toward the future. Immersive in its rich detail, it gathers momentum to its affecting and powerful conclusion. A remarkable novel by an author I plan to follow for years to come."

—Charles Yu, author of *Interior Chinatown* and *How to Live Safely in a Science Fictional Universe*

"*The Son of Good Fortune* . . . sympathetically illuminates the tenuous lives of undocumented immigrants, those who are 'not really here.' . . . Tenorio's characters are humorous and loving, in spite of the exclusion overshadowing their very existence."

—Shelf Awareness (starred review)

"*The Son of Good Fortune* is a deeply compassionate and richly imagined novel about the families we make and the families who make us. Lysley Tenorio peels back such labels as 'American,' 'Filipino,' 'immigrant,' and 'undocumented' to show us a mother and son in all their bright humanity—and the forms of love, connection, and survival available to them in a broken country. Tenorio is a master storyteller, and—like his brilliant collection *Monstress*—this is a gorgeous, searing wonder of a book."

—Mia Alvar, author of *In the Country*

"You know the feeling of picking up a book and realizing within ten pages that what you're reading is something . . . special? Something different? Well, that's what it's like reading Lysley Tenorio's novel. . . . A funny and kind novel about home and identity."

—*Omnivoracious*

"Propulsive prose, captivating characters, and vital details of immigrant life. . . . A masterfully constructed story of identity and ambition, and an authentic portrait of one unforgettable Filipino family."

—*Kirkus Reviews*

"Tenorio, author of the short-story collection *Monstress* (2012), the *San Francisco Chronicle*'s Book of the Year, is back with a highly anticipated debut novel. . . . Tenorio creates an unusual perspective on Filipino culture and inspires readers to reflect on what it means to be an undocumented American. . . . Thoughtful."

—*Booklist*

"Living with this extraordinarily human undocumented family will make you laugh, weep, and think, sometimes all at once. Tenorio brilliantly makes these characters so original that they're nearly tangible."

—James Hannaham, author of *Delicious Foods*

THE SON OF GOOD FORTUNE

THE SON OF GOOD FORTUNE

A NOVEL

LYSLEY TENORIO

WITHDRAWN

An Imprint of HarperCollinsPublishers

HarperCollins books may be purchased for educational, business, or sales promotional use. For information, please email the Special Markets Department at SPsales@harpercollins.com.

Ecco® and HarperCollins® are trademarks of HarperCollins Publishers.

A hardcover edition of this book was published in 2020 by Ecco, an imprint of HarperCollins Publishers.

FIRST ECCO PAPERBACK EDITION PUBLISHED 2021

Designed by Paula Russell Szafranski

Library of Congress Cataloging-in-Publication Data has been applied for.

ISBN 978-0-06-205959-8 (pbk.)

21 22 23 24 25   LSC   10 9 8 7 6 5 4 3 2 1

Mom—nowhere and everywhere

Dynamite is loyal to the one
who lights the fuse.

—Dean F. Wilson, *Skyshaker*

THE SON
OF GOOD
FORTUNE

PROLOGUE

Maxima in the dark. Half-lit by a Virgin Mary night-light and the glow of a screen saver, a slow-motion sweep of stars and planets—Jupiter, Saturn, Earth. Dressed in denim cutoffs and a Mickey Mouse tee, she doesn't shiver, despite her wide-open bedroom window and the cold night beyond. She sits at the foot of her bed, cleaning her nails with the tip of a switchblade. "*May bakas ka bang nakikita sa aking mukha?*" she sings. "*Masdan mo ang aking mata.*" Like all her favorite Filipino love songs, this one is about heartbreak.

An alarm goes off. The digital clock glows red—10:10 p.m. She closes the switchblade.

She stands and stretches, takes quick jabs at the air—*one-two, one-two, one-two*—then flips on the desk lamp and sits, turns on the ball-shaped webcam atop her monitor. A tap to the space bar and the galaxy vanishes; now her face fills the screen. Using it as a mirror, she puts on maroon lipstick and dabs with a Kleenex, smiles wide to check her teeth. She undoes her ponytail and shakes out her hair, a long black wave, then turns her face side to side, searching for her best angle. She could easily pass for thirty but is somewhere in her fifties; her true age, she swears, is a mystery, even to herself. Her parents, long since dead, kept no birth certificate; the grandmother who took her in never bothered to learn her actual birthday.

Eyes closed and fingertips on the keyboard, she whispers to herself, so softly that a person standing next to her would have no hope of knowing what she says. She takes a deep and slow breath, opens her eyes, types and clicks until another browser window opens.

There is a man on the screen.

"My love," he says.

"No," she says. "In Tagalog."

"Sorry. Hello, *mahal*."

"That's better." She blows him a kiss.

"Oh, mahal, please don't tease. It's been a lousy few days."

She leans into the screen. "Ano ba? What happened, Henry?"

"Where to start." He removes his glasses, the stubbly flab of his cheeks moving up and down as he rubs his temples. He pours a shot of Jack Daniel's into a coffee mug and recounts his terrible week—more layoffs at the plant and all the guys blame him, his ex-wife trashed the Miami time-share but won't pay for repairs, his Benz is still in the shop and the best rental he could get is a three-year-old Camry, and just today an invitation to his high school reunion—"My freaking fortieth!" he says—arrived in the mail. "But the real downer"—he gulps the whiskey—"is the weather. End of spring and I'm still shoveling snow."

"Snow, snow, snowy snowy snow," she sings in a made-up tune. She puts her elbows on the desk, rests her chin on clasped hands. "My whole life, I never see snow."

"Come to America. To North Dakota."

"One day. If God is good."

"God is always good." He pours another shot, doesn't drink. "Come closer. I want your face to fill my screen."

She leans into the webcam, so close she could kiss it. He says she is the most beautiful woman he has ever seen.

These past three weeks of talking online, he says, are the best he's had in years. A twice-divorced balding white guy on the edge of sixty doesn't hope for much, but when he found her profile on Good Catholic Filipinas and saw that her favorite food was sweet-n-sour chicken, that her favorite singer was Shania Twain, and that her lifelong dream was "to live in joy with a good man in God's country," he convinced himself to send her a message. "It's silly to reminisce," he says, "but life before you seems so long ago. I didn't realize how lonely I was."

"I was lonely too," she says.

"And I think that maybe, well, probably, that I might be"—he takes a deep breath, takes the shot—"falling in love with you."

She pulls away from the screen.

"I'm sorry," he says. "Too much, too soon?"

She shakes her head. "Not too soon, mahal. I think, maybe, that I am falling in love, too."

"With . . . me?"

She laughs. "Yes, with you. Tanga!"

"*Tanga?*"

"It means 'stupid.'"

He lets out a breath, slaps his chest twice. "My heart. It's racing."

"'Heart.' In Tagalog, *puso.*"

"Puso." He writes the word down. "That means 'heart.' Got it."

"Soon, you'll speak Tagalog. Then you can visit me in the Philippines, di ba?"

"Or you visit me first. Maybe you can be my date to the reunion?" He sets the scene: He enters his high school gym to the tune of his old prom song, "We've Only Just Begun" by the Carpenters, and though he hasn't aged as well as his classmates, there's no question that he has the sexiest, most gorgeous woman in the room on his arm. The other women are jealous of her, the men envious of him, and the bullies from his freshman year just stand to the side, giving him the thumbs-up. "And the whole night," he says, "you and I just dance."

He leans into his webcam. His whole head seems to inflate on Maxima's screen. "When can we meet?"

"Philippines to America," she sighs, "not so easy trip." The lines in Manila for passports and visas take hours, she says, sometimes days (that's just to apply), and never mind the near-zero chances of government approval. Their best hope for being together is to pray, to keep faith in God, and to wait. "And when I come to North Dakota," she says, "will you show me the snow?"

"Count on it."

"Okay. But one condition only: I don't shovel."

He laughs, which makes her laugh, harder and harder until she's hunched over, laughter becoming gasps for air. "Mahal," he says, "you okay?" She shakes her head, takes a breath and says it's nothing, then keels over again.

"It's definitely not nothing," he says. "What's wrong?"

She looks straight at the camera. "I'm hurt."

"Hurt? Hurt where?"

She clears her throat, takes a breath. "Don't worry, Henry. It's nothing, okay?"

"Stop saying that. Just tell me."

She looks at him for a moment, as though wondering if he can be trusted with something as private as pain. "If that's what you want, mahal"—she stands up—"then okay." She lifts her shirt slowly, adjusting the camera to make sure he sees, then turns in a slow circle to reveal a wound, a crusty gash that spans from the top of her hip to the middle of her abdomen. She explains: It happened in the typhoon two months before. A snap of bamboo, sharp as a spear, sliced across her body in the high-velocity winds. "I lost so much blood," she says. "But I'm thinking, okay lang, it's just a cut, bahala na. Pero now, I have an infection." Her own grandmother, she tells him, died from an infected cut, but God's good grace will keep her alive, she's sure of it.

She lowers her shirt and sits. "But every day it hurts."

"What can I do? How can I help?" He slumps in his chair. "I hate this. I *hate* being so far from you." Before she can speak, he says that maybe the day to meet should come sooner than later; what if this is God and the universe telling them that he should be the one to fly to her and, depending on the current round-trip airfare from Grand Forks to Manila, now is the time to come together? But Maxima says no and promises him that there's a better day ahead for them to meet, one when she is healthy and strong. For now, all she needs are his love, faith, and prayers. Nothing else.

"But there is one thing," she says.

"Tell me."

"Medicine. Ointments and creams with all the antibiotics. The best hospital in Manila has them. Pero"—she bites her lip, fighting tears—"walang pera."

"*Walang pera?*"

"No money." She shakes her head. "There's never money."

Henry puts his glasses back on. "Well, how much do you need?"

"Bahala na, mahal, it's okay. Please don't worry."

"How much. Tell me."

"I can't accept." She swivels her chair away from the screen. "I'm too ashamed."

"Just tell me. Please."

She takes a deep breath, nods. "Twenty-two thousand pesos."

"Pesos? How much is that?"

"Four hundred dollars." She turns back toward the camera. "USD."

Henry says nothing, just listens.

"Half the money for the doctor, the other half for the medicine," she says. "In the Philippines, if you have no insurance, medical care is very expensive, it's almost impossible, talaga. It's not like in the States." She dabs her eyes with her pinky and, with her other hand safely out of camera view, reaches for the switchblade next to her computer. She flicks it open and twirls it between her fingers, a thing she does when anxious or uncertain, when the inevitable is on the edge of finally happening.

On-screen, Henry is motionless, his face a blank. "Mahal," she says, "are you there?"

Finally, he moves. "I'm here," he says, "sorry. The screen froze for a sec. Where were we? What were you saying?"

"Money. For the medicine."

"And how much was it? Five hundred?"

"Five, yes," she says, nodding. "Five hundred. USD."

He looks toward the ceiling and blinks, like he's adding up figures in his head. "Let's make it six hundred, okay?"

"Six?" She shakes her head, says no, no, no, starts to weep. "It's too much, mahal, too much—"

"Sshhh," he says, a finger to his lips. "There's no price on love, *di ba?*"

She laughs. "*Di ba!* Yes, that's right." She wipes her eyes with a Kleenex, says it's almost one p.m. in the Philippines, time for her to go. She gives quick instructions when and how he can wire money to an online account, tells him she'll let him know when the payment goes through. "This will help me so much, so much. Thank you, mahal, thank you," she says. "And soon, one day, I promise, we will meet."

Henry nods. "Yes, mahal. And when we do, we'll sit in the country-side, put on some Shania, and then"—he leans into his camera, filling her screen again—"we're gonna fuck like bunnies." He winks and kisses the air, and the blade spins faster in Maxima's hand.

They say good-bye and Henry signs off, disappears from the screen. But Maxima is still there, and for a moment she watches herself, tilts her head slightly, like her face is one she recognizes but doesn't quite know.

She turns off the webcam.

She lifts her shirt, carefully peels away the wound, a trick of rubber and glue, then jots down quick notes in a small spiral notebook. She picks up the switchblade and opens her closet, where on the inside of the door she's tacked up a human target, the kind found at a shooting range. She steps back, stands against the opposite wall.

She raises the blade, aims, and throws. She misses the heart, not by much.

1

Excel is not a child. The man behind the ticket counter says he looks like one.

The man opens a binder, flips through laminated pages, then quotes Greyhound bus policy. "'All unaccompanied minors between the ages of twelve and sixteen must have written consent from a legal guardian to ride the bus alone.' So unless you've got some ID, a license, or a passport . . ."

"If I had a driver's license," Excel says, "why would I take a bus?"

The man spits bits of sunflower shell into a paper cup. "Beats me."

Excel searches his wallet for some kind of ID but finds nothing, not even a library card. He kneels on the ground and unzips his backpack, digs through rolls of shirts, underwear, and balled-up socks, feels around for a thin piece of plastic, an old high school ID. He pulls it out, sets it on the counter. "This was four years ago" he says. "I was fifteen then, I'm nineteen now."

The man takes the card, holds it up to the light. "You look the same to me. Could be a fake."

"What would I do with a fake high school ID?"

"People have their reasons."

"It's real," Excel says. "I swear."

The man shrugs, spits out more shell.

Excel takes back his ID. The one-way ticket from El Centro to San Francisco costs $70; the $340 crammed into his wallet is everything he has. He decides to spare five more. "For the ticket"—he sets three twenties and a ten on the counter, then holds out a five—"and for your help."

"You're bribing me. With five bucks."

"No, sir. It's just a tip." Excel tenses up, feels sweat slide down the back of his neck. "Should it be . . . more? Or a little less?"

"Kid, if you're going to bribe someone, especially at five a.m., aim higher." He types up Excel's travel information, takes the seventy dollars. "I'm going on good faith that you are who you say you are"—he prints the ticket, hands it to Excel—"and that you're just going where you need to go."

Excel has never traveled like this before, and the black, all-capital letters of his name, last then first—MAXINO, EXCEL—surrounded by reference numbers and the dark lines of a bar code, make him feel official, as if the journey ahead is a mission, not just a long ride home.

"Thanks," Excel says, "and please please don't call me kid."

He steps out of the station and onto the bus, a handful of passengers already aboard—a sleeping couple, young and white, pierced all over; a trio of men speaking Spanish in low voices; a ponytailed guy reading a *National Geographic*. Excel passes them all and takes a seat in the rear by the bathroom, the air a mix of Pine-Sol and urine; nobody, he thinks, will sit back here. But as soon as he's settled, an old woman in a checkered flannel and overalls—she looks like a lumberjack—

boards, sits across the aisle from him. She smiles at Excel, but he just nods, turns away, and shuts his eyes, hoping to sleep off as many hours as he can. The bus pulls out, and barely thirty minutes into the ride he feels a tap on his shoulder. He turns and sees the woman standing over him, holding out an egg. "Hard boiled," she says. "Want one? I got plenty."

Excel shakes his head, says he's fine.

"Oh. You looked hungry. Never mind."

Excel turns back toward the window. He closes his eyes, wakes an hour later at the next stop (he doesn't know the name of it), and finds in the empty seat beside him a paper sack with a sticky note attached that reads "When you do get hungry." Across the aisle, the seats are empty.

Inside is a sandwich, pretzels, a wax paper bag of carrot sticks, a hard-boiled egg. He's never taken food from a stranger; what if it's poisoned? First time ever on a Greyhound, he doesn't know what kind of people ride buses across the state, departing from middle-of-nowhere stations. Whoever they are, he's one of them (for now, anyway) and he's packed no food of his own. He takes a small bite of the sandwich (ham and cheese) and chews slowly, making it last another two stops. Later, the pretzels get him from Los Angeles to Valencia, the carrots to a town called Solvang; the egg he saves for later, just in case. He finally sleeps, then wakes at the Greyhound station in downtown San Francisco, where he deboards and heads to Market Street, catches the final BART train to the Colma station. From there, he walks the two miles to the locked front gate of the La Villa Aurelia apartment complex then realizes: he has no keys.

He walks halfway down the block. Bags slung on his shoulders, he climbs the low wall of Old Hoy Sun Ning Yung cemetery. He zigzags around tombstones and graves until he reaches the far end, squeezes through a hole in the chain link fence into the complex. He goes to

the back of the last building, climbs atop the Dumpster and onto the
fire escape. His bedroom window is two floors up, but moving closer,
he hears what sounds like weeping and sees the faint light in the open
window next to his. He thinks: *Of course.*

He doesn't move, waits for the conversation to end, then steps toward his window. It doesn't budge, and when he peers into Maxima's,
he finds her standing with a hand held high, a switchblade aimed right
at him.

"Stop," he says, hands up like he's surrendered. "It's me."

Maxima steps forward. Nine months have passed, their longest
time apart, and though he didn't think she'd look any different, he's
caught off guard by how much she resembles the way he often imagines her—weapon in hand, ready to strike.

She looks him up and down, like she can't quite tell if he really is
who he says he is, or someone else entirely. "You're back," she says.

"Yeah. Just arrived." He lowers his hands. "Could you put that
thing away?"

She closes the switchblade, tosses it onto her pillow. "I didn't know
you were coming."

"I meant to call. Couldn't get a signal in the desert. Couldn't get
one on the bus either."

"Nine months, no signal? Ano ba, your phone's from 1977?" She
folds her arms, makes no gesture to welcome him back.

It's pointless to apologize for his months of silence; she wouldn't
accept it, he wouldn't mean it. "I don't have my keys," he says. "I meant
to go through my window, but it won't open."

"I keep it locked these days."

"Well, could you unlock it? I would've gone through yours, but you
were"—he pauses, unsure of the word for what Maxima does.

"Working," she says.

"Right," he says. "Working."

She takes Excel's backpack and duffel bag, brings them inside. "I'll unlock your window, you enter through there," she says. "Gutom kaba? There's Panda Express in the fridge."

"Sure," he says, then thanks her, tells her that he's headed to the roof for a few minutes; after eighteen hours on a stuffy, stinky bus, he could use the air. "I'll be back," he says, "I promise," but before he can go, Maxima takes his wrist, her grip so tight he feels her fingers against his bones.

"It's good that you're home, Excel. But next time"—she squeezes harder—"don't spy on your mother."

What she means by *next time* he doesn't know. That he'll lurk on the fire escape tomorrow night, and nights on after? That he'll leave again to make a life, but automatically fail and inevitably return?

"I won't," he says, and she lets go.

He continues up the fire escape two more flights, steps onto the roof. He hasn't been here in over a year and everything is the same: the never-working satellite dish wrapped in ivy that somehow sprouts from rooftop gravel; the washing machine on its side, a pile of yellow rubber gloves still inside it; the pair of ripped and rusted lawn chairs. As a kid, Excel would come here without telling anyone, stay for hours, sometimes until dark and well beyond. *I'm hiding and hiding*, he'd tell himself.

He pulls his cell phone from his pocket. Almost twenty hours before, when Sab dropped him off in front of the El Centro bus station, she'd said no calls, not for a while. Instead of kissing him good-bye, she just touched his face, a gesture that might have been tender had it not made him feel almost ghostly, like he wasn't really there. So before her phone rings, he hangs up and decides to text her instead, but doesn't know the right thing to say. Maybe he'll just let her know he made it back, that he's safe, and that he misses her. Maybe he'll remind her to get some rest, for her sake and the sake of the baby. Or should he say *our* baby? *Unborn* baby? He knows he shouldn't say the word *baby* at all: Sab made it clear—no decisions, not yet.

He puts his phone away. No call, no text.

He walks to the edge of the roof. Of La Villa Aurelia's three buildings, his is the tallest, four stories high. From up here, the view is the 280 freeway on one side with Old Hoy Sun Ning Yung on another, and the rest is Colma, town of seventeen cemeteries, a handful of car dealerships (Lexus, BMW, Toyota, Dodge), and a cardroom called Lucky Wishes, where old Filipinos play and never win. To the north are two Targets, one on each side of the freeway (one in Colma, one in Serramonte), their signs a nightly red and white glow. Who needs two Targets so close together? Once, out of pure boredom, Excel walked from one front entrance to the other, counting his steps along the way—1,084, just to get to a place exactly the same as where you started.

It's June. Colma is cold, the sky hazy and gray. Excel closes his eyes, remembers the desert at night. Clean and cold air. Silence. What you saw when you looked up.

He crosses back and descends the fire escape, pauses at the bright, wide-open windows of the third-floor apartment above Maxima's and his. He's never met the tenants, but from the nonstop Bed Bath & Beyond coupons left atop their mailbox, he knows their last name is Sharma, and their apartment is nothing like the one directly below: Instead of cramped side-by-side bedrooms separated by a thin wall, the two windows look into a spacious living room with shiny dark wood floors, white built-in shelves, and a corner fireplace framed in marble; the space is so large it fits two sofas, one on each side of a glass coffee table.

He pokes his head through the window, hears no sounds of movement, climbs in. He walks over to the shelves, notices that the books are leather bound but have no titles or authors, and the framed black-and-white photographs are all of the same scene—floral-patterned tapestries flapping in the wind beside a river. He goes to the mirror above the fireplace, thinks of what the man at the Greyhound station said—*You look the same to me*—takes out his high school ID. He was fifteen, small for his age (he's caught up a bit, just shy of five feet six now), his face back then as round as a dinner plate. But in the mirror, he can see how nine months in the desert have hollowed out his cheeks and narrowed his face, and how almost forty-eight hours without real sleep has made his eyes bloodshot and murky.

There is another face in the mirror. Excel turns around, sees a small boy in striped pajamas standing in the living room doorway, holding a toy airplane in his hand. The Sharmas' son, he guesses.

The boy stares at Excel, oddly calm, as though the sudden appearance of a stranger in his home happens every day.

Excel moves quietly to the window, a finger to his lips. "I'm not here," he whispers, and just like that, he's not.

2

When he was gone, Excel thought Maxima might turn his room into something else—storage space or a home gym, maybe a sewing room, though as far as he knew, she'd never sewn a thing in her life. It's what you did when someone left, he thought, made use of the space left behind. But the room is still the same—the gray army blanket spread over the twin mattress, the milk crate nightstand, the top two drawers of the dresser half-open and empty. The place feels like a crime scene, everything untouched and kept in place.

He removes his shoes, sets them by the bedroom door. He pulls out a roll of T-shirts from his backpack, suddenly fears the implications of unpacking. Does it mean he's back for good? That he'll stay longer than he intends?

He thinks: ten thousand dollars. That's how much he needs to leave Colma, to get back to Sab.

He crams the shirts into his backpack, zips it up.

Excel flips on the living room light and sees Maxima everywhere.

Above the couch on the wall: two eight-by-ten photographs, one of Maxima in midair and midkick, a sword in each hand; the other of her in a shimmering gold gown, holding a rocket launcher.

On the cinder block bookshelf: a Polaroid of Maxima knee-deep in jungle water, flanked by men in army fatigues, wielding machetes; another where she sits on an overturned jeep, blowing a kiss to the camera, wearing a wedding gown spattered with blood.

Atop the TV, on a stack of old IKEA catalogues (why does Maxima save them? She never buys furniture), sits a gold statuette of a stick of dynamite, a star at the end of its fuse, with an engraving on its marble base that reads:

MOST PROMISING ACTION HEROINE

STAR OF TOMORROW

DYNAMITE-STAR! MANILA MOVIE AWARDS

He picks the trophy up, surprised by how light it is—the whole thing is plastic, the marble too—sets it back down.

He goes to the kitchen. On the wall above the table is a framed movie poster of *Malakas Strike Force 3: Panalo Ako, Talaga!* Excel translates: "Strong Strike Force 3: I Win, Really!" Something like that. The poster is an illustrated collage of the movie's big-drama moments—jeep explosions, big-muscled thugs firing machine guns, and curvy ladies in tattered blouses, desperate and on the run. Maxima's role in the film was small and uncredited—an assassin disguised as a nurse, her one scene a death scene—but she's there at the bottom of the poster, staring straight ahead, swaddled baby in one arm and a pistol in her hand, aimed right at you.

Before he left, the walls were blank; it was a way, Maxima said, to make the dinky box of their two-bedroom apartment look less small, which, to Excel, sounded like they were living in an optical illusion. But maybe his absence made the walls too blank, the apartment too big, so that she had to crowd it with pictures from a former life. Years before (pre-Excel, pre-America), Maxima had starred in a handful of action flicks made for cheap in Manila; "lowest of the low-budget, talaga," one critic called them. But Maxima was always proud. "I could have been the Michelle Yeoh of the Philippines, believe me," she used to say, and in darker moods, she'd watch her bootleg VHS copy of *Malakas Strike Force 3: Panalo Ako, Talaga!* on an all-night loop, hunched forward on the couch like the story meant something new with each viewing. Once, when Excel was watching a TV show about the world's deadliest birds, Maxima stormed into the room, grabbed the remote and put in the tape, said she needed to check something in *Strike Force 3*. "Check *what?*" Excel said, but Maxima brushed him off, muttered things in Tagalog that Excel couldn't keep up with. "You're barely in the movie," he said. She turned, shot him a look of instant anger or genuine hurt. He apologized immediately, left the room and went to the roof, where he decided he wasn't really sorry, not at all.

"I found that poster online," Maxima says, entering the kitchen. "Ten bucks. And for a collector's item like that? On that *Antiques Side-show*, it's ten times that amount, believe me."

The poster is slightly tilted; Excel straightens it out. "It looks nice," he says, "the living room, too. The pictures, the trophy. You've never displayed this stuff before."

She shrugs, opens the refrigerator, rummages through. "I thought it was time to decorate, 'make a house a home.' And it's better to look at pictures of me than of other people. You can't miss somebody who's still here, di ba?"

"Guess not," he says. But on the refrigerator, held up by a Domino's Pizza magnet, is a photograph of Joker, Maxima, and himself. They're standing in the sun at Evergreen Lawn Cemetery, a pair of concrete sphinxes in the background. Joker waves hello, his silver hair slicked back into a stubby ponytail; Maxima stands beside him, arm around his shoulder. They're both smiling, but Excel looks removed and a bit oblivious, slightly smaller, even dimmer, like he's standing in shade two steps behind them, an accidental bystander in the background. Excel hasn't seen the photo before, can't remember when it was taken or, even more puzzling, who took it. But he knows from the hunch in Joker's shoulders and the knockoff Louis Vuitton fanny pack at his waist that it's a few months before he died, just shy of his seventy-fifth birthday, almost two years before, when Excel was seventeen. Heart attack, out of nowhere.

A stranger might call it a family portrait, three generations in a single moment, and though Joker could pass as a grandfather, he wasn't. "Grandmaster Joker," was what they called him instead, a term Excel was embarrassed to say aloud ("It's like we're living in a kung fu movie," he'd complained), though Maxima had insisted it was the correct one. "That's who he is," she said. Back in the Philippines, long before Excel was born, Joker had been Maxima's grandmaster in the Filipino martial art of escrima. She was his top pupil, a village girl who he believed could one day become a grandmaster herself. But when she was nineteen, a Manila movie talent scout with an eye patch (a fashion statement, not a necessity) who'd seen Maxima perform a hand-to-knife demonstration approached her with an offer. "Stunt work today, action star tomorrow" was his promise; Maxima fell for it, then for him. For Joker, there was zero chance of compromise; low-budget action movies out of Manila would cheapen everything he'd taught her. Not long after, with no other students and no family of his own, Joker moved to California to join his brother, and for almost fifteen years had no communication with Maxima, not until the day she called him from Manila, telling him she was pregnant with no job, no family, and nowhere to go. "I broke the old man's heart, and he still took us in," she'd said. "We owe Grandmaster everything," which made life itself seem like one long debt they could never repay.

Maxima closes the refrigerator, a Tupperware of fried rice in one hand, a Panda Express takeout box of chow mein in the other. She dumps them into a bowl, pops it into the microwave. "I haven't had dinner," she says, "but there's enough, if you want." For ninety seconds, they stand in silence against the microwave's hum; in someone else's life, Excel thinks, his return would come with triumph and cheers, a home-cooked meal during which he'd tell stories of his travels, then distribute souvenir gifts thereafter. But they are not those kinds of people, not even in the photo on the refrigerator.

The microwave beeps; Excel speaks up. "I should've called before I came back. I meant to. Things just got busier than I expected."

Maxima brings the food to the table, sits. "Bahala na, Excel," she says, a phrase he's never been able to completely understand. *Oh well. Don't worry. That's life. Fuck it.* What it means when followed by his name, he doesn't know.

He joins Maxima at the table, is about to scoop up the mix of rice and chow mein when Maxima slaps his hand. "Pray first," she says. They're not Catholic—they're not anything, really—but for all his life Maxima and Joker chanted what they called *orasyones*—"martial arts prayers," was how Excel understood them. There were orasyones for heightened senses in combat, protection against sudden ambush, ways to weaken your enemy; an orasyon could even reach the dead, which Maxima said kept Joker's spirit close by. But most seemed made up on the spot; once, right before a sparring session with Joker, Maxima recited an orasyon calling for an earned and respectful victory over her opponent, then asked that the lottery scratchers she'd bought that morning bring more than just a lousy five bucks.

What she prays for now she keeps to herself. Head bowed, eyes closed, she mouths her orasyon; mostly it just sounds like breathing. Excel keeps one eye open, looks at the illustration of Maxima in the bottom corner of the poster. He knows that scene well, but the first time he ever saw it—he must have been three or four years old—he thought that the baby in her arms was actually him, and that at some point early in his life, Maxima cradled him as she shot down enemies blocking their way. He remembers how let down he felt, when he finally understood it was just a movie.

Maxima takes a breath and lifts her head, eyes blinking open like she's waking from sleep. She runs her fingers through her hair, pulling it back, and Excel notices that it's blacker now, her eyebrows too. Far as he knows, she's never dyed her hair before. Maybe he'd just forgotten how dark it is, after all the time away.

She scoops food onto Excel's plate. "So tell me. How was it? Did you make important discoveries?"

He smushes the rice with his fork. "Discoveries?"

"You said you were going to the desert to make"—she quotes with her fingers—"'important discoveries.'"

Excel has lied so much in the past nine months that it takes a moment to remember the one he'd told Maxima. "Discoveries," he says, "right." Nine months before, he told her that he'd found a job digging for an archaeological excavation in the California desert, that evidence of a lost civilization might be recovered. Room and board covered, $2,500 a month in cash. He told her he'd be gone for two.

"That job is still going on," he says, "but I needed a break. Guess I'm feeling a little aimless right now."

"Aimless. Not knowing." She shakes her head. "No purpose, then no life. Just la, la, la. So American."

Let her talk, he thinks. It only makes leaving easier.

"And your friend?" she says, "is she still making important discoveries too?"

"Sab is not my friend. She's my girlfriend."

"Well, I never got to meet her."

"She's still out there. But we might be on a break right now, too."

She nods, sighs. "It happens. Even when it's true love. If I was smart, I would have broken up with that eye patch–wearing son of a bitch a lot sooner."

Maxima almost never mentions his father, and Excel never asks. Why wonder about someone you've never met and never will? His whole life, he's imagined the man exactly as Maxima describes him, and taken it as the truth: that he sits at some roadside cantina in the Philippines countryside, drunk and playing gin rummy all day, an underage girl on his lap.

"If you'd left him sooner," he says, slicing through clumps of chow mein with the edge of his fork, "I wouldn't be here."

"Don't say bad things like that, Excel." She hits his shoulder with the back of her hand, harder than necessary. "No matter what, you'd be here"—she slaps the table twice—"one hundred percent."

"Maybe," he says, and hopes it isn't true.

3

A dark morning, nine months before, September. Maxima was leaning against the arm of the couch, hands deep in the fraying pockets of her pink terry cloth robe. Excel was at the front door and down on a knee, tying the laces of his Converse high-tops. "Triple knot, triple knot," she said, "so you don't trip and fall."

"Double's enough," he said, but he tripled it anyway, biding his time in what he knew were the last minutes before leaving home for good; he had no clue how moments like this were meant to go. He tied one shoe and started tying the other, noticed a tiny tear in the mustard-brown carpet, revealing the grain of what looked like dark hardwood. He'd never seen it before, and he felt a sudden urge to rip it further, to see what else might be hiding underneath.

Excel got to his feet. "Well," he said, "guess I'll be going," and Maxima moved toward him for what he suspected was a good-bye hug, though neither of them was a hugger. But instead of reaching out to pull Excel in, she took an envelope from her pocket. "Cash," she said, handing it to him. "Just in case."

The gesture caught him off guard. Maxima had been silent for days and pissed off for weeks, ever since Excel told her about the job in the desert. "It's just a couple months," he'd said, "maybe a little longer," and she said, "*Leaving? So soon after Joker?*" But Joker had been dead for a year, which seemed enough time to heal, or at least endure, and wasn't that how he was raised? You fall, you get up. Someone hits you, you hit back. Someone dies, you still have to live.

He took the envelope—there were five twenties inside—tucked it in his front pocket. "You didn't have to," he said, "but thanks."

"I hope it helps." She retied the sash of her robe so tightly she looked like she was trying to cut off air.

"Well," he said, slinging his bags over his shoulders, "bye." He opened the door and almost stepped through when something slammed so hard against the back of his knee that he dropped to the ground. He tried getting up but fell back down, his arm suddenly twisted behind his back, and Maxima's chin pressing down hard against the top of his skull. "If this happens to you," she said, grip tightening, "what do you do?" He tried untwisting his arm, getting to his feet, his whole body squirming and stuck. He knew this move: the Maximattack, she'd called it. There were tricks to breaking free but he could never get them right, and by now had forgotten them all.

"Let go," he said, "*now.*" He heard her whisper something—an orasyon to keep him down, he assumed—until she finally released his arm and stepped away.

She offered a hand to help him up; he refused, stood on his own. "Nothing will happen to me," he said, then walked out the door.

He hurried through the complex and out the front gate, saw Sab's Corolla parked at the curb. He opened the door and threw his bags in the back, leaned in to kiss her when he noticed purple streaks in her brown hair; the day before, they'd been blond. He took a strand, rubbed it between his fingers. "Bad?" she asked.

He shook his head. "Even better."

They kissed, then drove off, and at the final stoplight before getting on the freeway, Excel took out his apartment key and flicked it out the window, the morning still so early and quiet that he heard it clink against the asphalt, the sound of everything he no longer needed.

THEIR DESTINATION WAS A BLANK ON THE MAP. THE CLOSEST landmarks were a city called El Centro and a dot of a town called Whyling, near the bottom of California. Once there, they'd head east, to a place called Hello City.

Sab drove; she had the license, the car. Excel's job was to navigate. He unfolded the California road map and spread it over his lap, then realized he'd never read an actual map before—when you go nowhere your entire life, nothing is more useless than a map. Their flip phones wouldn't help if they got lost, so Excel tried making sense of all the grids and lines; under the dim car light, the whole state just looked like an arm bent at the elbow, the crisscrossing freeways like networks of veins. But he finally found San Francisco, then Colma, then the 280 freeway, and, finally, maybe, himself: he put a finger on what he estimated was their current position, checking back and forth between the map and the road ahead. He felt like he was tracking his own movement, a kind of out-of-body experience that made him dizzy. His first road trip ever, he didn't want to get carsick, so he put down the map, told Sab it was a straight shot south for a few hours more and reclined his seat, looked out the window. They passed nothing scenic or memorable, not yet, but he took in every lit-up sign for every strip mall, gas station, and fast food chain they passed, like a tourist determined not to miss a single thing. How could he not:

barely an hour outside Colma, Excel was farther from home than he'd ever been before.

They'd met in June, three months before. Excel was lying on the grass next to Joker's grave when a girl holding a ziplock bag filled with what looked like gray powder approached. "Want some?" she asked.

He sat up. She was wearing an army jacket, a black skirt that reached her Doc Martens. Her hair was barely held together in a loose, straggly bun, and her lipstick was gray, nearly black. He thought she was selling him drugs.

"It's for your monkey face," she said, shaking the bag.

"For my what?" It was an overcast Saturday, the cemetery nearly empty, which was how he wanted his day off from The Pie, the pizza place where he'd worked since high school.

"Your *orchid*," she said. "It's called a monkey-faced orchid. Look." She picked it up by the small clay pot, held it to Excel's face. He hadn't known the flower was an orchid, much less a specific kind. He'd simply found it on top of the Dumpster behind the cemetery flower shop, thought it was alive enough to lay at Joker's grave. Up close, he could see how the petals' maroon splotches, combined with the bulbous flap in the center of the flower, might resemble the face of a monkey, but one that looked surprised, almost panicked.

"Deer eat the flowers at night," she said. "But if you sprinkle some pepper, they stay away. So"—she offered the bag again—"want some?"

He shrugged. "Why not."

She took a pinch, sprinkled it over the orchid. "I work at the cemetery flower shop. I put pepper on the flowers a few times a week."

"I thought you were selling me drugs."

She shook her head. "My drug mule is on vacation."

It didn't register with Excel, not until he saw the slight lift of her eyebrows, signaling the joke. Silence was his default response to any stranger who spoke to him, like he was someone who didn't know the language. Back in school, teachers had nagged him to speak up, would call him out by name to force his class participation. He had few friends, and the guys he did hang out with, Vic and Truong, weren't so much into conversation as they were into *Grand Theft Auto*, and he hadn't spoken to either since graduation (Vic left for some college in either North or South Carolina; Truong joined a branch of the military, Excel couldn't remember which). Staring at this girl with a bag of ground pepper in her hand, he realized he hadn't had a real conversation with anyone in months, maybe longer.

"Well"—he took a breath—"it's tough to find a good drug mule these days."

She laughed. "I'm Sab," she said. He could tell she was mixed—part Asian for sure (he guessed Japanese or Korean), maybe some white, Mexican, or African American, too. She looked like she could be everything.

"Excel," he said. "Like the spreadsheet."

"Excel? *Excel.*" She said his name like it was a word she'd never heard before.

"It's weird, I know."

"Totally. I like it." She held up the ziplock bag, asked if he wouldn't mind helping her put pepper on the rest of the flowers; the sooner she was done, the sooner she could go home.

He got to his feet. She'd looked taller when he was sitting, but standing up he saw they were about the same height. Looking her in the eye took no effort.

They walked the rows of graves. Most had no flowers, and those that did, Sab pointed out, belonged to the more recently deceased. "Nobody bothers if you've been dead for a long time. If my mom had been buried instead of cremated, I'd bring her flowers every day." It caught him off guard, that a total stranger could reveal something so personal to another, and he wasn't sure if he should just let the comment slip by, or ask a question so that she could tell him more.

"Sorry for your loss," he said.

She sprinkled pepper on a sunflower and looked up at him. "Sorry for yours."

They finished just after five p.m., and without realizing it, Excel walked back to the cemetery flower shop with Sab, stood outside the door as she closed up, then walked her to her car. She thanked him for his help, and before he could find something to say that would prevent them from parting, she said, "Do you like Denny's?" then took out a two-for-one coupon from her purse. "My treat."

They drove to the nearest Denny's, were seated in a family-sized booth in a far corner of the near-empty dining room. Excel couldn't remember the last time he'd eaten in a restaurant with actual menus, and too many options and categories overwhelmed him (breakfast, lunch, and dinner served at the same time, Fit Fare versus Deluxe Dinners, and what were all these *slams?*). "I'll just have toast," he said. But Sab said absolutely not, that ordering toast was a disgraceful use of a two-for-one coupon. "We're getting patty melts," she said. The food came quickly, and Excel ate while Sab talked: she'd come to Colma two months before, to live with an aunt in Colma Isles, a trailer community just off the freeway ("Even more glamourous than the press says," she said). Her mother died when she was seven, her father was a drunk somewhere in Nevada. She had been raised by one grandmother in San Diego, then raised by the other in Sacramento, lived with aunts and uncles some years in between. She had so-so grades but no money for college, so the four-hundred-dollar-a-month bedroom in her aunt's trailer was, at this point in her life, the best situation she could find.

"And how's that turning out?" he asked.

"Better today than yesterday." She reached for his plate, took a fry. He reached for hers, took an onion ring, and said, "Me too."

After, Sab drove him home, but as they neared the front gate of La Villa Aurelia, she asked, "Would it be okay if I just kept driving?" and Excel could see how tight her grip was on the steering wheel, like fists clenched ready for a fight, but slightly shaking too. He put a hand on hers, felt the faint vibrations of the moving car coursing through her fingers into his. He didn't know how to drive (neither Maxima nor Joker ever had a car), and to be moving like this, to be going somewhere, anywhere, felt foreign, a small and quietly thrilling risk. Here was a day, finally, that wouldn't play out exactly as he'd predicted.

They drove to the movie theater in Daly City but stayed in the car, talked for an hour, then another, often looping back to their discontent. Sab was sick of changing cities, but couldn't find one that felt like home. Excel thought he'd be in Colma forever, but wasn't sure how to leave, where to go.

Later, they realized the parking garage was nearly empty. "Midnight," Sab said, checking her watch, "maybe we should kiss?" "Maybe so," Excel said. He leaned in, caught a glimpse of a tattoo just below her ear and behind the corner of her jaw—a tiny black lightning bolt. He traced it over with his finger, kissed it, then kissed her.

It was nearly three a.m. when he finally got home, and though Maxima was on the other side of the wall chatting online with faraway strangers, he slept better than he could remember. The next morning before work, he dropped by the cemetery and saw that Sab was right: the orchid was still at Joker's grave, intact and untouched, the monkey's face speckled with pepper but perfectly clear.

He saw her later that day, every day after. The first time they had sex (he was her second, she was his first) went well enough that they did it again the next night, an experience so incredible to Excel that he said out loud, "I think that changed my life," which made them both laugh. Soon they were spending all their free time together, which required zero adjustments to other parts of their lives; they had each other, and he felt lucky for it. But Colma, Sab made clear, was tempo-rary. At some point, she was moving on.

That point came sooner than expected. Almost three months after they met, while sitting at Joker's grave, Sab told Excel that her aunt was moving her boyfriend, a mechanic with pet tarantulas, into the trailer. "The guy's a creep," she said, "so I'm moving out." A cousin named Lucia, who owned a small organic soap company near the bottom of California, might have a job for her, a cheap place to stay. "It's a little out of the way, near the desert. Or maybe *in* the desert? She said it was 'off the grid,' whatever that means. It's my best option, and it would be nice not to go alone. We could get the hell out of Colma, try something new . . ." She trailed off, plucking out blades of grass, as though she feared his answer would be no, as if there might be any reason for him to stay behind.

ANOTHER HOUR SOUTH ON THE FREEWAY, SAB TURNED OFF THE radio. "So," she said, "how'd she take it?"

Excel's seat was reclined all the way back; the only thing he could see was the morning sky, darkness fading to light. "Fine. Good. She wished us well."

"Liar."

He took a few moments, then told her what he'd told Maxima.

"'Excavation'?" Sab said. "'Lost civilizations'? Who are you, Indi-ana Jones? Does she believe you?"

"She does."

"And she thinks this is temporary. But what if a month goes by and she's expecting you back? Then two months? Then five or six?"

"She'll be fine."

"What if she waits for you her whole life?"

He imagined Maxima rocking in a chair on the porch of some house in the middle of nowhere, staring at a long, empty road, waiting for Excel to appear in the distance. "She'll get used to it," he said. "People get used to it."

"That's fucked up."

"It's not fucked up," he said, "it's life." He meant that *not* telling Maxima he was leaving forever was the natural order of things, the way the world sometimes worked. Maxima had left the Philippines the same way—she'd lived a life and found another, no deliberations or discussions. If instincts were hereditary, then Excel's way of departure was coded into his DNA, a thing meant to happen sooner or later.

"It's better this way, believe me," he said. "If I'd told her I was leaving forever, she would've made it hard. Maybe impossible. You don't know what she's capable of."

"Then give me an example."

She'll make a man fall in love with her, then take his money—that was the first thing that came to mind, and though Sab and Maxima had never met (Excel made sure of that), he felt a need to protect Maxima, a sudden loyalty; he didn't want Sab's sympathy for Maxima to become judgment.

He said, "She slashed a guy's tires once."

"Well, at least she didn't slash the guy."

"She made me act as lookout."

"That's kind of terrible. But also kind of funny."

"I guess." He tried smiling, like someone looking back on how silly life could be, but he was thinking of what he didn't tell Sab—that he had been only eight years old at the time, that he was the one who'd done the slashing. It would look less suspicious, Maxima said, if a kid was caught crouching between cars, rather than a grown woman. She never explained who the man was, or why his tires had to be slashed ("He's a bad guy," was all she said, fingers massaging the knuckles of her other hand, like she'd just punched someone out or was about to), but she spent the day teaching Excel how to handle the knife, the right way to puncture a tire. Even Joker gave advice on the best technique ("Jab-jab! Quick-quick!" he said, demonstrating with a plastic spoon. "Like a strike to your enemy's face!"). Excel had no idea who the enemy was or what he looked like, but he did as instructed, and imagined the moment of attack was like popping a balloon: a tire one second, a scrap of rubber the next. When the time came to finally do it, in the parking lot of Big 5 Sporting Goods, where the guy worked, Excel threw his whole body, the entire force of himself, into the knife. He slashed one rear tire, the other, then ran as fast as he could to the adjacent Burger King, where Maxima waited and watched. When he reached her, she squeezed his shoulders and said, "Mission accomplished," then bought him a vanilla milkshake. But Excel remembered looking back at the tires as he ran, how solid they were, how perfectly intact. Despite all his strength and training, he wasn't sure he'd made any impact at all.

He looked over at Sab, noticed a new piercing, a fourth, at the top of her ear, a tiny blue hoop. He reached out to touch it, then placed his hand on the back of her neck, and promised he'd contact Maxima when the time was right. "For now," he said, "let's just drive."

NEARLY FOURTEEN HOURS LATER AND DESPITE EXCEL'S CLUMSY NAVigating (they missed three exits, twice went west instead of east), they entered Whyling. They passed a market, a post office, a gas station, a store with a sign that read SUPPLIES, then continued down the two-lane road until there was no road at all, just gravel, then dirt. Excel put away the map, meaningless now, and read the directions Sab had printed from an e-mail and taped to the dashboard.

- drive through Whyling until the end
- continue straight (a mile or so?), look for the boulder, turn right
- keep going, going, going—look for an Airstream with soap on it—that's ME!!

THE SON OF GOOD FORTUNE   35

He looked up from the directions. Everything was dry, endlessly flat, the sky as colorless as the earth below. "It's like *Mad Max*," Sab said. He put his hand on her lap and squeezed, as if reassuring her that all was going according to plan, though he'd done no planning himself. They drove on, passed a scatter of RVs and trailers, tents clumped in groups and tents standing alone, then, about twenty yards ahead, saw a white boulder the size of a small car, the message THIS IS HELLO CITY painted across in black, blocky letters. A blond guy in pigtails, shirtless and in flip-flops, stood beside it, holding a peacock by a leash, its jewel-blue tail sweeping the dirt as it paced back and forth.

"Poor bird," Excel said.

"It's okay," Sab said, making the turn. "I don't think they can fly anyway."

Another mile and they found the Airstream, a pink bar of soap painted on its side. In front of the trailer was a sitting area with a wicker couch and two matching chairs, a small firepit in the middle, all of it on a stretch of bright fake grass. They pulled up and parked, and a woman in a fedora and lacy tank top stepped out. She looked a little like Sab but more Japanese, was maybe about ten years older. "Lucia," Sab said. She walked over to her but Excel stayed by the car, watched as they hugged and swayed. He'd never seen a reunion before, the actual moment when family came together after so much time apart. He felt out of place and intrusive, so he looked away, pretended that there was something in the distance that caught his eye.

He heard his name, turned and looked back. "I don't know you," Lucia said, still holding Sab, "but welcome home."

"HELLO CITY WAS MEANT FOR BATTLE," LUCIA SAID, THEN POPPED open a bottle of champagne. After World War II, the US government acquired the land to use as training ground for air combat, but the plan went nowhere and the military moved out, leaving behind four hundred acres of unwanted desert. In the mid-eighties, groups of ex-hippies and the occasional former felon began arriving, living in vans and tents on whatever bit of land they claimed for themselves. Those people were still there, but the current population—almost two hundred, the last time anyone counted—was a mix of artists and retirees, a contingent of midwestern and northeastern seniors, even a couple of legitimate tech millionaires who'd made all the money they needed, then bailed out of capitalist society to live free and be left alone. Now, the only proof of a former military presence was the few dozen helicopter landing pads dotting the land, concrete circles with a yellow H painted in the center.

"H for 'helipad'?" Excel said.

Lucia shook her head. "H for 'hello,'" she said, then poured champagne into three tin cups and toasted their arrival.

She served dinner on the patio, sandwiches and salad on orange metal plates. "Fig and prosciutto on sourdough with massaged kale tossed in beet pesto," she said. "Hope that's okay?"

Sab said it was perfect and Excel agreed, though he'd never had figs, prosciutto, massaged kale, beets, or pesto in his life. "Neat plate," he said.

She rolled her eyes. "Those are Sven's."

"Sven?"

"My ex. The Swedish bastard. The reason I'm here." They'd met three years before in an L.A. yoga class ("My clinically depressed law school dropout period," Lucia said), and after two months together, Sven convinced her to move to Hello City, challenged her to live her truest, freest life. "And I thought, screw it, why not?" she said. "So we moved here, learned to make organic soap, and a year later he gets ants in his pants and starts applying to law school behind my back, when he *knew* that it was law school that triggered my depression in the first place. Would've been so much easier if he'd just slept around instead. So anyway, Sven the Liar gets into Yale, gives me a half-ass invite to go with him so long as I'm willing to get my own place *off campus*. So I said screw you, kept the trailer and the plates, and here I am, off-the-grid businesswoman and owner of Pink Bubble Organic Soap." She poured herself another cup of champagne, got up from the couch, and put an arm around Sab. "And now my favorite cousin is here with me." She looked over at Excel. "What about you? Why are you here?"

He took an extra-big bite of the sandwich and chewed slowly, biding his time for the right response; there was no single defining reason he could nail down, no specific incident he could recount to explain why he'd come. *Life*, he thought, *is that a good answer?* What came to him instead was a feeling, something between a sharpness and a deepening ache. It was his leg, he realized, the spot behind the knee where Maxima had kicked him. Though it hurt in that moment, it had been fine the entire drive down. Maybe it was all the hours sitting, or maybe the cool desert air, but the pain was clear to him now.

"I'm here for her," he finally said. He reached for Sab's hand, held it until the throbbing in his leg subsided.

They finished eating, and just before they gathered their dishes Lucia told them to look up, and Excel saw a sky he'd never seen—the blackest black with folds of the darkest blue, streaked with light that he learned wasn't just stars but whole galaxies. "Whoa," Sab said, and Excel said, "Yeah," though what he actually felt was amazement, followed by an unexpected stupidity. How could he not already know such skies existed? The best he'd seen before was from the roof of his apartment building, lit by a pair of Target signs, and the planes flying away from San Francisco International Airport, their tiny red and green lights flickering in the dark, reminders that he'd never really been anywhere before.

After dinner, Lucia took them to a converted school bus, which sat on a small patch of dirt ten minutes beyond the Airstream. Lucia owned it, had been renting it out for the past year, mostly to weekend tourists wanting to experience Hello City. "Lookie-loos and gawkers," she said, "so obnoxious." This was where Sab and Excel would live now, for two hundred dollars a month. The bus was narrow and shorter than the average school bus, about eight paces from end to end—but Excel's whole life had been spent in the crammed box of the La Villa Aurelia apartment, so the space seemed livable enough. The bus had been gutted, refloored with green linoleum, and furnished with a two-person table, a short bookcase, a green metal trunk for storage, a minifridge. All that remained was the steering wheel and the rearview mirror above.

"Home sweet home," Lucia said, then stepped out of the bus.

In the back, sectioned off behind a shower curtain patterned with raindrops, was a mattress and box spring. "Our bedroom," Sab said. They lay down and kissed, held each other, too tired for anything more.

"What do you think," Sab said.

"About what?"

"This place."

He'd only ever lived in Colma. He didn't know how to figure out if a place was right for him or not. "What do *you* think?" He waited for an answer, heard only breathing.

"Where else would we go," she finally said.

EXCEL WOKE THE NEXT MORNING, THE COLDEST HE'D EVER BEEN. His ears, his face, the back of Sab's neck when he kissed it—any part of them not under the blanket felt like it had been chilling in a refrigerator. Puffs of breath appeared every time he exhaled, and the ceiling of the bus looked like a long slick of ice, shiny and Arctic blue, like the inner dome of an igloo, or the walls inside one of those ice hotels he'd seen on the Travel Channel, in Finland or Norway, one of those countries he knew, without question, he'd never see.

Sab shifted in her sleep, pulled the covers over her head. Excel slipped out of bed, put on pants and shoes, zipped up his hoodie, stepped out of the bus. Outside was warmer than in, but the morning was dark enough to look like early evening, and the still-rising sun silhouetted everything before it—trailers scattered in the distance, a row of low tents. Beyond, tall cacti looked like crucifixes, or people raising their arms in half surrender. He moved farther out, was startled back a step when a desert mouse—the first he'd ever seen—cut across his path. Then, suddenly, the ground beneath his feet was not dirt but concrete, and he realized he was standing on the edge of one of the concrete helipads Lucia had mentioned. In the middle of it was a faded H, the size of a pickup truck, large enough to be seen from high above. He imagined a sky filled with helicopters, their pilots looking down, and wondered what it might mean to them, to see someone like himself standing on the H.

Hello.

Help.

Here.

4

Excel wakes to the sound of a dying heart.

Ba-bum. Ba-bum. Loud and heavy, slow.

He gets out of bed and goes to the living room, finds Maxima throwing one-two punches at The Bod. The Bod is her electronic cardio boxing dummy, all head and torso, the color of blue toothpaste, with a dozen diamond-shaped points of contact meant to light up when you hit them. "The stronger the blow, the brighter the glow," the manual said. Maxima had bought The Bod at a garage sale, but after one workout, the little diamonds went dim forever. "Maybe I hit too hard," she had said, and put him away soon after. Excel hasn't seen The Bod in a while, had forgotten its facial expression, two dark squares for eyes, a short black line for a mouth.

Maxima punches twice more—*ba-bum, ba-bum*—takes one step back and delivers a kick to The Bod's neck. "Good morning," she says, "it's late."

The VCR clock says 10:07 a.m. "Guess I was more tired than I thought," he says. *The Price Is Right* is on TV, muted. A blond girl in a Stanford sweatshirt is choosing between a pair of Jet Skis or a cruise to Puerto Vallarta.

"There's coffee. Pan de sal if you want, but no butter."

"Maybe later, thanks."

"What's your plan?"

"My plan? You mean, for today?"

"For today. For life. Either one."

He sits on the arm of the couch, suddenly tired again. "Shower, get dressed. I was going to stop by The Pie, get my old job back."

"Wow. A home *and* a job to come back to, anytime you like. If I went back, you think I'd have those things waiting for me? You're lucky, talaga." She turns back to The Bod, goes for the abdomen now, and Excel tries to picture a moment when Maxima steps off a plane and onto Philippines ground. All he's ever seen of the country comes from clips from her movies; every scene is a martial arts attack, a shoot-out, some degree of destruction. Whenever he imagines her in the Philippines, she is always fighting her way through.

The Stanford girl wins the Jet Skis. "What about you. What's your plan for the day?"

"Just working."

"Working." He nods, looks at the TV. "Right."

"Excel," she says, tone sharp as a warning. "Your face."

He straightens up, looks at her. "What about my face?"

"You should see yourself. You look like this." She raises a brow, rolls back her eyes, and scowls.

"I don't look like that."

"Yes you do. When I said 'working,' that was your face. Like you're judging me. Like you're ashamed." Before Excel can try to deny it, Maxima goes to the kitchen and returns with a Christmas card, two candy cane–licking elves on the front. "Read it," she says. He opens the card.

Maxima and Excel:

Maligayang Pasko and Happy New Year! Kumusta ka? Best wishes to "you and yours" this season. Beginning <u>JANUARY 1</u> *your rent will be increased to $1000 (ONE THOUSAND), still better than "market rate" (like rent control, di ba?). Rent due in cash by 1st of EACH month. God bless!*

Regards,

Benedicto Anonuevo

Property Owner

Excel had never known the full name of Joker's brother, had always referred to him as Uncle Bingo, a formality he'd hated. Awful enough referring to the landlord as family, even worse knowing what he thought of Maxima and Excel: a pair of freeloaders leeching off Joker. Bingo owned the apartment—Bay Area real estate was his business— but out of familial respect for his oldest brother, he let Joker live there for free. But when Maxima and Excel moved in, Bingo started charging five hundred a month; after Joker died, they thought Bingo would kick them out, but he let them stay for eight hundred dollars a month. "In honor of my brother," he'd said.

"'Maligayang Pasko, I'm raising your rent.' Grade-A asshole, talaga," she says. "I looked for another apartment, a room in a house. Somebody even asked seven hundred dollars for a bed in a garage, no heat."

He imagines Maxima curled up on a cot in an empty garage, wearing layers of coats to keep warm. *You should've called.* That's the right thing to say. But how would he have helped? In Hello City, he'd made just enough from odd jobs to get by, not much else. "You've been able to pay it? In full, on time?"

"Barely. I cleaned houses, washed cars. But it's not just rent and utilities. Auntie Queenie needs a part-time nurse now, so I'm sending money back to the Philippines for that. Plus, her medicine, di ba?" Maxima's sister, Queenie, had been a live-in maid in Saudi Arabia for decades, though from the way Maxima tells it, she was more like a slave; after she suffered a stroke, she was let go. Now she's back in the Philippines, in the village where they'd grown up.

She turns back to The Bod, raises her fists. "I have many hardships, Excel. So when I say I'm 'working,' and you make a face like this"—she crumples her face—"just remember, even if you're gone, life still happens here."

On the TV, a heavy guy in a lime green polo shirt and cargo shorts charges to the stage—his nametag says JAKE—waves hello to the camera. A panel slides open, reveals a brand-new truck, white and gleaming. Jake jumps up and down, pumps his fist, and though the TV is on mute, Excel can almost imagine his voice—earnest and hopeful, confident but quivering, with so much to win or lose.

MAXIMA STARTED TALKING TO THE MEN SIX MONTHS AFTER JOKER died.

Excel had slept on the couch his whole life, but with Joker gone, Maxima insisted Excel take his room. "It's too sad," she'd said, "to have that empty space so close." Excel obeyed, but the mattress was thin with poking springs, and Joker's smell—a mix of aftershave and Bengay—hung in the room, like he'd just been inside it and was still somewhere nearby. One night, unable to sleep, Excel heard Maxima weeping on the other side of the wall. It happened again the next night, though the weeping was followed by laughter, and then the sound of what was, unmistakably, a second voice—low and deep but smaller and faraway, like a man calling long distance on a bad connection. Excel guessed that Maxima had met someone, a possible boyfriend maybe, but was too embarrassed to admit it; what few romances she had always went bust. But as the nights went on he heard more voices—all men—saying things like "sweetheart," "darling," "my love." One evening, after a double shift at work, he found a box of Converse high-tops atop his dresser, a twenty-dollar bill tucked into each shoe. She'd never given him an out-of-nowhere gift before, and though he wanted to be grateful, all he felt was suspicion.

He went to Maxima's room, entered without knocking. "Something's not right," he said, holding up the shoes. She was sitting on her bed, looking at an IKEA catalogue. "Who are you talking to?"

She sighed and rubbed her eyes, like they'd been arguing for hours and she'd finally had enough. "I'm talking to men."

"What men?"

"From the Internet."

"Internet. Like online dating?"

"*Dating.* Me?" She let out a laugh, shook her head. "No. I'm not dating."

"Then what's going on? Tell me."

She looked back at the catalogue. "I have a profile on some websites. Sometimes men find it, and if they like what they see, they contact me. If they seem nice, we talk on camera." She pointed to a webcam on her desk. Excel had never seen it before, and he stepped back, suddenly worried someone could be watching from the other end.

"What do you talk about?"

She shrugged. "Lots of things. Life, I guess? The ups and downs. The good days and the bad days. And sometimes, if there's a connection"—she looked up at Excel, then away from him—"I ask for help."

"What kind of help?"

"Money."

He looked back at the camera on the desk, imagined Maxima sitting in front of it. "Is this . . ."—he trailed off, not knowing the right way to phrase a question he didn't want to ask—"a sex thing?"

Maxima shot up from her bed and shoved him against the wall, kept him there. "I do *not* do that," she said, the force of her hand crushing into his chest. He could not believe how strong she was.

She stepped back, took a breath. "Ano ba? Why should I defend myself? Why should I explain?" But with no prompting from Excel, she told him about OK Filipinas, A Kiss across the Ocean, Pacific Catholic Romance, websites where men—most of them middle-aged and American—searched through profiles of women from Thailand, Vietnam, Japan, the Philippines. "They want the perfect Asian wife. And you know what 'perfect' means. Hardworking. Housecleaning. Loyal. A maid in the day, a whore in the night. These men, that's the kind of thing they say, believe me." The men assumed she was in the Philippines, someone looking for a way to America, via marriage. Once she felt a connection was made, mutual trust established, she'd make up an elaborate tragedy or hardship, something that only money—both small and large amounts—could fix, and the ones she could convince would wire the cash.

"I only take what I need," she said. "Enough to make rent, pay the bills. Anyway, it's my business, nobody else. You don't have to like it, but you have to live with it." She sat back on her bed and opened the catalogue, flipped to a page showing an all-white kitchen, plates stacked perfectly next to the sink.

"Fine," he said, "but I'm not wearing these shoes." He left the room.

Later, he asked Maxima to at least keep her voice low, but there were still nights, even some days, when he heard her through the wall—flirting and giggling, cheesy lines she'd use again and again ("I am a simple woman who believes in the two L's: the Lord and love."). Sometimes he'd learn the names of men and where they were from, their hobbies and interests, the thing that they loved: Jermaine from Saint Louis lived for the Yankees, Werner from Milwaukee collected German beer steins, Roberto from San Antonio loved the US of A. Maxima could indulge them all, could make them believe she loved the same things too, and somehow find the perfect opportunity to pivot the conversation toward that moment when Maxima would go from giggles to heartache, and reveal a tragedy (a typhoon that devastated her village, the sudden death of a sibling, even a cousin held hostage by Muslim insurgents) that would require her to ask, with shame and humility in her voice, for a little money ("Life in the Philippines"—she'd say, right before breaking—"is hard."). Excel would listen with his ear to the wall, embarrassed and ashamed, but also, admittedly, riveted— how convincing could she possibly be? How did she come up with the perfect sadness to make the men believe her, want to help her? But for all of Maxima's stories and lies, he learned that a bit of truth could sometimes slip into the conversation, as he did on the night before he left for Hello City: stuffing clothes into his backpack, he could hear Maxima through the wall, weeping about the son she lost, the broken heart that would never heal. When the man on the other end asked, "What can I do, mahal? How can I help?" Maxima had no requests— not for money, not for prayers—then told him there were some things in the world that simply could not be fixed.

ON *THE PRICE IS RIGHT*, JAKE LOSES THE TRUCK, BUT HE'S STILL SMIL- ing for the audience, fists in the air like he's a winner. "He lost," Maxima says, "why is he celebrating? Dummy." Excel rereads the Christmas card, and remembers, suddenly, that he didn't send one to Maxima. He hadn't called at that point, but he'd meant to write a card, had even made sure that Sab saved an extra stamp for him to use. He doesn't know what Maxima did for Christmas, if she did anything at all. He hopes, if nothing else, there was someone online for her to talk to.

He puts the card down, tells Maxima that if he can get his job back, he'll try to help out with rent. "Bahala na," she says, punching The Bod, "I can manage."

5

It's a twenty-minute walk from the apartment to The Pie Who Loved Me, a spy-themed kiddie pizza parlor with games, rides, and animatronic animal characters dressed in trench coats and fedoras. An online reviewer called The Pie Who Loved Me "the Chuck E. Cheese of the damned, where pizza goes to die" and in high school, being voted "Most Likely to Work at The Pie" wasn't so much funny as it was cruel: it meant that your classmates thought you were doomed, that whatever qualities you displayed, none was more apparent than your lack of ambition, your zero potential. Excel doesn't know who won it the year he graduated, was just relieved it wasn't him—an upside of nobody knowing you, he thought.

A new sign hangs above the entrance—the red lettering is bright and cheery, the *o* in *Who* and *Loved* is a pepperoni pizza—but the rest of the storefront is as grim as before: gray stucco wall, cracking red-tile roof with missing tiles all over, the one window a small dark square on the door. It's almost business hours, but when Excel enters, half the lights are off, no kiddie music plays, the cash registers sit unmanned. But a familiar stink of industrial mozzarella and oven cleaner is in the air; someone is prepping for the day. He goes to the dining room, notices the Spy Ring Hip Hop Players is missing a member—Ivanka Iguana on bass—and the ones remaining look maimed or dead, heads hanging to the side with half-closed eyes and half-open mouths, like someone tried decapitating them but gave up halfway. Sloth the Sleuth is in especially bad shape, both arms dangling from their sockets by wires and tubes, his gray, shaggy fur matted and crusty. In Hello City, there were artists who could take a broken animatronic body and repurpose it into furniture or make it part of a sculpture. Something functional and new.

Somebody says, "X?"

Excel turns around, sees an elderly man in a floppy baseball cap alone in a booth, a small dictionary on the table. He walks over, sits across from him. "It's good to see you, Z," Excel says. For the first time in days, he smiles.

"You return," Z says.

Excel nods. "I return."

"But you leave forever."

"That was the plan."

"Something wrong happens?"

Excel understands that Z's English—always clipped, always in bites—renders everything he says in the present tense. But the way he says it—*something wrong happens*—makes life sound like an endless loop of mistakes, never what it's meant to be. Z arrived from Serbia a few years before, at the age of seventy, brought here by his son. The plan was to collect Social Security, an extra income to help other family back home. He knew almost no English, and had trouble pronouncing Excel's name, so settled for X instead. In return, Excel calls him Z, short for Zivko.

Excel taps the dictionary. "What's a new word?"

Without missing a beat, Z closes his eyes and waves a finger in the air, drops it on a random word in the middle of the page. "This one," Z says.

Excel leans over, tries reading the word upside down, but it's so unfamiliar he has to turn the dictionary toward him. "'Planet stricken,'" he says, the word as foreign to him as it must be to Z. "'Adjective. Affected by the supposedly harmful influence of the planets.'" He turns the book back toward Z, suggests picking another word, one he can actually use in real life.

Z shakes his head. "Any word. I can use." He rereads the definition, concentrates. "Today I wake, maybe sick"—he checks the word again—"but not sick. Only *planet stricken.*" He looks up from the page, the face of someone who doesn't know if he's right or wrong.

"Perfect," Excel says.

"When you leave. I have few words. Now, many." He closes the book. "X. Why are you back?"

"Things didn't quite work out as planned."

Z sighs, nods slowly. "Yes, I know."

"I need a job. Is Gunter here?"

Z leans forward, all the lines on his old face pulling together with worry. He says something in what Excel guesses is Serbian, then pats Excel's wrist. "Okay," he says, "my grandson, over there." He points to the game room. Excel slides out of the booth, stands up straight, takes a breath. "Wish me luck," he says, and Z looks at him blankly like there's no such thing, then moves on to learn another word.

GUNTER STANDS ON THE TOP RUNG OF A METAL LADDER, SCRAPING a web of pink chewing gum from the ceiling with a butter knife. How this keeps happening, nobody knows, but Excel once caught a kid standing atop the mini-carousel, stretching out his chewed-up bubblegum like it was pizza dough, then coiling it around a low-hanging light fixture. The kid's parents merely watched, as if witnessing an artistic genius in the making.

Gunter reaches, scrapes off the last strand of gum, lets it fall to the floor. "Bastard fucks," he says, and when he looks down to descend the ladder Excel accidentally makes direct eye contact. Before he bought The Pie, Gunter was a bouncer for a string of San Francisco strip clubs, and he looks more like a brawler than ever before; his neck is thicker, his chest bulges, and his T-shirt sleeves are so short they show new tattoos, a ring of blazing skulls around each bicep.

Excel takes a breath, steps forward, says hello.

Gunter looks down, squints at him, and tilts his head. "Well, son of a shit"—he gives a half laugh—"look who's back."

It's a warmer response than Excel expects. "The place looks nice."

"Then you got anuses for eyes." Gunter folds his arms, feet still firm on the top rung, unafraid to fall. "That gum down there? Been on the ceiling for three months. And nobody here does shit about it, so I'm the one that's gotta climb the goddamn ladder and clean it up. Is that how a CEO should start a business day?"

Excel shakes his head.

"We agree. So this makes me wonder: Are you here to scrape shit off the ceiling?" Excel takes that as his cue and nods, is about to ask for his job back, but before he can speak, Gunter wants to know where Excel gets the nerve to show his "jackass asshole face" after all the "bullshit toxic slander" he said the day he quit. Excel tries to answer but Gunter says, "No dickweed, I ain't done yet," and he lets out more profanity and names, some of which might almost be funny ("shit-wipe" is a new one), except for the fact that Z sits just one room away, trying to learn the language. Excel imagines walking out and taking Z with him, to a place where he can read his dictionary in peace.

"I'm sorry," Excel says.

Gunter folds his arms, biceps flexing. "For?"

"All of it. For everything I said."

"And?"

"And"—Excel gives himself a moment, a last chance to walk away, but knows he can't—"I'd like my job back."

"No."

"You're understaffed. You've got no cashiers. Maybe I can help."

Gunter puts a finger—his middle—on his chin, makes an exaggerated thinking face, says no again.

"You have a right to be angry with me," Excel says. "I was out of line."

"'Out of line.' Hm. Tell me *specifically* what was out of line."

"Everything. All of it."

"You want a job? Then climb up here"—he gives the top of the ladder a quick pound of the fist—"and you tell me to my face what you said."

The ladder is two-sided, sturdy enough, Excel hopes, to bear both their weight; if not, at least they'll come crashing down together. He climbs up slowly, and when he's one step away from being face-to-face with Gunter, he looks at the toes of his sneakers and imagines that the ground twelve feet beneath them isn't the red industrial rug of The Pie but actual earth instead—rocks and pebbles, burnt-orange dirt, the terrain of Hello City. He pauses for a moment, then ascends the final rung and looks at Gunter, tells him again what he'd told him nine months before—that he'd found a way out of Colma, a real opportunity, so no longer needed this dead-end, dumbass job, that three miserable years working for a prick like Gunter were finally—hallelujah! (it was the first time Excel had ever said the word)—over and done with. "What else?" Gunter says, and Excel looks down again, the ground seemingly farther than before. "And then I called you"—Excel takes a breath—"a man without a future." That was the line meant not merely to sting but to outright hurt, like the kick you give to someone already down: Gunter was forever lamenting his life, all the opportunities the universe denied him. "Here I am," he had once said, "surrounded by booms. Internet boom. Dot-com boom. Even this bullshit slow food boom. But what about me? Where's the Gunter boom, huh? What is it with people like us?" He'd said this at the start of a staff meeting, and by the time he finished, everything he said was a weepy blather. "I have no future," he said, his last coherent words. The entire staff was silent, unsure whether to comfort a boss they feared or get back to work and laugh behind his back later. Excel just stared at him and thought, *Don't let that be me.*

"And I guess that's it," Excel says. "That's what I remember. And I'm a shitty person for saying all those things. But I need my job back. So I'm sorry. Really."

Gunter looks up at the ceiling, licks his thumb, and wipes away a smudge of dirt, and the skulls on his arm seem to stare down at Excel. Below, two small boys enter the game room, divvying up a handful of gold tokens.

"You can have your job back," Gunter finally says. "Same pay as before."

Excel squeezes the sides of the ladder, a mix of relief and a sudden fear of heights. "Really?"

"Yeah. But it's like probation."

"Understood."

"And no overtime."

"Not a problem."

"And any tips, you split with me."

"Will do."

"You're gonna work weekends."

"Of course."

"And I get to hit you."

There's no smile on Gunter's face, just a look that says take it or leave it.

"Just one time," Gunter says. "In the gut. That shit you said the day you left, nobody ever talked like that to me. *Nobody*. Kinda knocked the wind out of me, tell you the truth. Seems like justice that I get to knock the wind out of you." He moves three rungs down, skips the rest and jumps to the ground, the thud of his landing reverberating through the ladder.

"Come on down," Gunter says. "Let's get this over with." He cracks his knuckles, and Excel thinks of his $10,000 debt to Hello City, figures this is the start of paying them back.

He begins his descent. Below, the two boys each drop a token into the Skee-Ball game. One looks Excel's way quickly, then gets back to the game. Excel has been hit before—he thinks of Maxima's spankings when he was growing up, the occasional smack to the head the times he got mouthy. But a punch to the gut, the fast full force of it— Excel has no idea what could happen. Maybe his breath—one single body-filling breath—will gush out, leaving him hollow, full of nothing but pain. Or maybe Gunter's fist goes so deep that Excel's organs— just for a moment—collide and squish together, all that cushioning blood and air between lost. Maybe he'll puke or bleed or both, hurt so much he'll weep. But all those scenarios are in the future; for now, Gunter has him against the wall as he pulls back his arm, making a fist, and there's nothing Excel can do besides stand there and take it, so he repeats to himself a thing he used to say in a moment such as this, a sad truth of life that might, for the time being, mean an escape from it. "Not here," he says, so softly he can barely hear himself. "I'm not here. I'm not really here."

6

Excel's tenth birthday began as all the ones before it: he blinked awake and found Maxima standing over him. "You're older," she said.

He knew the celebration ahead: A picnic by the sphinxes at Evergreen Lawn Cemetery. Subway sandwiches and Doritos. A single candle sunk halfway into a Hostess cupcake. He got up from the couch. "What time are we going to the cemetery?" he asked.

"No cemetery. Not this year."

He thought he was in trouble, that he'd done something wrong. "Then where?"

"San Francisco," she said.

Just ten miles from Colma, and Excel had been there only once. He must have been five or six, and despite a promise to ride the cable car, he ended up sitting all morning by a watercooler in the waiting room of some downtown office, while Maxima and Joker met with someone—they didn't say who or why—in another room. When the meeting ended, they went straight to the BART station and went back home, Maxima's face like a stone the whole ride over, and for days after that.

"Eat breakfast," she said, "then get dressed. Wear nice clothes, okay?" She patted his head, then walked over to the window, stared out.

He toasted a pan de sal and ate it with margarine and sugar, then went to Maxima's room and changed into a white polo shirt and blue corduroys, the best clothes he owned. He went to the bathroom and as he brushed his teeth he heard what sounded like Joker scolding Maxima in Tagalog so fast that Excel could follow only one phrase, which Joker said over and over. *Ang bata, ang bata.* The child, the child.

They stopped talking when Excel returned to the living room. Maxima was by the door, dressed in a black sweater and jeans, hair up in a small, tight bun, the red strap of her purse like a line across her body. She looked serious, like today was about business, but Joker was still in his pajamas and slippers. "You're not coming, Grandmaster?" Excel asked. Joker shook his head, then handed him a ten-dollar bill and a dollar coin, his usual birthday gift. Before Excel could thank him, Joker took hold of his shoulders, squeezed hard, and pulled up slightly, like he was trying to make Excel taller. He said something in Tagalog, looked at Maxima, then let him go.

They took BART to San Francisco and got off at the Powell Street station, took a long escalator up to street level, where dozens of tourists were already lined up for the cable car. "Can we?" Excel asked, pointing to the ticket booth, and Maxima said, "It's your birthday. Of course." They bought the tickets, waited in line for nearly an hour, then finally boarded a cable car so packed there was room for only Excel to sit; Maxima held on to a pole and stood on the edge.

The ride began slowly, flatly, but Maxima looked anxious, her lips moving, just barely; Excel guessed she was whispering an orasyon to herself, which made him think there was some kind of trouble ahead. *Stop looking like that*, he thought, and nearly said it, until the cable car suddenly jolted, and Excel could see how steep and high they were; if the brakes gave out, they would all slide backward downhill to their deaths.

The cable car climbed on, the whole city tilting and askew behind the straight line of Maxima. "Don't let go," he told her, holding the red strap of her purse, and she gave him a look that said, *Me? Let go? Puwede ba?*

The end of the line was Fisherman's Wharf, and they were the first to step off. The main drag was monotonous with souvenir shops and seafood restaurants, and Excel stopped only to look at the outdoor tanks crammed with lobsters and crabs, their claws bound in thick yellow rubber bands. For his birthday lunch, Maxima bought them two clam chowders served in bowls made of actual bread, a thing Excel had never seen. They ate on the curb, watched a man disguised as a bush reach out to scare unwitting passersby, as tourists laughed and took pictures. "Idiots," Maxima said. "You can see his feet under the leaves. How can anybody fall for that?" But Excel laughed at all the people who did, and Maxima even let him drop a quarter into the man's tip jar.

The chowder was fine but the bread bowls were soggy; they tossed them in the trash and moved on to Pier 39, pushed through crowds to get to the center, where a double-decker carousel started up, organ music loud and lights blinking. Excel noticed some of the horses had fish tails from the waist down. "I want to ride," he said.

"Later," she said, "first, we need to talk."

The feeling returned, that he'd done something wrong. "It's my birthday," he said, "I don't want to talk," but she took his wrist and led him to the other side of the pier, to an empty spot on the far end, overlooking floating platforms packed with sleeping sea lions.

They stood side by side against the metal rail. "You're ten years old now, so I'm going to tell you something," Maxima said. "And I don't want you to complain or whine or cry. Understand?"

"I don't cry," he said.

She looked over both shoulders, making certain no one was nearby, then back at Excel. "We're not really here," she said.

"Who's not really here?"

"You. Me. Us. We're not supposed to be here."

"Be where?"

She paused, like she couldn't name the place. "America," she finally said. "You and me"—she bent down to meet his face—"are TNT."

He pictured a stick of dynamite, the lit fuse, the explosion to come.

"It's what you call a Filipino who's not supposed to be here," she said. "TNT. It stands for 'tago ng tago.'"

"I don't understand you," he said.

"'Tago' means 'hiding'; 'ng' means 'and.' Tago ng tago. Hiding and hiding."

"We're not hiding."

"We are. Always."

"From who?"

She sighed, as though there were too many ways to answer. "Police. Government. Immigration."

"But I was born here," he said.

She shook her head.

"I was born *there*?" He meant the Philippines. She shook her head again.

Not here and not there meant nowhere. "But we have"—he searched for the term—"green cards. Inside your desk." He'd seen his before. A thumb-size photograph of his face, the numbers with endless digits, the Statue of Liberty, faded like a ghost.

"Peke," she said.

Another Tagalog word he didn't know. "'Peke'?"

"Fake."

He thought for a moment, like this was a problem he could solve. "Your passport. Don't you have a passport?"

"Sa Pilipinas lang," she said. "Doesn't mean anything in the States."

He looked out at the sea lions. "We're not American."

"No."

She looked suddenly tired and rubbed her eyes, tried to explain: she was eight months pregnant when she got rid of the eye patch–wearing son of a bitch for drinking away half her savings, then blowing the other half on the Manila cockfight circuit. Despite her films, despite a Dynamite-Star! Manila Movie Award, there were no more acting jobs for her, no stunt work, nothing. "And my only family was your Auntie Queenie, but she was a live-in maid in Saudi Arabia. Do you know how they treat Filipina maids out there? You think I'd do that to myself? To you? No way." Staying in the Philippines, unmarried and pregnant, was unacceptable.

Her best option was to call Joker. "Fifteen years, we didn't talk, and you know what he said when I called? 'Come to California. I'll help you.' That's *true family*, believe me. He wired the money for a plane ticket, and a week later I'm on my way to California. Thank god for Joker. My only hope. Like Princess Leia and Obi-Wan, di ba?" She smiled, like that was supposed to make Excel feel better and salvage what was left of his birthday.

"Then what happened?" Excel asked.

"You," she said. "You happened."

He was meant to be born here. "I wanted a hospital room with a view of the Golden Gate Bridge," she said. "Like in a movie I saw once.

But no. You"—she jabbed his shoulder softly with her pinky finger—
"you couldn't wait. You were born on the plane."

"On the plane?" Excel said.

"In the sky. Above the ocean."

He knew how the world worked: if you were born in America, you
were American; if you were born in the Philippines, Filipino. "So what
am I?" he asked.

"You"—she looked at him for a moment, blinked a few times,
as though she wasn't completely sure who she was speaking to—"I
don't know. I don't know what you are. Not yet." She brought up
the last visit to San Francisco, that day he'd spent in an office waiting room. She and Joker had met with a lawyer, hoping the circumstances of his birth might make him a citizen. "We paid that asshole
seven hundred dollars," she said, "just to tell us no." Excel's citizenship,
technically, was like Maxima's—Philippines. "But that's not home,"
she said, "this is."

She told him being TNT was why she couldn't get a driver's
license or a decent-paying job, why they couldn't leave the country
or cross California into another state, why their lives were the way
they were. And Excel wanted to tell her to close her mouth and stop
talking, that she was ruining his birthday, and she should go stand
somewhere else and let him watch the sea lions on his own.

Then he remembered his arm.

"Is that why"—he lifted his short sleeve, pointed to the raised puff
of hard skin just below his shoulder, the scar left from a bad fall on his
bike two years before. The cut was small but deep and bled nonstop,
and he reminded Maxima that she hadn't taken him to the emergency
room.

"I wanted to," she said, pulling down his sleeve, "but I couldn't.
Joker was in L.A. with his brother, and if I took you to the hospital
by myself, and if they asked for ID or a Social Security number or
something I didn't have, what if they found out? What if they took

you from me? I was scared." Excel had never heard Maxima admit she was scared, but he remembered the fear in her face as she sterilized the needle over the stove, then threaded it with dental floss, which she said would keep the wound shut. She pushed the needle through his skin, and when he screamed for her to stop, she told him to keep still, and what he thought was sweat running down her face was actually tears. The cut healed, eventually, and Joker said the scar was evidence of bravery, proof of strength. "A warrior wound, di ba?" he said, and Maxima nodded, tried to smile. But whenever he saw the scar he knew: *This isn't right*. Now he knew why.

He stepped away from the railing and turned to leave (where to, he didn't know), but Maxima took his wrist, pulled him close.

"Listen to me," she said, "and do as I say. No matter what, never tell anyone you're TNT. Understand?"

He sighed, nodded.

"*Understand?*" She took his other wrist, squeezed them both to the point of pain.

"I understand."

"You'd better. Because you don't want to end up like Lola NeeNee, the cookie lady. Remember her? She's here for thirty years and one day she makes a right turn on a 'No Turn on Red' sign, the cops pull her over, they see she has no papers, no green card. Nobody has seen her since." He'd almost forgotten her, the old Filipino woman who went door to door selling homemade coconut cookies out of a small, foil-lined laundry basket. She'd sometimes stop by and have coffee with Maxima and Joker, one of the few visitors they ever had. Now he imagined her alone on a curb somewhere, an empty laundry basket at her feet.

"If you tell," Maxima said, "we're all in trouble."

He promised he wouldn't. Then he asked, "Why did you bring me here?"

"For a better life. What else?"

"No. To San Francisco."

She loosened her grip, let go of his wrists. "I wanted you to have a nice birthday."

Below, the sea lions rolled off the platforms and into the water, one by one. "I want to ride the carousel," Excel said.

She gave him five dollars. He charged ahead and bought a ticket, got in an already-moving line and stepped on, curved around the carousel until he found a half horse, half fish. But instead of climbing on he just stood where he was and leaned against it. The ride started up, the revolutions of the carousel faster than he'd expected. He kept a firm hand on the line where the horse became fish, his arm rising and falling as he spun, and he looked out to see Maxima—there, not there, there, not there—until he just closed his eyes, and everything was gone.

They went back to Colma. Joker was on the couch when they entered the apartment, fighting sticks on his lap. "Alam ba?" he asked Maxima. "Yes, Grandmaster," Excel answered for her, "I know." He said nothing else, walked straight into Maxima's room and climbed out the window onto the fire escape, stepped onto the roof. *I'm hiding and hiding,* he thought, *TNT,* and he stayed there until sundown and well beyond.

Every few days for the next few weeks, Maxima, at random points in the afternoon and evening, would ask how school had gone, what he'd eaten for lunch, whom he'd spoken to, then finally get to the point. "Did you tell anyone?" It was like an endless quiz composed of the same single question with the same correct answer: "No." Eventually she stopped asking, but by then the question was wired into his brain, became its own kind of paranoia: because being TNT was the last thing he should ever confess, it remained at the forefront of his mind. He was a quiet kid who became quieter, often to the point of silence. In class, he spoke just enough to confirm his presence, learned the strategy of playing group games (dodgeball, kickball, freeze tag) without talking to other kids. Some days he'd skip lunch and sit at the far corner carrel in the library with a comic book, finish schoolwork in advance, or just put his head down and rest. What took effort and strategy became, as years went on, instinct and habit, a way of moving through the world. Tolerable, predictable, alone.

AT THE START OF NINTH GRADE, IN ENGLISH CLASS, EXCEL SHARED a desk with a Filipino kid named Renzo. He'd moved to Colma from L.A., was wiry and tall with black spiky hair tipped dark blue, and wore a leather wristband with metal studs; Excel wondered if he belonged to some kind of punk rock street gang. They never spoke, not until the day Excel saw, on the upper corner of Renzo's notebook, a sticker of an armadillo in a varsity sweater wearing a backpack.

"That's Junichi," Excel said, stunned that someone else knew of *You Don't Say, Junichi!* an obscure Japanese cartoon about teenage armadillos, infamous for its bad dubbing and awkward English translations.

Renzo looked at Excel right in the eye. "Shall we play *balls?*" he said, quoting one of the show's taglines. They started laughing, and that no one nearby understood what was so funny only made them laugh harder. "I've got the graphic novels in my locker," Renzo said, "if you're interested." Excel shrugged and said okay, and after school they went to the Target café and read through them, then continued to hang out afterward, cracking each other up with their favorite lines from the show ("You're giving us *happy time*, Junichi!")

They developed a routine. Three or four times a week after school, they'd split a two-for-one hot dog meal at Target, then walk around the store to screw with the merchandise (they'd stuff a pair of women's panties into a four-pack of men's underwear, stash toothpaste in the freezers behind the ice cream). Though Excel never invited him into the apartment, he'd occasionally bring Renzo to the roof, where they'd concoct their own Junichi story lines while watching planes taking off from SFO or throwing bits of rooftop gravel at the Old Hoy Sun Ning Yung headstones, four stories below. Sometimes they'd just sit without speaking, a silence that didn't bother Excel at all.

On the last Friday night before the end of ninth grade, Renzo, out of nowhere, thanked Excel for a good year. "I didn't have a lot of friends in L.A.," he said, "didn't think I'd have any up here."

They were sitting on the edge of the roof, legs dangling over the edge, and Renzo's honesty made Excel a little tense; mostly, their time was spent making each other laugh. He stood up, pretended to stretch his back. "For sure," he said. "It's cool you moved up here."

Renzo nodded, went quiet. "What if I told you something," he finally said, "something nobody knows."

"Nobody?"

Renzo shook his head.

Excel bent down and picked up a piece of gravel from the ground, wondering about the moment to come. Of course he knew there were other TNTs in the world, but he'd never actually met another before, and to have that person be his friend—his closest? his only?—seemed almost fated, that rare bit of luck that never seemed to come his way. Renzo's confession would prompt his own (it only seemed fair), and he wondered how he'd say it, if he'd look him in the eye, or maybe stare at one of the departing planes as he spoke the truth.

"Okay"—Excel took a breath—"but if you do, then I need to tell you something, too."

"Deal," Renzo said. He took several breaths deep breaths, as if about to plunge himself underwater.

Someone like me, Excel thought, *finally*.

"I think I'm gay," Renzo said.

Excel said nothing.

Renzo turned to face him. "Does that bother you?"

Excel threw bits of gravel into the air. He thought for a moment; it didn't bother him, not at all. And he was glad that Renzo had confided in him when he'd confided in no one else. But Renzo's coming out felt like a letdown, an opportunity lost; this was not the trade of secrets Excel had hoped for, the truth he'd needed to hear. He knew a deal was a deal, that it was his turn to tell the truth, but he could feel himself reverting back to the promise he'd made to Maxima, who was only two floors below.

"It doesn't bother me," he said.

Renzo looked almost expectant, like there was more Excel should be saying. "Okay then," he said, "your turn."

"It's nothing." He shook his head. "I have nothing to tell."

"*Nothing.* After what I told you?" He stood up. "What were you going to say? Tell me."

Excel picked up more gravel, wishing for more time to figure out the best thing to say. "I wasn't going to say anything. I only said that to get you to talk. That was lame, I know. But I'm glad you told me, and if you want, I won't tell anyone. Your secret's safe, okay?"

"Oh." Renzo looked at the ground and nodded, paced back and forth a few times. He bent down and instead of a single pebble he grabbed a handful of gravel and threw it at the sky. "This game is pointless," he said, then climbed down the fire escape.

Renzo didn't call that weekend, or the rest of the week. When Excel finally reached him, Renzo said he was busy with a summer job, and that he'd be spending the second half of the summer down in L.A. "To spend time with my friends," he said. The conversation would be their last, and Excel spent the rest of the summer alone, watching TV, sleeping late, hanging out on the roof. Near the end of summer, Excel tried calling Renzo once more, but his father answered, explained that Renzo would be transferring to Saint Bishop's in Oakland for the fall, a school so prestigious and rigorous that he wouldn't have time for socializing with old friends. But in the last week before school began, Excel spent a few afternoons in the Target café hoping Renzo might show up, *Junichi* graphic novels in hand. He never did. The following Monday, Excel was alone again, a sophomore.

He was, more than ever, resolved to never tell anyone he was TNT. The fear of telling the truth had wrecked his only friendship, and what would have come of it anyway? Even if Renzo had been TNT himself, what would they have done? Started a club? Joined forces and marched on the capitol steps in Sacramento, demanding their right to stay? Maybe it would have been better if Renzo had kept the secret to himself. Or, instead of the truth, Excel should have made up a secret, said he was the son of Filipino gang members, had an incurable disease, or said he was gay too. Maybe then, Renzo would still be here.

And yet he couldn't forget the feeling, that surge of fear and possible relief that had come with almost saying it: *I'm TNT.* It was a peculiar energy that sometimes possessed him, made him want to run down the street as fast as he could, scream his head off, punch and take down whatever stood in his way.

Now, with Gunter's big hand pressing hard into his chest, pinning him to the wall, Excel is desperate for that energy again. There's no point in fighting back—Excel would go down in a second—so he just waits to be hit, for the very center of himself to collapse from the force of the blow to come. "I'm not really here," he says to himself, lips barely moving, but loud enough for him to hear.

Gunter's fist stays frozen in midair, just above eye level.

"Nah," Gunter says, "not even worth it." He drops his hand, steps back. "You can have your job back. Shift starts now. Here"—he hands Excel the butter knife—"there's more gum on the ceiling. Finish where I left off. And welcome back." He walks out of the game room and Excel stays where he is, his racing heart slowing down, when suddenly bells go off and a red light whirls and wails like a siren. Excel looks up and sees that the boys playing Skee-Ball are scoring big points, the prize tickets snaking out of their slots and coiling on the floor. They're high-fiving each other, jumping up and down, celebrating in a language Excel doesn't know, but he thinks he understands what they're saying—*we win, we win, we win.*

7

Gunter makes Excel work a double shift for a single shift's pay. "Consider it part of your atonement," he says, overenunciating *atonement* like it's a new word acquired from Z's dictionary. Excel follows him to the break room, where Gunter loans him a uniform, a black polo shirt with a picture of a spyglass on the back. "You'll have to order your own, at your cost of course," Gunter says.

"No problem," Excel says, then notices the name embroidered on the left front pocket. "It says 'Lydia.'"

"Better than your real name." Gunter points to the clock. "Bathrooms are waiting. Chop chop."

Gunter considers The Pie Who Loved Me's "A" grade from the Health Department one of his great achievements (though he'd written over a dozen fake Yelp reviews himself, praising the restaurant's cleanliness—"every toilet is FIVE STARS!"), and on the day he quit, Excel swore he'd never clean a bathroom for Gunter again. But for the next three hours, he scrubs every urinal and toilet, the floors, the walls, and the doors of each stall, even the inside and outside of the toilet paper and paper towel dispensers. When he's done, he heads to the kitchen to do more of the same. Three guys are already working when he enters (two on food prep, one at the sink). Excel doesn't know them, but from their glances and whispers, he's guessing they know him—the big-mouth hotshot who'd tried putting Gunter in his place nine months before.

Someone in dark glasses and headphones singing "Little Red Corvette" enters, stops when he sees Excel. It's Reynaldo, the assistant manager and Gunter's second-in-command. He was there when Excel told Gunter off the day he quit, and Excel remembers the smirk on his face as he shook his head, like he knew Excel would one day be crawling back.

"S'up, Excel," Reynaldo says, "back for more?" He gives a slight kick to the toe of Excel's shoe, walks away, and laughs.

EXCEL'S SHIFT ENDS AT NINE BUT HE WORKS UNTIL TEN, AND ONCE outside, he can smell the day on himself—ammonia and bad cheese, Windex, a hint of what he swears is expired pepperoni. He wants to stand like a scarecrow in the middle of the parking lot, let the wind air out his clothes. But Colma is too cold tonight. He puts on his hoodie and zips it all the way up, starts toward the apartment.

He checks the time on his phone—10:19 p.m.—and figures, since his phone is already out of his pocket, maybe it would be okay to call Sab. To say hello and how are you—he'd be fine with that. Leave a voice mail, if nothing else.

She picks up on the fourth ring. "I was asleep," she says.

"Oh. Sorry." He thinks of Sab's back against his chest, the two of them cocooned in a blanket in the back of the bus.

"Okay, I lied. I'm in bed, but sitting up. I just said that to make you feel bad. Did it work?"

"Kinda."

"Well, now I'm the one who's sorry. Where are you?"

He walks down Serramonte Boulevard, night traffic loud enough that he has to plug his other ear to hear Sab. "Walking back to the apartment," he says. "I just got off work."

"You got a job already? Where?"

"The Pie."

"You're kidding."

"It's money. Gunter even let me work extra hours."

"I thought you said Gunter was a grade-A asshole tyrant."

"He still is. But it's my only option right now. It's a little tougher for me, getting a job." He reaches the intersection, misses the walk signal. "It's weird, knowing that you know."

"You regret telling me?"

"You regret knowing?" He'd told Sab he was TNT when she'd told him she was pregnant. Was it the best timing? The worst? Maybe it was just inevitable. What else could he have said , other than the one thing Sab didn't know about him?

"If it's the truth," she says, "then I should know."

"Then I don't regret telling you."

"So that's settled. But I thought we said no calls. I haven't made a decision, and I don't want any pressure. Not even a discussion, not yet."

"I'm not pressuring. I just wanted to check in, see how you're feeling."

"I'm fine. Same as when you last saw me."

That was two days before, when she dropped him outside the Greyhound station in El Centro, the morning so dark he can't quite remember her face in their last moment together.

"What about you?" she asks. "How is it, being back?"

"It feels wrong. But I'll survive."

"Well, I'm glad you made it back safely. How was the bus ride?"

"Long. Boring. A woman gave me a hard-boiled egg."

"Did you eat it?"

"I meant to, but I left it on the bus. I hope no one sits on it."

Sab laughs a little, then yawns. Or does she pretend to yawn? He's seen her do it before, those nights when Lucia would yammer on and on, and Sab would pretend she was suddenly exhausted so they could get away. "I'm sleepy," she says, "for real this time. I'm going to hang up, okay?"

The traffic lights change, walk signal missed again. "Okay," he says, "you hang up first," and she does.

EXCEL REACHES THE FRONT GATE OF LA VILLA AURELIA, REMEMBERS he still has no keys. For the second time, he walks down the block and climbs over the wall of Old Hoy Sun Ning Yung, tripping over stubby headstones as he crosses the cemetery to the back fence. He finds the tear in the chain link, squeezes through, and by the time he climbs the fire escape and crawls through his window, he's ready for bed.

But there are voices in the kitchen. Maxima, someone else.

"Hindi ko alam. Siguro panahon. Ayoko na."

"Sigurado ka? Paano kung gumanda ang buhay?"

"Siguro. Hindi natin alam kung ano ang nangyayari sa hinaharap. Hindi ka makakasiguro sa buhay."

They talk so fast that Excel can't keep up—something about life and unpredictability? About knowing when enough is enough? Mostly he listens for his name, the way he would whenever he'd catch a whispery conversation between Maxima and Joker; to hear "Excel" in a stream of Tagalog usually meant some kind of trouble. But nobody says it, and when he's 100 percent sure that the conversation has zero to do with him, he goes to the kitchen.

Maxima is at the table, drinking key lime wine coolers with Roxy, whom, for a second, Excel almost doesn't recognize. Her face is thinner, more angular, and though she's dressed in a loose blouse and jeans, Excel sees that she now has cleavage and breasts.

She'd arrived in America as Rocky, but has been Roxy for as long as Excel has known her, and had started bringing up medical transitioning in the past few years. "That's the dream," she'd said. Though trained as a nurse in the Philippines, she couldn't get hired in the States, and her cocktail waitress job couldn't pay enough for the changes she'd hoped to make. She always said she came to America to become herself; now she looks happier than he's ever seen her.

"Look who's back." Roxy stands, hugs Excel. "Pogi pogi still," she says, patting his cheeks. "Baby face, di ba?"

Maxima finishes the rest of her wine cooler, wipes her lip with her knuckles. "He's not a baby."

"You look great, Roxy," Excel says.

"It's the lip gloss." She laughs, then points with pride at the places on her body where she's had work done. "Work in progress, right?" She says she owes it to Maxima, who convinced her to go for it, gave her money to help her get started, and helps pay for her hormone therapy now.

He thinks of the money he needs himself. "That's really generous of her," he says.

Roxy nods. "Without her . . ." She turns to Maxima and squeezes her arm, eyes suddenly teary.

"Tama na," Maxima says, handing her a tissue. "There's enough tears in the world."

Roxy dabs her eyes, perks up. "Excel is going too, right?"

"Going where?" Excel asks.

Roxy nudges Maxima. "Ano ba? Show him the paper."

"Fine." Maxima pulls a piece of paper from her purse, gives it to Excel. It's a flyer with Philippines and American flags side by side, clip art of a movie projector in between. "3rd Annual Full-On Filipino Film Festival (F.O.F.F.F.)," it says. "Celebrating the BEST in Filipino Film Cult Classix!"

"Look what's showing the last night," Roxy says.

Excel looks at the bottom of the flyer. "*Ang Puso Ko VS. Ang Baril Mo*," he reads, doubtful of his pronunciation. "That means, *My Heart VS.—*"

"*Your Gun*," Maxima says. "That was my biggest movie, and they're doing a screening, first time in the States. Maybe you want to come with us. Maybe not. It's up to you."

Roxy gives him a look like there's only one right way to respond.

"Of course," he says. "If I'm not working, I'll definitely go."

"Request the day off in advance," Roxy says, the same look on her face. Excel nods, says he'll do that.

Roxy points to the microwave oven clock, says she needs to get home. She reaches into a canvas tote bag on the floor, gives a quick look at Excel, then at Maxima, who says under her breath, "Ya ina, it's fine," then pulls out a stack of manila folders, sets them on the table. Maxima takes out a letter-size envelope from her purse and hands it to Roxy, then takes out a Safeway paper bag, fills it with daikon radish and Japanese eggplant from the refrigerator, tins of sardines from the cupboard, gives the bag to Roxy. Roxy refuses but Maxima insists, says the hormones are making her too skinny, and points at the thirty-pound sack of jasmine rice on the floor. "Excel, take that to Roxy's car?" He says sure, picks it up and hoists the sack of rice over his shoulder, and follows Roxy out the door.

He loads the groceries into the trunk, and just as he's about to say good-night she takes a cigarette from her purse, tells him to wait. "I have a question," she says. "Talagang asshole kaba?"

He thinks she's joking at first, but her face is serious. "Excuse me?"

"*Why. Are you. An asshole.*" She lights up, takes a drag. "Nine months. No visits to Maxima. No calls."

"I didn't have cell service."

"No e-mails."

"I e-mailed."

"Two times? Three? That's the same as never."

"It wasn't easy to communicate back there."

"Bullshit. So many nights, she waited by the phone. She thought you were lost in the desert, or that you were kidnapped by gangs. She even thought maybe you fell in quicksand! And where's this 'back there' anyway? What happened to you?"

"Nothing happened to me."

"Then why did you *disappear?*" She exhales smoke and the word seems to linger in the air with it, demanding a response, as though Excel had literally vanished and not simply left. He imagines himself, there one second, gone the next. Or he just fades away, like a signature written in disappearing ink, growing fainter and fainter, until all that remains is paper.

"I'm going to be a father," he says.

Roxy takes a longer drag this time. "Oh. Well, shit."

"Yeah. It's a lot to handle."

She steps closer, lowers her voice. "Who's the mom?"

"Sab. My girlfriend."

"Does Maxima know?"

He shakes his head.

"Ano ba? You have to tell her."

Excel had considered it, on the Greyhound back to San Francisco from El Centro, in a moment when he was missing Joker, and thinking how much Maxima missed him, too. But he worried she'd use the baby to their advantage, a means to a green card, a way toward citizenship. She's said things like that before—*Find a girl, get married, then you'll be okay.* Like it's up to Sab—or this baby—to fix the mess they're in.

"I'll tell her," he says, "but not yet."

"Who else knows?"

"Just you."

"Just me? Oh, I don't like this secret-secret thing, Excel." Roxy looks in the direction of the apartment. "But okay. I won't say anything. For now."

"It's why I'm back," he says. "I need to make money, need to prepare. This baby's going to change everything."

"Are you staying in Colma?"

"We haven't figured that out."

She finishes her cigarette, flings it into the street. "Why are you telling me this?"

"I don't know. Maybe because you called me an asshole. You were being honest, thought I'd be honest too. Maybe I just wanted to say it out loud."

"I get that." Roxy reaches into her purse, takes out the envelope Maxima gave her. "Here," she says, pulling out bills. "It's not much, but it can help."

"She gave you that," Excel says. "That's yours."

"That was payment, actually. I help her out with, you know, her business."

"The files?"

"The files. The accounts. Money transfers. I'm like her secretary. Or her accountant, maybe?" She laughs at the thought, then holds out five twenties.

"I can't take that."

"Don't be an asshole. Take it."

He waits a moment, feigning reluctance. "Okay, you win. Thanks." He takes the bills and folds them, puts them in his pocket.

A car approaches, high beams shining, momentarily flooding the two of them in light.

"I was wondering," Excel says, "how much money does she have? How much does she make off these guys?"

Roxy looks suddenly uncomfortable. "I don't really know. Some months are good, some not. You're planning to ask her for some?"

He shakes his head. "I'll figure this out on my own."

Roxy nods, though she looks unconvinced. She reaches into the envelope, offers another twenty-dollar bill, and Excel accepts.

BACK IN THE APARTMENT, EXCEL FINDS THE MANILA FOLDERS STACKED neatly on the kitchen table directly under the light, as if meant to be read by whoever might find them. He runs his thumb down the edges of the folder tabs, flicking through the names—Akers, Chavez, Daubmann, Foley, Haschemeyer, Horack, Kamm, Livings, Ng, Roderick, Shea, Tigay, Watkins.

Excel checks the hallway, hears Maxima belting out a Tagalog love song in the shower. He goes back to the folders and opens the one on top, finds a sheet of paper that looks like a questionnaire.

NAME:	Donald "Donny" Akers
AGE:	53
START:	2/23
END:	5/20
CITY:	Tampa, Florida
OCCUPATION:	Quality control (motherboards? Computer parts?)
EDUCATION:	Junior college (2 yrs)
STATUS:	Divorced (3 Xs!!!)
CHILDREN:	None
OBJECTIVE:	"Lake house retirement—Adderondax (???)"
DREAMS:	To find true love
TRAGEDY:	Lost first house in hurricane
FAVORITE FOOD:	Pepperoni pizza
FAVORITE FILM:	"Field of Dreams"

FAVORITE TV SHOW:	"MacGyver" (???)
FAVORITE MUSIC:	Classic rock
DEFINITION OF LOVE:	"It all starts with trust"
GREATEST FEAR:	Die alone
GREATEST HOPE:	"Hit the jackpot" (lottery)
MOTTO:	NONE
LOOKING FOR:	Filipina, 25–35 yo, never married, no kids, "virgin would be nice" (asshole)

He flips to the next page, the top of which reads "NOTES/ COMMENTS."

FEB 28

2nd meeting. Better than 1st. More open this time, not so nervous (the beer helps?) Says what he wants: young, Catholic. "God comes first." Some education is good but not a req. Next time: quote bible? In Eng and Tagalog?

MAR 5

3rd meeting. D has three beers in one hour. Loose and easy. Likes to tell gay jokes (asshole talaga!). Tells salary—$70k a year (CONFIRM!!!) . House cost $200k. Has BMW and Mercedes. "Mid-life crisis." Mayabang talaga!

MAR 9

Same, same.

MAR 17

He laughs if I laugh. He cries if I cry. We are <u>CONNECTING</u>. First wife is Barb. He cheated but she was "loveless" so not his fault. Married when they were 17, divorced 14 years later. Barb was not "true love." D says: love is not a luxury. Love is a necessity. Tries to turn this into debate. Ano ba? Whatever. Let him win

MAR 22

Cont. discussion on love: luxury or necessity. So boring. Asks to
see my tits. Asshole. I say no way. I'm not like that. I'm a good
girl. He says he respects that. "Just testing you."

APR 2

Sleepy, tired. Had a fever but let him talk, let him talk, then good-
night, good-bye, I love you and he believes

The notes go on for pages and pages, the whole folder like a
psychological profile, or what Excel imagines could be a therapist's
notes—brief summaries of sessions with patients, annotated with her
own analysis. He wonders if Maxima keeps a folder about him, what
kinds of notes might fill the pages inside. What would it mean to her
that he has a recurring dream of getting bitten by a white cat? Or that
once, in tenth grade, on an unexplainable impulse, he stole cash from
his teacher's wallet? Or that his goal in life is to live in a bus in the
California desert? What are the annotations for those facts? What is
the final analysis?

"That's mine," Maxima says. Excel turns, sees her standing in the
doorway in a 49ers T-shirt and striped pajama bottoms, a red towel
turbaned on her head.

"They were sitting right there. I was curious, sorry." He closes the
folder. "You've gotten organized."

"Too many men," she says, "too hard to keep track. The files help."

"Why did Roxy have them?"

"She types them up."

"Types them up? For what?"

Maxima looks impatient with his questions, though he's asked so
few. "I take notes by hand. She types them for me, and I review them
before important talks. And for all that, I pay Roxy. I need the help,
she needs the money. Ano ba, Excel? Am I under arrest? Is this an

interrogation?" She pulls the towel from her head and snaps it like a whip, hangs it on a chair to dry. "You moved to the desert, to make"— she uses finger quotes again—"'important discoveries.' But you're not the only one. I can make discoveries, too." She opens the refrigerator. "Gutom ka ba? Roxy brought Taco Bell."

He didn't think he was hungry, but realizes that he hasn't eaten since this morning, and Taco Bell actually sounds good. "What'd she bring?"

"Three Seven-Layer Burritos, two Mexican Pizzas."

"Mexican Pizzas. Joker's favorite."

"We'll bring one to him tomorrow."

"To who?" He knows what she means, but asks anyway.

"To Joker, of course. We're going to see him tomorrow."

"You mean, see his grave." He hates the way she says it—*We're going to see him*—as if he'll be there on the grass, waiting to welcome them.

"No, smart mouth. I mean Joker. I don't visit grass and dirt. I visit *him*. And you're coming too. Nine months without visiting him. That's a sin."

He wants to say no, that he wants to see Joker by himself. It's not a fight worth having. "Strange," he says, looking at their photo on the refrigerator. "I don't remember taking this."

She looks at the photo. "We didn't."

"What do you mean? We're standing right there."

"You weren't there that day. Just Joker and me. A stranger took that picture for us." She reaches for the photo, holds it up to his Excel's face. "Photoshop," she says, "I asked Roxy to put you in. I wanted a picture together, the three of us."

"This moment," he says, looking closely, "it never happened?"

"Never," she says.

He takes the photo from between her fingers, holds it up to the light. "I thought it was real," he says, then puts it back on the refrigerator.

"Tomorrow," she says, "we'll leave at nine a.m. sharp."

"Can we do ten?"

"Fine, whatever, ten o'clock." She takes the Seven-Layer Burritos and pops them in the microwave, says nothing as the food heats. But then she looks at Excel, squinting, as if he's out of focus and not quite there, just like in the picture. "Ano ba," she says, pointing at the name on his work shirt, "why are you 'Lydia'?"

The plan was to devote the first full day in Hello City to cleaning, unpacking, settling into life inside the bus. Sab swept and mopped, Excel wiped down windows, inside and out. Their clothes fit easily into the metal trunk, and they figured out how to use the generator and the propane stove, learned to tolerate the outhouse.

They moved the two-person table to the middle of the bus, next to the bookcase, which Sab filled with things Excel didn't know she owned—a stack of vinyl records (he'd heard of Johnny Cash and the Cure, but didn't know who the Ramones or the Sex Pistols were) and a Spice Girls CD; a copy of *The Anarchist's Cookbook* ("It was part of a costume," she said) and a Lonely Planet guidebook for Kyoto, the city where her mother was born ("One day," she said, "we're gonna go," and Excel just nodded); a skull candle holder and a Princess Leia action figure, which she'd shoplifted from Toys "Я" Us when she was ten. She'd packed them all in a large shoebox and was about to break it down when she froze. "My mom," she said, scanning the bus. "Her picture." She went through her emptied bags, searched through the trunk, checked in and around the bed.

"I forgot it," she said. "How could I have done that?"

Excel had seen it before, a small black-and-white photo of her mother as a high school senior back in Japan, dressed in a school uniform, diploma in hand. "You'll call your aunt and have her send it," he said. "It'll be here in a week, okay?" He pulled her close and kissed her temple, then noticed the time on the alarm clock on the floor beside the bed. It was just past eleven a.m., the bus looked bare and clean, yet they'd unpacked everything they'd brought. He wondered what he might have forgotten too, if there was a lost or misplaced thing he couldn't remember. He thought of their fourteen-hour drive from Colma to Hello City, imagined a small box somehow tumbling out of the trunk and rolling onto the freeway, still there.

At noon, Lucia came by with BLTs and a map. "Eat, then explore," she said. The map was a xeroxed copy, hand drawn and nowhere near to scale, and Hello City looked like a diamond made up of four smaller diamonds, north and south, east and west. Most people were in North Diamond (Lucia included) while South Diamond was full of artists, living in group trailers and minicommunes. West Diamond was the way in, the welcome sign at its tip. East Diamond, which was also called the Outerlands, was a few hours' walk from there, and populated by those who came to Hello City with no desire to be part of it. "It's all drug users, sex offenders, general weirdos," Lucia said. "Keep your distance, they'll keep theirs."

In the center of the map was a black square, the symbol for the Square, the town center of Hello City. "You want to fit in? You want to belong?" Lucia said, as if issuing a challenge. "Then go there. Get to know the place. It's the way to be a good Hello City citizen." She wasn't looking at Excel when she said it—*citizen*—but he felt self-conscious, a twinge of guilt. He'd meant to tell Sab he was TNT before they left for Hello City, had even planned to tell her at Joker's grave—what better place to tell a person what you were, than in the exact spot where you'd first met? But when the moment came, just two days before leaving Colma, the sight of Joker's tombstone, knowing all he'd done to give Maxima and Excel the life they had, made telling the truth too risky, the aftermath too uncertain. Sab, he knew, wouldn't tell anyone, but the lingering possibility was undeniable: What if she did?

He wouldn't tell her, not yet. Out of practicality, out of safety. And maybe out of loyalty: to admit what he was, was to admit what Maxima was, too.

THE SQUARE WAS LIKE A CROSS BETWEEN A FARMERS' MARKET AND A garage sale. There was a booth that sold onions, potatoes, and a dozen different kinds of squash, another that sold supermarket rejects—dented canned goods, expired boxes of pasta and cereal. A larger booth called the B&Q sold everything, no matter what it was, for a buck and a quarter. On the other side was a long row of assorted junk spread out on blankets laid on the ground—light fixtures, doorknobs, souvenir shot glasses from all fifty states. One blanket was covered with doll heads and bullet casings, nothing more. There were two food carts (Sammy's sold sandwiches, Hot Food sold hot food), and an outdoor Internet café called Beans!, which had four computer terminals that looked like they were from 1992. There was a library (a green tent full of paperbacks on shelves made of milk crates), a wellness center (a massage chair tucked under a beach umbrella), and a booth with a sign that simply said REPAIRS, though what kinds of things could be fixed wasn't clear. On the other side of the Square was a small stage, a raised platform covered in Astroturf with strings of lights crisscrossing above.

The day was warm, already too bright. Excel bought a twenty-five cent coffee and sat in the shade at Beans! while Sab went to the B&Q. She picked up random items—a rusted desk lamp, an iron, a boomerang—and inspected each one, like an appraiser trying to determine its value. She was wearing what she'd worn the day they met—army jacket, black T-shirt—and for a second, for reasons he didn't know, he imagined not knowing her. Would he guess she was a citizen of Hello City, or assume she was new, that she'd arrived only yesterday? Arrival, he realized, was utterly foreign to him—he'd never really come from somewhere else before.

He thought of Maxima's first days in America. How the new weather felt on her face, her skin. What the change in time zones did to her sleep. If her first time in a supermarket overwhelmed her, if she understood the value of US dollars versus Philippine pesos. Except for the two trips to San Francisco, he'd only really seen her in Colma—at the cemetery, walking along the strip malls, in the cramped rooms of their apartment.

One of the Beans! computer terminals was free. He went to it, opened the browser, and composed a quick e-mail.

I'm here now. I'm fine. More soon.

It was his first time e-mailing Maxima—he'd never been gone before—and he wasn't sure if the message was enough, if it was too direct, or all she needed to know.

He looked up and saw Sab approach. He hit Send, closed the browser.

"Look what I bought," she said, then held out what looked like a small metal octopus the size of a lemon, its tentacles made of tiny bent spoons. "It's a cool souvenir, right?"

"Right," he said, though Sab, he thought, was wrong. He'd never traveled, but it was his understanding that you bought souvenirs from places you visited or passed through, not from the place you meant to call home.

In the middle of the Square was a posting board, where people placed ads for upcoming events, ride shares into towns, even personals (someone had written "I like sex, you like sex, call me" on a hot pink Post-it). But most were help-wanted ads, various odd jobs available in Hello City, and Excel needed one fast; they'd arrived with less than five hundred dollars between them, and Sab would be making only $150.00 a week helping Lucia with Pink Bubble. They had enough to start, but not much beyond that.

There was a help-wanted ad for solar panel installation, another looking for assistance with Internet hookup. Someone needed hypnotherapy and life coaching, someone else was looking for a person to simply hold them for occasional thirty-minute sessions ("Not that one," Sab said). All the jobs paid in cash, none required specific experience or even a résumé, and, because this was Hello City, no form of ID was required. During high school and in the summers between, Excel would apply for the most straightforward of jobs—restaurant busboy, salesclerk, bowling alley custodian—and the few he was actually offered were invariably sabotaged in the actual hiring, by all the forms of identification he couldn't provide. Only once did he try to fight: he'd applied for a sales position at Kadabra's, a magic shop that opened in Colma at the start of his senior year. No magic experience required, and any sleight of hand necessary for in-store demonstrations could be learned on the job. During the interview, the storeowner, an older gentleman with thick silver hair and jet black eyebrows, mentioned he was from Jordan, a country Excel had heard of only the week before, when he happened to see a TV documentary on the ancient city of Petra. "I visited Jordan once,"

Excel lied. "Petra is awesome. *Everyone* should visit Petra before they die." The storeowner smiled, impressed with Excel's worldliness, and called that evening to offer him the job. Excel showed up at the store the next morning and filled out the W-4 form, but paused at the box asking for his Social Security number. He considered writing a phone number down instead, or the numerical dates of important historical events; maybe inputting those numbers into whatever computer the IRS used might let the form somehow pass through undetected. But Excel chickened out, left it blank. "You forgot," the storeowner said, pointing out the missing Social Security number. "I didn't," Excel said, "I just don't have one." The storeowner looked confused, asked why not. "I just don't," Excel said. The storeowner suggested speaking to his mother or father about it, in case he was mistaken, but Excel shook his head, said, "Nope, no mistake," and continued filling out the form anyway. "They're just numbers," he said, sweat building on his neck. The storeowner reached out, put a calming hand on Excel's shoulder, then gently took the W-4 form from his hand. He gave Excel a look that seemed to say, *I understand what you mean*, but there was nothing he could do to help. "It's just a number," Excel repeated. "I can do this job without a number. Please?" He didn't know why the job mattered so much—he didn't care about magic or illusions—but he'd somehow convinced himself that getting this job might be a sign of good things to come, the critical pivot toward a more promising future.

"You try again," the storeowner said, "next time." As a kind of consolation, he gave Excel a pair of X-ray glasses, and wished him the very best of luck.

Standing in the Square, looking through the various kinds of help people wanted, Excel didn't think he'd need that kind of luck, not here. All anybody wanted was for you to show up, do the work asked of you and do it well, get paid for it.

At the bottom of the posting board, Excel saw a green piece of paper with "ASAP" written on it. He bent down, read the rest. "E-mail SouthDRed@hotmail.com if interested. Lift stuff, move stuff, I'll give you $$."

"I can do that," Excel said.

9

The mattress springs of Joker's bed poke Excel's back, no matter which way he tries to sleep. He's awake all night, even by dawn. He sits up, looks out his window. There's no sunrise to see from here, just the slow lift of gray from the headstones of Old Hoy Sun Ning Yung. Those first days in Hello City, he'd wake early enough to watch everything go from pitch black to a day almost unbearably bright.

He lies back down, finally dozes off when Maxima pounds on his door. "It's almost ten!" she says. "Who sleeps this late? Nobody, that's who. Wake up!"

He showers, gets dressed. Maxima is by the front door, all in black, and she gives Excel an up-and-down look of utter disapproval. "You can't see Joker looking like that. Ano ba? You look like a home-less. And why is the happy face drunk?"

"I don't look like 'a homeless.'" He looks down at his black Nirvana T-shirt, the yellow smiley face logo with X's for eyes and a hanging tongue, bought at the Square for $1.25 at the B&Q. "My clothes got a little worn in the desert. I wasn't exactly going to four-star restaurants out there."

She mutters in Tagalog, something about Excel and what he knows or doesn't know, he's not exactly sure. She buttons her jacket, grabs her purse. "We'll stop at the good Target on the way, get you a shirt there. Let's go."

They leave the apartment, make their way toward the Target in Colma (Joker and Maxima had always called it "the good Target" since it was closer, the bathrooms were supposedly cleaner, and for a time an elderly Filipina woman working the express line gave them discounts on nondiscounted items). When they get to the store, she gives Excel a fifty-dollar bill. "Joker wants us to look nice when we see him. So buy something with long sleeves. Something dark and *clean*. And bring me back my change. We'll meet out here in thirty minutes."

"I'll be done in twenty." He takes the money, walks off.

Target always makes Excel think of Joker. Joker loved the store, could spend hours, sometimes half a day, pushing a cart through each department, up and down every aisle. He liked keeping track of which items were new and which were discontinued, and he especially liked comparison shopping, pitting name brands against the generic Target brand, and reporting his findings. "Old Spice shaving cream?" he'd say. "Four dollars and ninety-nine cents. Rip-off, talaga. Pero the Target shaving cream? Two dollars. And guess how much, the eight pack of Charmin?" He would even point out pricing inconsistencies to the red-vested Target employees, explaining to them that he was a "concerned consumer," though he rarely bought a thing beyond the essentials; an occasional bag of Kit Kats or Starburst for Excel was Joker's only splurge.

There's just one clearance rack in the men's department. Excel searches through, finds a gray button-up shirt with long sleeves, a men's small. He takes it off the hanger, walks over to the three-way mirror and tries it on. Though it feels all right in the chest, the shirt sags over his shoulders and the sleeves run past his knuckles, the shirt-tails droop to his thighs. In the mirror, reflecting from three sides, he looks like a boy playing dress-up.

He rolls up the sleeves, tucks in the shirt. Good enough.

He walks back toward the entrance, passes racks of kids' clothes, when he sees the Nirvana drunk smiley face, same as his own T-shirt, but brand-new and tiny. He picks it up, sees that it's a one piece ("novelty onesie" the tag says), and possibly the smallest piece of clothing he has ever held. 0–3 MONTHS, the tag says. Strange, Excel thinks, that clothes can be sized according to how much time you've been alive.

He slides the onesie from the hanger, lays it flat against his palm. So tiny, nearly weightless. Excel has never held a baby, isn't sure he's ever wanted to. But if Sab wants to have it, and if he and Sab get back together, he can imagine the baby wearing the Nirvana onesie, and maybe Sab could get a matching shirt, too. The three of them together, drunk smiley faces on their chests.

Carefully, he puts the onesie back on the hanger, returns it to the rack. *Father*, he thinks, walking toward the entrance, the same route he'd once walked with Joker. *I am a father. Might be, should be. Maybe.* Ahead, he sees the brightening day beyond the sliding doors, and just as he's about to exit an alarm goes off, a high-pitched beep so loud his chest almost buzzes. "Sir!" someone shouts, and a balding guy with a Target nametag and a sagging necktie comes charging toward Excel. "Sir!" he says again, louder and scolding, and Excel has no idea what he's meant to do. For all the years Maxima warned him about being TNT, the plan, should there ever be trouble, was to call Joker. But Joker is gone, and he has no backup plan, no prepared lines to recite that might keep him safe or buy him some time. "I didn't do anything," he says, but the man snaps his fingers and points, says, "The shirt, the shirt," and Excel looks at himself, sees a price tag dangling from his sleeve. He's still wearing the shirt, realizes he didn't pay for it. "It's a mistake," he tries to say, but the man pulls him by the arm toward the cash registers, and Excel remembers all the cautionary tales Maxima tried drilling into his brain—about the TNT who was caught when trying to cash a winning lottery ticket, or the TNT discovered not by Immigration but by a collection agency, after two missed credit card payments. He thinks of Lola NeeNee, wonders if she's even alive.

All those stories and for what? He learned no lesson from them, just fear. They do him no good now.

Then Maxima comes running.

"Is there a problem here"—she looks at the man's nametag— "*Wilbert?*" Wilbert points to the shirt, to the security tag affixed to the back of the collar. Excel tries speaking, but Maxima cuts him off. "He gets confused," she says, "abnormal sometimes. He's been living in the desert." She places a hand on Wilbert's forearm, leans into him. "He was *a homeless*," she whispers, "but he's trying to be normal again. So can we pay for the shirt now? Is that okay, Wilbert?" She keeps patting his arm and saying his name, then carefully places a rolled bill into his palm. "Just a misunderstanding, Wilbert," she says, in a low and soothing voice, "di ba?"

Wilbert looks at Maxima, then at Excel. "I guess it is," he says. "But you need to pay for that shirt." He steps back, waves Excel toward cashier number 3. Excel nods, apologizes for the error, goes to pay.

Later, after they've left Target and are standing at the intersection waiting to cross, Maxima finally speaks. "Stupid, kaba? What's in your head, trying to steal like that?"

"I wasn't stealing. I was distracted and forgot to pay. Anybody could've made that mistake."

"You're not *anybody*. You don't know that by now?" She looks at the red light, presses the pedestrian crossing button over and over.

"Why did you say those things in there?" he asks.

"What *things*?"

"About me being homeless in the desert."

"It's called an *alibi*. And it worked. You should be thanking me instead of all this critique-critique."

"Fine. But just so you know, I had a home in the desert." She presses the button again, irritated and impatient with the unchanging traffic light; Excel has no idea if she heard him or not, if she even understands what he said. "Finally," she says, red light turning green. She steps off the curb. He watches her cross to the other side.

10

Joker didn't raise Maxima. He trained her. "Big difference," she said.

She always claimed that she'd raised herself. True, there was a grandmother who took in Maxima and her sister, Queenie, after their parents' typhoon death, dragged away and drowned in the Pasig River. Maxima was nine and Queenie was twelve, but the old woman's idea of child-rearing was snapping the backs of their legs with a wire flyswatter if they overcooked the rice or slept past seven on a Saturday. Queenie was older but Maxima was her constant defender, which was how Joker came to discover her power: Walking home from school one afternoon, Maxima and Queenie were followed by a trio of boys who called out, "Orphan girls, hey orphan girls," while trying to lift the backs of their skirts with the ends of their bamboo fishing poles. "Sons of whores!" Maxima shouted back. "Stop it!" But the boys kept going, and Queenie tripped and fell, skinning a knee and muddying her good school dress. Maxima spun around, snatched a fishing pole from one of the boys, and smacked another in the head. The third boy lunged forward, wielding the pole high like a sword, but Maxima just socked him in the face and grabbed his fishing pole, too. One in each hand, she slammed the bamboo sticks hard against their knees and backs, sent them home crying. Joker, who'd been filling plastic jugs at the village water pump, witnessed the whole thing. "Small girl, big talent," he said when he'd told Excel the story. "Total untapped potential. Malakas, talaga." Maxima, who was doing push-ups on the kitchen floor, translated: "'So strong,'" she said, "'for real.'"

Joker, a grandmaster in arnis and escrima ("No arts are deadlier!" he always said), approached Maxima's grandmother about training her ("If it's free, what do I care?" she said). Within two years, Maxima was a formidable grappler and disarmer of weapons; by age fourteen, she could engage in hand-to-hand combat with anyone in the province and defeat them all. She mastered escrima fighting sticks (short and long), edge weapons, could even wield a poison-tipped stingray tail. Though Joker had no children of his own (despite a few romances when he was younger, he was a lifelong bachelor), he never mistook her for a proxy daughter. "I was more than that," Maxima said after Joker died, "I was his protégé."

When Maxima was nineteen, she attended the annual Batangas City Merry Christmas Martial Arts Gala-Extravaganza, performing a hand-to-knife fighting demonstration with Joker. It was there that she met Excel's father, the eye patch–wearing son of a bitch. He approached her after the show, offering a tryout for a Manila action flick he was coproducing, a women-in-prison drama that he predicted would be the next big Asian action movie megahit, a hundred times bigger than Jackie Chan. "I'd never been anywhere, not even Manila," she'd said. "And that eye patch was sexy, what can I say?" But the audition was the next day, when Maxima and Joker were already scheduled to do a second fighting demo. "Joker said, 'I forbid you to go with that eye patch–wearing son of a bitch to Manila!' and I said to him, 'I'm not asking your permission!'" The next morning, she rode all the way to Manila in the eye patch–wearing son of a bitch's motorcycle sidecar, believing that the argument with Joker the night before was just that, a slightly heated disagreement, that they'd see each other again in a day or two. "I didn't know I'd spend the next fifteen years in Manila," she said. "I didn't know I'd break Joker's heart."

It was an old story, but after Joker's death, Maxima retold it several times. Excel didn't know why. Maybe it was a way of keeping him grateful ("We owe him everything," she always said), a way to honor Joker's memory. Maybe it was a cautionary tale, to warn him of the hurt caused when you leave the one who loves you behind.

EVERGREEN LAWN HAD BEEN JOKER'S FAVORITE CEMETERY, BUT HIS brother Bingo had buried him instead in the cheapest plot at Meadow of Life Memorial, near the end of a long row of graves, along the edge of a wire fence. Walking toward him, Maxima plucks random, still-good flowers from bouquets left at other graves, so that when they reach him, she has a jumble of carnations, roses, a single bird-of-paradise. She takes a rubber band from her purse and binds them together, kneels down, and lays the bouquet on his tombstone, a simple concrete rectangle embedded in the grass.

She kisses her palm, presses it against the tombstone, right over Joker's name. "Grandmaster," she says, "nandito na kami, okay? We're all here, together again. Ako at ang bata."

Me and the child.

Maxima takes out the Taco Bell Mexican Pizzas from a small paper sack, sets them on the grass. She turns, looks at Excel. "Say hello."

He tenses up, feels his face go stiff, mouth sealed tight. He hates that she forces him to talk to Joker out loud, hates that he must act as though Joker exists on some spiritual plane where he can actually hear them.

"Hey," she whispers, then grabs Excel's wrist and brings him to his knees, "say *hello*."

"Hello Grandmaster, how are you?" He pauses, thinks of more to say. "I'm sorry it's been so long since I've visited. I've been gone but now I'm back." He closes his eyes, feeling stupid, feeling sad. Joker has been dead for nearly two years, and Excel can't remember the exact way he and Joker used to speak, if their conversations flowed easily, if they'd fallen into a habit of understanding each other with the fewest words possible.

Maxima turns back to Joker, bows her head, and immerses herself in an orasyon. Excel slowly rises and quietly steps back, retreats to another row of graves.

JOKER AND MAXIMA FOUGHT THE DAY HE DIED. THEY WERE IN THE living room, a blue training mat spread over the rug, and she was on the offense. Joker, in his raggedy YMCA sweatshirt and a terry cloth headband, blew the whistle around his neck and called out, "Laban! Laban!" But he easily blocked every combo punch she threw, then accused her of holding back, the ultimate disrespect to any honorable opponent.

"Ano ba?" she said. "My opponent is seventy-four years old with two bad knees and high cholesterol. What do you want me to do?"

Excel was on the floor by the window, slogging through CliffsNotes for the *Iliad*, his earplugs failing to drown their sparring out. When he was younger, Maxima had tried training Excel in escrima; even if she'd never become an actual grandmaster as Joker had hoped, she could at least pass his teachings on to Excel. But Excel was a disaster, as klutzy with the fighting sticks as he was with his fists, prone to getting hit despite plenty of time to dodge. It was stupid, he thought, pointless. Why train for battle when there was no enemy to fight?

Maxima and Joker switched; now he was the attacker. He took the fighting sticks, held them high as if ready to strike, and just as Maxima called for the fight—"Laban!"—he froze, his battle face pale and weak. He put his hand over his chest—he looked like he was about to recite the Pledge of Allegiance—then stumbled back, falling to the couch.

Maxima knelt in front of him, took hold of his shoulders. "Grandmaster," Maxima said, "*Joker. Iyong puso?* Your heart?"

Joker kept his eyes closed, face calm but teeth gritting.

Excel was still on the floor. He thought of the scar on his arm, the deep cut Maxima tried to fix herself. He wondered what she might do to Joker, if she would try to save him on her own. "We should call an ambulance," he said.

Maxima removed Joker's headband, fanned him with a magazine. "911," she said to Joker, "okay?"

He opened his eyes. "*911? Tanga kaba?* It's my *blood sugar,* don't you know? Look"—he pointed at Excel—"*ang bata.* He looks like he'll pee his pants. You're scaring him." He caught his breath and straightened up. "I just need to eat." Maxima looked skeptical and mentioned 911 again, but Joker slammed his fist on his thigh and reminded them that *he* was the grandmaster, and that they should abide by what he knew was true. It would be stupid, he said, a huge waste of money, to call an ambulance when all he suffered from was hunger. "Come on," he said, "I want to go."

"Go where?" Excel said. "What for?"

"To celebrate," Joker said. "I won the fight today." He held out his hand for Maxima to take, and she pulled him gently to his feet.

Joker wanted the $9.99 buffet at Sizzler ("All you can eat," Joker would say, "that's the best cuisine!"). He put on his one good blazer and his San Francisco Giants baseball cap, grabbed his knockoff Louis Vuitton fanny pack, and they all walked (slowly) to the restaurant, arrived just after five p.m. They paid, picked up their trays, and

slid them down the buffet. Excel scooped pasta and red sauce onto
a plate, while Joker loaded two plates with double portions of every
item (he'd made sure Excel brought Tupperware in his backpack).
Maxima lingered behind, her eye on Joker.

"I think he's okay," Excel whispered to her, "look at him." They
watched Joker charge ahead to the soft serve machine and take two
servings of bread pudding, then head into the dining room to a corner
booth.

"Get us drinks," Maxima said, then followed Joker.

At the drinks station, Excel got 7UP for Joker, root beer for
Maxima and himself, and before he turned around to go join them,
he envisioned the moment to come—the three of them in the corner
booth, their table crowded with plates piled high with greasy, fatty
food. They would eat in relative silence, which was nothing new—
sometimes, there just wasn't much to say. And this image of them was
so ordinary and familiar that he believed life—their life, his own—
would be okay. Not special or remarkable, but enough.

Drinks balanced on a tray, he walked to the dining room, found
Joker slumped in the booth, clutching his chest as Maxima rubbed his
back in circles with one hand, fanning him with his baseball cap with
the other. He was in pain but still conscious, still able to talk, and he
whispered to Maxima things Excel couldn't hear, not until the end,
when Joker told her, "Go, go."

She hurried to the front of the restaurant. Excel stayed standing,
tray still in his hands. Joker looked up at him, pointed in Maxima's
direction. "Follow," he said. Scared, unsure what else to do, Excel set
the tray on the table and obeyed, walked out of the dining room and
found Maxima talking to the cashier. "There's a man over there," she
said. "He's alone and needs a doctor. Can you call 911, please?" She
was focused and calm, like a bystander wanting to help, an ordinary
concerned citizen.

The cashier went to check on Joker. "You're lying," Excel whispered. "Why'd you say Joker was alone?" He tried returning to Joker but Maxima grabbed his arm and pulled him close. "When they come," she whispered, "don't say anything. If you do, we could be in trouble. Understand?"

He tried pulling away. She squeezed his arm harder. "You're hurting me," he said. She waited a moment, finally let go.

Maxima and Excel stood at the booth across from Joker when the paramedics came, watched as they put a breathing mask over his face and hooked him up to machines. A few other customers watched but said nothing, returned to their food.

"Excuse me," Maxima said to one of the paramedics. "May I ask where you're taking him?"

"Are you with the gentleman?" he said.

She shook her head. The paramedic said nothing, asked her to please stand aside so they could do their job.

The paramedics placed Joker on a stretcher, wheeled him quickly away. Maxima and Excel followed (not too closely) behind, stood by the front door as the ambulance drove off, the sirens blaring. Maxima called Bingo to tell him what had happened, pacing back and forth as she explained, replying meekly to everything he said on the other end. "Yes, sir. No, sir. I'm sorry, sir." Excel realized he was still wearing his backpack, then remembered the Tupperware inside. He went back in and went straight to the buffet, filled one Tupperware with fettuccini alfredo, the other with Chinese chicken salad, slipped them into his backpack.

Outside, Maxima was off the phone and sitting on the curb, Joker's baseball cap on her lap. "What do we do," Excel said.

"We wait." She looked up at him. "Why did you go back inside?"

"Grandmaster didn't eat," he said. "I packed up some food. He'll be hungry later."

They stayed that way for a while—Maxima sitting on the curb and Excel standing behind her, staring ahead at nothing. Finally, just before dark, he held out his hand to help her up, and the two of them went home.

No word came from Bingo that night or the day after, and Excel went back and forth between calm and panic—one moment, he pictured Joker in a hospital room recuperating, undoubtedly complaining about the crappy food; in the next, he imagined Joker lost amid rows and rows of beds, hooked up and plugged into machines, no way of getting home. "We're just sitting here," Excel finally said, "let's call somebody, or check all the hospitals if we have to." But Maxima just sat on the couch and stared out the window. "That's not the plan," she said.

The following night, Bingo came to the apartment to tell Maxima and Excel that Joker had died from cardiac arrest and they were not to attend the funeral. He was younger than Joker by a decade, was dressed in a suit with two cell phones holstered at his waist, and the entire time he stood by the living room window, hands on his hips. "My brother created many burdens by keeping the two of you," he said, which made Excel feel like they were stray animals Joker had taken in. "We are prominent Pinoys in the community, and if you attend, people will wonder who you are, why you're here. They will say, 'Sinong babae yan? Ang bata? TNT, di ba? TNT?' and point-point-point at you. All that tsismis. We don't need it."

Maxima stared at the floor, nodded.

Bingo discussed logistics: though they always considered the apartment Joker's, it was actually owned by Bingo, and he agreed to let Maxima and Excel stay, on the condition that they pay rent and utilities directly to him, in cash, on the first of every month. Should anyone ask, they were to identify themselves as family friends from the Philippines, here on tourist visas, and, for the sake of property value, he reminded them to be tidy.

"Of course," she said, fists clenched on her lap. "Thank you, sir." If she wanted, Excel knew, Maxima could knock Bingo to the floor in two seconds.

Bingo walked to the door. "Is it true," he said, turning back to Maxima, "artista ka raw? Sa Pilipinas?"

"For a time. Small parts, lang, sir."

"TNT movie star," he said, then shook his head with a laugh. "Puwede ba?"

Bingo left. Maxima stayed on the couch for several moments, then got up and picked up one of Joker's fighting sticks, slammed it hard against the living room wall, again and again. Excel got up and went to Joker's room, climbed out the window, up the fire escape to the roof.

Those first visits to Joker's grave, they went together, and Maxima, without fail, would weep. But Excel didn't, not one tear. He had no right, he told himself, after he'd acted like a total stranger, in those last moments he had with Joker.

Maybe that's why it troubles Excel even now, almost two years later, that Maxima expects him to speak to Joker out loud, with casual *hellos* and *how are yous*, like two people who've been apart forever, simply picking up where they left off. "Excel," she calls out, getting to her feet. "It's time to go. Come tell Joker good-bye."

He walks back slowly. He won't say good-bye, he decides, won't even speak. Instead, when he reaches Joker's grave, he takes a packet of black pepper from his pocket and tears it open, sprinkles it over the flowers Maxima gathered from other people's bouquets, saving them from the deer to come.

11

SouthDRed@hotmail.com was the e-mail address of Red, an artist from South Diamond in Hello City. He lived in a commune called Infinity Inc., a cluster of RVs and tents that served as live-work spaces for painters, sculptors, and performance artists, the entire perimeter surrounded by a white picket fence looped with barbed wire. Excel showed up at eleven thirty for a noon appointment, waited by the front gate. He watched a woman with a long green braid and paint-splotched overalls dipping small appliances—a toaster, a coffeepot, an iron—into an inflatable kiddie pool of what looked like pink liquid rubber. They made eye contact several times, said nothing.

Just past twelve, a guy in a long red beard and camouflage pants approached. "I'm Red," he said, "you're Excel?" He kept the gate closed between them, gave a quick up-and-down look, as though doubtful Excel could do the work. "You read the ad, right?"

Excel straightened up, pulled back his shoulders, tried not to feel his actual height; in bare feet he wasn't quite five foot six. "I can lift a lot," he said, "more than you think. I was in the weight-lifting club in high school."

"There's a club for that?" Red said, looking skeptical. "Well, just remember to lift with your legs." He unlatched the gate and stepped out, told Excel to follow.

Red called himself a semi-site-specific installation artist. Junk was his medium, especially big discarded things that aggressively took up space. "Someone left a grand piano in Hello City once," he said. "I smashed it up and made a giant mobile sculpture." They climbed into Red's truck, a beat-up Chevrolet with a missing rear windshield, drove out of Hello City and through Whyling, then onto the freeway toward El Centro. Had he known the job meant leaving Hello City, Excel might not have taken it; departing a place so soon after you'd moved there felt wrong, a waste of arrival.

Red flipped on the radio, searched through stations but found nothing, turned it off. "So," he said, "what happened to you?"

Excel thought Red meant his face. He checked the passenger side mirror for a rash or bruise. "Nothing happened to me," he said.

Red shook his head. "I mean, *what happened* that brought you to HC? Something must have happened. Or didn't happen."

"Neither," Excel said. "Just looking for a change. New opportunities."

"Opportunities. Huh."

"What about you? Did something happen?"

"Everything happened. Booze and drugs. Two bad breakups, two arrests. Then I turned thirty-five and got clean, realized all I cared about, all I could afford to care about, was creating. No better place to do that than HC. Still here, eight years later."

Excel glanced over, noticed a spread of what looked like cigarette burns on the inside of Red's left arm. He wasn't old, but he looked weathered and tough from his years of living in Hello City. Excel wondered how the years to come might change him, too.

They exited the freeway, drove through El Centro to the edge of the city, pulled into the small lot of an old warehouse filled with refrigerators, enormous desktop computers, cash registers, even old electronic slot machines. The only person there was Barb, a short woman with a tennis visor and cargo shorts, who greeted Red with a high five. "It's all back there," she said, then led them toward the back, where dozens of television sets lined the floor. They were boxy and old, with channel dials and antennas; some were flat screens, sleek enough they looked brand new.

"Perfect," Red said. He looked at Excel. "Let's get to work."

Red bent down, picked up a television set in a kind of bear hug, loaded it onto a dolly. Excel did the same, one after another. They said little as they worked, though on occasion Red would make random observations out loud, like how a crack in a television screen looked like the number seven, or how the missing keys of an old keyboard were the *K*, *E*, and *Y*. "Cool," Excel would say, but felt the pressure to be more perceptive, to find something that no one else would notice or know, but all he recognized was the moment itself—here he was, loading TV sets onto a truck with a "semi-site-specific installation artist," bound for the desert, a million miles away from Colma and The Pie—nothing in the world seemed more random than that.

They fit about twenty sets onto the truck and drove them back to Hello City, unloaded them behind Red's trailer, returned to El Centro for another load. They made five trips in all (they stopped at a taco truck on the third, Red's treat), finished just before dark. Red thanked Excel for his help, gave him fifty dollars, ten more than originally agreed. "Wow," Excel said, "that's so nice," and he meant it: he couldn't remember the last time anyone had been so overtly generous.

He folded the bills in half and put them in his pocket, thanked him. "And what about all that?" he asked, pointing to the television sets. The entire day, Red never said what his plans were for them, and Excel didn't think it was his place to ask. Now, with more than a hundred of them scattered about, the question only seemed natural, a fitting end to the day.

"All that," Red said, looking back, "no idea. But if I ever figure it out, I'll let you know."

EXCEL RETURNED TO THE BUS, FOUND SAB SITTING ON A LAWN chair on the helipad, still in her apron, a metal pail of beers on ice at her feet. "A welcome gift from Lucia," she said.

He sat beside her, reached for a bottle. The brand was Cerulean Spark, an IPA. "I don't understand this beer."

"It's some local craft beer from San Diego. She said we should pay attention to its 'stone fruit notes.' That's like the name of a shitty band. I would've been happy with a six-pack of Bud Light."

Excel grabbed the bottle opener. "How's the soap industry?"

"I learned lavender is technically part of the mint family." Sab yawned, leaned back in her chair. "There's a lot of boiling, lot of mixing. Lucia says I'll need to develop my stirring technique." She looked at the splotches on her apron. "Maybe a cemetery flower shop wasn't so bad after all."

"Hey"—he put a hand on her arm, gave it a squeeze—"we just got here. You'll get used to it."

She shrugged, took a bottle from the pail. "How was lifting and moving?"

"I lifted. I moved." He thought of telling her that he'd lied about being in the weight-lifting club, but was too tired to go into it. "It was a good day," he said.

"Then we should toast," she said. "To your good day."

She raised her beer to Excel's. The last time he'd toasted was the day of Joker's funeral. The morning of, Maxima had drawn the curtains and built a makeshift shrine on the dresser in Joker's bedroom, then got on her knees and whispered orasyones all day, as Excel knelt beside her, head bowed. In the evening, they split a foot-long Subway sandwich that neither of them touched, but Maxima insisted they drink the last of Joker's Ginebra gin, which he'd always kept on his milk crate nightstand, between the alarm clock and a small Tupperware of Nilla Wafers. "This stuff is strong," Maxima said, "but drink it down." She poured shots into paper cups, raised hers high. "To Grandmaster," she said. "Please guide us. Please forgive us. Please tell us what to do." Maxima teared up but Excel held himself together and took the shot, which tasted like a mix of vinegar and the smell of gasoline. He took another shot, then a third. Later, after Maxima had finally fallen asleep, he went to the bathroom and puked so much he wept.

He raised his beer, clinked it against Sab's, grateful to be there, grateful to be gone.

New money in his pocket, Excel suggested they treat themselves to dinner. They grabbed a flashlight and put on double hoodies (it was a colder night than expected), made their way to the Square. It was just past eight o'clock and though most things were closed (the sellers were gone, only the food carts and Beans! were open), the Square was more alive at night than in the day, lit up by tiki torches and crisscrossing Christmas lights above, and a crowd of about thirty, maybe even more, were gathered, sitting on benches and lawn chairs, in small circles on tarps laid on the ground in front of the stage. Lucia was there too, hunkered on a low stool and wrapped in blankets, sharing a joint with a blond dreadlocked guy in a parka and a long skirt.

The smell of curry came floating from the Hot Food cart; Sab and Excel walked over, stood in line. Excel reached into his pocket for the cash, then saw something that he hadn't noticed before, about twenty yards away on the edge of the Square: a large metal cage sitting on a wooden table, an owl inside. Excel moved closer, saw a gold-framed sign propped against the base of the cage. It read:

> **This is The Oracle.**
>
> **She is the Wise One of Hello City.**
>
> **Ask a YES or NO question.**
>
> **If she hoots, it's a YES. If not, it's a NO.**
>
> **25¢ per question.**
>
> **All donations go to The Square.**

"Guess how old she is," someone said. Excel turned, found Red standing beside him, a steaming mug in his hand. He looked back at the owl, guessed five years old, maybe ten. "Thirty-three," Red said. "She's a great-horned owl, life span of about fifteen years. But in captivity, she could live to be fifty, even older." The owl was perched on a broken branch that stretched beyond the cage on either side, like an arm reaching through the bars of a cell.

"Have you ever asked her a question?" Excel asked.

"Yup. And I got the answer I wanted." He took a sip of whatever he was drinking, walked off. Next to the cage was a mason jar half-filled with quarters. Excel reached into his pocket and felt a mix of coins, but decided he had no questions, not yet.

THEY ORDERED LENTIL CURRY AND WALKED OVER TO LUCIA, JOINED her on the tarp. Someone took the stage, held up a metal triangle, and clanged it like a dinner bell, which, Lucia explained, meant a Hello City Town Council meeting was about to begin. "It's half to-do list, half shit show," she said, "but this'll make it more entertaining." She lit another joint and passed it to Sab, who took a drag then passed it to Excel. He'd smoked pot only twice before, with some of the kitchen guys at The Pie; all it did was make him feel slow, his shift even slower. He took a drag, managed not to cough, tilted his head back and let out smoke, watched it momentarily fog up the starry night sky.

A woman in a cowboy hat and an old, matted fur coat took the stage. "Hey folks, me again, Rosie, HCTC chair, for those who don't know, and I'm calling this meeting to order, blah blah blah." She took the pencil tucked behind her ear, flipped through pages on a clipboard and read off a list of reminders—people were still leaving personal trash in the bins behind Beans!, artists in South Diamond were taking paint donations, the ride shares into Whyling were canceled for the week. "And now to the nitty-gritty," she said, "stop signs in Hello City." Excel wasn't sure if Rosie meant to rhyme, but he started repeating it, over and over: *Nitty-gritty, Hello City. Nitty-gritty, Hello City.* Sab looked over at him, started laughing, the smell of pot in the air around them.

People spoke out against the signs, called them a waste of money and time, the ultimate authoritarian symbols. "Stop sign in Hello City today, Starbucks in Hello City tomorrow," someone shouted. The few in favor were all parents, and two women took the stage together to argue their side. "Our kid is on his tricycle all the time," one of them said, "and he's almost been hit twice. Enough of this bullshit." There was applause, and as Excel clapped too, he realized that he hadn't seen a child since he arrived. It never occurred to him that there could be children in Hello City.

They went back and forth for another twenty minutes; in the end, they voted to table the discussion until the next meeting ("Shocking," Lucia said, rolling her eyes). Rosie went through reminders and announcements, then asked if there were any new arrivals in the audience and if so, for them to come up and introduce themselves. "But you got to follow the rules," she said. "First, tell us why you're here. Second, give Hello City a gift." The gift, she explained, had to be something nonmaterial—a line of poetry, a favorite joke, a verse or two from a favorite song, if you had the guts to sing. "Give us an experience," she said, "something to remember you by."

"We're new!" someone shouted.

A couple approached the stage, gray haired and in matching track suits. They stepped up, waved hello. The woman's name was Heddy, her husband was Ned, and they'd just arrived from Oroville, Washington, just miles from the Canadian border. They'd recently retired after fifty years in the hospitality industry, and were done with the northwest rain. "So now we're here, thanks for having us," she said. "And here's our gift." They walked to the front of the stage, bent down, and did side by side headstands for an entire minute. People applauded and Heddy and Ned got to their feet, took a bow, then left the stage.

"Who else is new?" Rosie asked.

Lucia waved her arms. "Them!" she said, pointing at Sab and Excel.

Excel smiled and looked at the ground, found himself saying it again—*Nitty-gritty, Hello City, nitty-gritty, Hello City*—and he closed his eyes, wondering how many times he'd have to say it until this moment passed.

He lifted his head, looked at Sab. She shrugged. "Might as well." She got up, stepped onstage. "I'm Sab," she said, "short for Sabrina. And I came here because"—she looked down, like she didn't quite know the reason, then smiled and looked up—"because, why not?" Then she searched the crowd, asked someone sitting near the stage for matches and a cigarette. "And here's my gift." She lit the cigarette, took two long drags and bent backwards, exhaled perfect smoke rings into the air. People clapped and Excel meant to clap too, but he kept thinking, *Sabrina*. Standing onstage, she looked as she often did—black jacket, torn jeans, Doc Martens, her hair a floppy bun of brown with purple streaks. But *Sabrina*? Did he know that was her real name? Had she mentioned it before? Maybe the pot was screwing with his memory, but he was almost positive that this was new information. "Sabrina," he said softly to himself, pronouncing the name like it was a foreign word, "Sabrina."

She took a bow, went back to Excel. "I'm really high," she said, then kissed Excel on the cheek. "Your turn."

He stood up, knees wobbly, but kept his balance and went to the stage. "My name is Excel," he said, "like the spreadsheet." Nobody laughed, but Sab nodded, encouraging him. "And I came here, to Hello City, because . . ." No reason came to mind, only Maxima, from a time he didn't truly know: that moment of her arrival in America, eighteen years before. What if she'd been given the chance to introduce herself, to stand up and explain why she was here? Would that have made life better, or given her a different one entirely? He couldn't remember the last time he'd stood in front of people like this, but knew how rare an opportunity it was; he wouldn't squander it with a lie. He looked at the audience, noticed that the ground beneath the benches, chairs, and tarps was a concrete circle, another helipad, the faint yellow of its fading H barely visible but clearly there. *H for hello*, he thought, *H for here*, *H for high* (which, he realized, he was). "H for hiding," he finally said. "That's why I'm here." The pot had taken full effect, his face and body filled with a surging calm. "I was hiding. Now I'm not."

No response. He turned to leave.

"Stop," Rosie said, "you owe us a gift."

He'd forgotten, then asked if he could have a moment to think of one ("I guess," Rosie sighed). He scanned the Square, saw a container of powdered nondairy creamer on the counter of Beans! He went to get it, then took the matches Sab had used, returned to the stage. "Here's my gift," he said. He lit a match, then tossed a bit of the creamer into the air. He'd seen the trick on TV; if timed just right, he would flick the lit match, igniting the powder, like fire bursting from air.

The fourth time it worked, a small quick flame. There was polite applause; someone said "Bravo." Excel took no bow, left the stage.

Rosie called the meeting to a close, and three older men—all with ponytails and beards—joined her onstage, unpacked a banjo, a guitar, a small drum set. Rosie took out a fiddle, and the four started playing a waltzy country tune. People got to their feet, cleared away the benches and chairs, so that the helipad was a dancefloor now, with Heddy and Ned taking the lead. Others followed, and Excel saw Sab swaying her head side to side, like she wanted to join. "Maybe," she said, holding out her hand, "just to fit in?" and Excel said, "Why not," and took it. He was never one for dancing; an eighth-grade school dance was his one public attempt, and even then he hovered by the speakers, where the color-changing lights couldn't reach. But on Monday, a kid in math class mocked the way he'd moved (one shoulder bouncing up and down, head bobbing back and forth) and only now, as he and Sab held each other and swayed near the stage, surrounded by all the other dancers, did Excel finally get it: sometimes, you're just more obvious when you try to hide.

"It's good to be with y'all tonight," Rosie called from the stage, "here in our lovely Hello City. Hope you'll stay a while, listen, and dance. Enjoy yourselves and don't forget, we don't care where you come from, we're just happy you came."

LATER, BACK IN THE BUS, IN BED AND IN THE DARK, SAB HELD EXCEL tight. "'Hiding,'" she whispered, "what did you mean?" Her voice was warm against the back of his neck, and though he tried focusing on only that, his high had faded; he was himself again. "It was the pot," he said, "that's all." He turned to face her, kissed her so that he wouldn't have to speak.

12

The Pie is a mob of birthday parties by eleven a.m., every table and booth in the dining room crammed with celebrating families. It's the best day for tips but Gunter won't let Excel work the tables. "No mercy for you, Lydia," he says, pointing at the name on his shirt. "Today, you're balls."

"Balls," Excel says. "No problem."

Few duties at The Pie suck more than ball pit–monitor duty. Barely ten minutes in, one kid elbows her brother in the eye, another gets his ankles caught in the mesh netting, shrieks like he's drowning. Later, a kid gets a bloody lip from an accidental kick, and his parents scold Excel for his failure to supervise the children more closely. Then a little girl's loose front tooth falls out and goes missing. She wails about the tooth fairy money she's sure to lose, and her father speed-walks straight to Excel. "We need that tooth," he says.

"I think it's in the balls," Excel says.

"That tooth is a *keepsake*," he says. "Dive in. Swim around. Find it. Isn't that your job?"

"There are *thousands* of balls in there," Excel says.

Gunter, standing nearby, comes forward. "Lydia"—he snaps his fingers twice—"find the tooth for our customer." Intentional or not, Gunter's arms flex, and the tattooed skulls stare at Excel again.

"Of course," Excel says. "Happy to do it."

Excel grabs rubber gloves and some plastic bags from the utility closet, returns and clears the kids out of the ball pit. He removes his shoes and climbs in, wades around and scoops his arms through the sea of balls. In fifteen minutes he fishes out dirty socks and crusty Band-Aids, an assortment of hair clips and scrunchies, near-fossilized pizza crusts punctured with tiny teeth marks. He thinks of the lie he told Maxima, knows that this is the closest he'll ever come to making *important discoveries.*

But still no tooth. How long, he wonders, until he's allowed to give up a pointless, impossible search? This is nothing but a show put on by Gunter, to prove The Pie's excellent customer service (the "Voted #1 in CUSTOMER SATISFACTION!" certificate, gold framed and hanging by the front door, is bullshit, a Word doc Gunter made himself). But the girl still sobs and her father lets out exaggerated, impatient sighs, like Excel is the reason for their terrible day.

It's almost one p.m., the ball pit line gets longer with antsy kids chanting, "Hurry up, Ly-dia! Hurry up, Ly-dia!" louder and louder and clapping in sync. He turns to shush them, then realizes that the girl with the missing tooth is gone, her father too. He wades through the balls and climbs out of the pit, sees a wad of chewed gum caught on the bottom edge of the mesh netting, a tiny tooth lodged in rubbery pink. Carefully, he pulls it from the net, the gum stretching in a long, oozy strand, drops it into a plastic bag.

He climbs out, goes to the break room's lost and found department—a laundry basket in the corner—drops the bag inside. He sneaks out the service door into the back lot for some air, but before he can cool off he takes out his phone and calls Sab. Six rings pass until she finally picks up, but instead of her voice there's just a yowling, a desperate cry that somehow sounds both faraway and intimately close. He thinks of a baby, not their baby necessarily, but of something small and alone. Then he hears a crash.

"What's happening," he says, "are you there?"

"Sorry," she says, "I dropped the phone."

"What's that noise?"

"Noise. You mean Zeus?"

"Who's Zeus?"

"The peacock."

"The one on the leash? I didn't know he had a name."

"He runs free now. But Lucia leaves out a bowl of tofu for him, so he's always hanging around. If the bowl's empty, he freaks out. I was refilling it when you called." Excel hears what sounds like wind, a scraping noise he knows are Sab's Doc Martens against the dirt. "Where are you?" she asks.

"At work. A kid lost a tooth in the ball pit."

"That's unfortunate."

"I found it. In a wad of gum."

"That's more unfortunate."

Two kids on skateboards come skidding into the back lot, doing clumsy spins and jumps. One falls, lands on an elbow. "There's a jar of my baby teeth somewhere in the apartment," Excel says. "Did I ever tell you that? They'd drop one by one, I'd clean them in the bathroom, then put them in a jar."

"That's . . . weird. Kind of creepy."

"I never went to the dentist as a kid."

"Never?"

"Nope. Actually, I've never been."

"Well, your teeth look fine to me." She says nothing for a moment, Zeus's yowling filling the silence. "Excel, why are you telling me all this?"

"I don't know. Maybe I just want you to know more about me. Tell me something I don't know about you."

"C'mon."

"I'm serious."

"In junior high I was in the school production of *Grease*. A Pink Lady. Worst experience of my life."

Excel has never seen *Grease*, but assumes it's awful. "What else?"

"Well"—she pauses, like she's thinking carefully of what to reveal next—"sometimes, when you thought I was running errands with Lucia, I was gone."

"Gone. Gone where?"

It was just a few times, she says, four or five, maybe more. Instead of making deliveries to the post office, she would drive through Whyling and get on the freeway, sometimes drive to El Centro, where she'd sit in a Burger King or a random donut shop, order something that came with free refills—coffee or iced tea—so that she could stay for a couple of hours. She would take out a notebook and pen, try to pass herself off as a college student, or some kind of working professional. "Sometimes I'd pretend I was a teacher," she said, "and that I was doing lesson plans." Other times she'd reread the books she'd packed, the guidebook to Kyoto especially. "Sometimes I just sat and made lists."

"Lists of what?"

"Just lists. Doesn't matter."

He's troubled by this, wonders about all those times she was somewhere else, in places Excel didn't know. "I never knew you were gone."

"I wasn't *gone*. I just left. Couple hours, here and there. I always came back, didn't I?" Zeus's yowling starts up again; Sab tries to calm him down. "He's butting his head against the door," she says. "I gotta go."

"Fine," he says, "but do me a favor. If you leave again, promise you'll tell me."

She doesn't promise, doesn't even respond. She just says bye, talk later, maybe soon.

He hangs up, turns back toward the door, and finds Z sitting on a crate beside the Dumpster, hunched over with his dictionary. He's in an employee shirt two sizes too big and his Pie baseball cap flops crookedly over his ear, like a kid in a grown-up's clothes. Gunter, Excel realizes, is putting Z to work, no doubt without pay. In a better world, Z would be in an air-conditioned RV in Hello City, playing cards with the other retirees, enjoying the day and all the years he has left.

Excel walks over, realizes Z isn't looking at his dictionary after all, but flipping through pictures in his wallet. Even in their plastic sleeves they look decades old, the edges yellow, the images faded. "My family," Z says, thumb pressing on a photo of himself as a young man back in Serbia, next to a woman and a teenage boy. His wife died almost thirty years before; his son, Gunter's father, was the one who brought Z over from Serbia, but died soon after Z arrived, for reasons Excel doesn't know and doesn't ask. He's buried in Colma's Serbian cemetery; on days when Z's energy is good, he'll walk the mile to his son's grave.

Z and his family stand in a line in the picture. Behind them is a tiny house, balanced on what looks like a stack of rocks rising from a lake. "Is that Serbia?" Excel asks.

Z nods, says it's called the House on the Drina. "Very famous, very beautiful. One day, X, you visit."

Looking at the photo, Excel realizes he doesn't have one of Hello City, and if he did, isn't sure what it should be of. The bus? One of the helipads? Zeus running free? "One day," he says. "Let's both go."

Z puts away his wallet, flips open the dictionary to a page that begins with *valence* and ends with *vanquish*, points to a word in the middle. "Valor," Excel reads. "Meaning 'great courage in the face of danger, especially in battle.' What's a good sentence, Z?"

Z sits up, thinks for a moment. He takes a breath, ready to speak, when Gunter pokes his head through the service door. "And what the hell is this? Are we playing school? Is this what I pay you for?"

"You don't pay me," Z mutters, his tone as plain as a fact, and Gunter responds in what Excel assumes is Serbian, loud with *k* and *sh* sounds. They go back and forth like this, and once or twice Excel hears his name mentioned, like when he'd eavesdrop on Maxima speaking with Joker or Roxy in Tagalog; it's strange to hear his name surrounded by a new language. "Stop," Excel says, getting to his feet, "don't yell at him. It's my fault. I took a break when I wasn't supposed to, and I wanted to test out some words with him."

"Words, huh?" Gunter says. "Here's some words for you: *Back to the ball pit, shit-lick*. And next time you guys play school, do it on your own time, not mine." He swipes the dictionary from Z's hands and goes back inside, door slamming behind him.

"Sorry about that," Excel says. He opens the door and holds it for Z, who mouths the word over and over as he passes through—*valor, valor, valor*.

EXCEL'S SHIFT ENDS AT SEVEN BUT GUNTER MAKES HIM STAY UNTIL nine thirty, no overtime. By the end, he's so wiped out that the twenty-minute walk to La Villa Aurelia takes closer to forty, but he won't need to jump the fence of Old Hoy Sun Ning Yung or climb the fire escape to his bedroom window; he has keys now (Joker's set, from Maxima) and can let himself in.

Everything is dark when he enters the apartment; Maxima, he knows, is working. But there's no line of light beneath her door, no voices coming from the other side. "Hello?" he whispers, knocking softly. He opens her door slowly and flips on the light, finds her gone.

On her desk, next to her keyboard, he sees the fake rubber wound, the one Maxima sometimes wears to show the men how much she hurts. He picks it up, presses it against the line of his forearm. It looks real enough, and he thinks of the scar just below his shoulder, left from the wound she tried to heal herself. Most of the time, he forgets it's there, the way people forget their tattoos—so meaningful when you get them, meaningless later in life.

Excel goes to his room—*Joker's* room—crouches on the floor, pulls a large shoebox from under the bed. He removes the lid and finds about fifty comic books inside. Excel wasn't a collector, but as a kid was a sucker for any team title—*The Justice League, The Avengers, The Legion of Superheroes*—DC or Marvel, didn't matter. Maxima, forever stressed about money, refused to pay for them. "Four dollars for one *Justice Avengers?*" she'd say. "No thanks, I'll buy a can of Spam instead." But Joker, on the sly, would buy a comic book once every few months and sneak it to Excel late at night, when Maxima was asleep. "Don't tell," he'd say, and Excel promised he wouldn't, the secrecy of it so thrilling he'd get giddy and laugh so hard that Joker would have to cover his mouth to shush him. This was their secret transaction for years, and even after Excel stopped reading them, he'd still laugh whenever he'd find a comic book stashed under the couch cushions, where Excel slept every night. In Hello City, the shoebox of comics was the one thing he regretted leaving behind.

He flips through the stack of comics, the slick covers bright with costumes and capes, power beams shooting out from hands and eyes. He puts the lid back on, slides the box under the bed. He doesn't need to read them, just needs to know they're still there.

Excel isn't hungry, but he goes to the kitchen and searches the fridge, settles on one of Maxima's key lime wine coolers. He takes a sip—it's nastily sweet—and looks at the photograph of Maxima, Joker, the photoshopped version of himself. It's real enough, and he's simultaneously disturbed and touched that a person would invent a moment in the past, just to make the present a little easier.

He goes to the living room, lights still off. He can't remember the last time he'd returned to find the apartment empty. Wherever he came from—school, work, Hello City—Maxima was always here.

Except once. Excel was nine or ten, asleep on the couch, and he woke to the sound of the front door unlocking. *Burglar!* was his first thought, and he flipped on the light, reached for the hammer under the couch (Joker had kept it there, just in case), raised it high above his head, ready to strike. "Stop," Maxima said, "it's me." She locked the door behind her, went to the kitchen. Excel followed, and though she was lit only by the freezer light, he could see how wrong she looked—the neckline of her dress stretched and loose, the downward smear of her lipstick, her ponytail nearly undone. "Were you gone?" he asked. "When did you leave?" She shushed him and pointed toward Joker's door, then opened the freezer and filled a plastic bag with ice, pressed it against the side of her face, her shoulder, the knuckles of her right hand. "What happened to you?" he whispered. "Bahala na, Excel," she said, "don't worry. I beat him. I won."

Joker came out of his room, entered the kitchen. Maxima told Excel to go to bed, nudged him toward the living room. He returned to the couch and pulled the sheet over his head, stayed awake to listen, their back-and-forth too low and fast for him to keep up with, but there were things he understood. *Police?* Maxima said. *Ano ang sasabihin nila? What will they do? I call and they find us. Ano ba?* They kept arguing, and at some point Excel couldn't stay awake.

He never knew where Maxima had gone that night, never asked. Wherever she is now, he's sure that she's fine, her absence tonight no different, really, than her absence during his time away in Hello City, when he was the missing one.

13

There were jobs in Hello City. Low pay, low commitment. Excel had posted his own flyer on the Square's posting board, kept the message simple. "I need work, please contact," he wrote, then listed his e-mail address. Those first two weeks, Excel spent a day and a half cleaning out Heddy and Ned's Airstream (thirty bucks), worked one full afternoon restringing lights in the Square (fifteen bucks), bathed someone's cats (the owner refused to give her name) on three separate occasions, ten bucks each time.

Days later, he received an e-mail from Red. Help? Tomorrow, 12PM? was all it said, and Excel replied, Sure.

He wasn't awkwardly early the next day, showed up just past noon. The television sets were exactly where they'd left them, and Red was staring at them, arms folded and silent. "I'm not seeing anything," he said, "just a bunch of fucked-up TVs. You?"

Excel stepped back, unsure what exactly he should be looking for, how to see something that wasn't there. "A bunch of fucked-up TVs?"

Red looked over at him, gave a defeated smile. "Let's get to work."

They went to Red's trailer, a long and narrow space crammed with floor-to-ceiling stacks of books, piles of old newspapers and magazines, cardboard boxes spilling over with random junk—metal door hinges, shampoo bottles, endless tangles of extension cords. One box was full of plastic snow globes and, without asking, Excel picked one up and shook it, watched tiny flecks free-float around a tiny Eiffel Tower. He wondered if it really did snow in Paris, if this truly was the way it fell. He'd never seen snow before; now, for the first time, he wanted to.

Red gave instructions: Excel was to go through as many newspapers and magazines as he could, then cut out from headlines any words or phrases that, for whatever reason, held a particular significance. "What kind of significance?" Excel asked, wishing he could just lift and move TVs instead.

"Beats me," Red said. "You'll be the one reading, so you make the call." He told Excel he'd be back in an hour or two, then left.

There was nowhere inside the trailer to sit; Excel couldn't find a single chair, didn't even see a bed. He brought an armful of newspapers outside, sat on a tarp on the ground. He started with a copy of the *Los Angeles Times*, dated August 17, 1977. He turned the pages slowly—they were yellow, almost brittle—read the headlines.

Carter to Name FBI Director
Pesticide Plant Sterility Still a Mystery
Presley Death Marks End of an Era
Worst of Storm Still to Come

He read them again, got nothing. He tossed the newspaper aside, flipped through the pages of a *Time* magazine from 1991 (Susan Sarandon and Geena Davis were on the cover), but the headlines and stories inside were meaningless, and though he understood there was nothing artful about the work he was doing—he was paid labor, nothing more—he felt unqualified to do it, incapable of finding a connection—intellectual or emotional—to the news of the world beyond. His own world, he realized, was simply too small.

He decided to make a game of it. He'd cut out a headline whose first word started with the letter *A*, then *B*, then *C*, and work his way through the alphabet. By the time Red returned three hours later, Excel was surrounded by little rectangles of text, a confetti of random words. Red picked up a handful and looked them over, muttered, "Interesting, interesting," under his breath. He had Excel collect them in a large shoebox, then told him he'd need help with the television sets. "Just moving and lifting," he said, "the easy work."

EXCEL LEFT INFINITY INC. WITH FORTY DOLLARS IN HIS POCKET BUT no understanding of Red's plans, much less his art. Still, he was glad to help, grateful for the money, and hoped for more work ahead.

It was just after four p.m., the day still bright but starting to cool. Excel went to the Square and bought a twenty-five cent coffee at Beans!, sat at a computer with a screen saver of goldfish swimming in the sky. He pressed the space bar to clear the screen, opened a browser to check his e-mail, in the off chance someone had responded to his flyer. He found his inbox clogged with the usual spam.

No More Viruses-EVER!!!
Want Better Sleep? Here's How.
It's me, ISABELLA! Can We Be Friends (Or More?)
THEFT: Your Identity May Be Compromised!

He scrolled farther down, stopped at a subject line that read, Hello. Maxima.

He took his fingers off the keyboard and pulled away from the screen, worried he might somehow open the e-mail and instead of a message find Maxima herself, weeping for the camera, already midway into a story so sad he'd be compelled to return to Colma—another sucker in the world willing to give her what she wanted. Just like that, his new life would be gone and he'd be back in the old, to endless days of hiding and hiding.

He looked over his shoulder, made sure no one was nearby who might read the screen from behind. He opened the e-mail. She wrote:

Hello. How are you. I'm glad you arrived safe.
What is it like, the place where you are.
It's fine here. I'm ok.
I hope we are talking soon.

He'd never received anything written from Maxima before, not an e-mail or letter, and she simply signed the prewritten messages in birthday cards she'd given. He tried to hear her in the words on the screen, to calibrate her voice to each sentence, each question; if he could, he might decode another meaning, an actual motive. But it wasn't like those scenes in movies in which, instead of seeing an actual letter, you hear the disembodied voice of the letter writer reading it aloud as the camera fixes on the recipient's face, eyes sliding side to side down the page, welling up at just the right moment.

Maxima's e-mail was just words on the screen.

He logged out of his account, closed the browser. He drank his coffee slowly, the sun nearly set by the time he finished, the strings of lights above the Square twinkling. The Oracle, Excel noticed, was inside her cage and wide awake, head twisting and bobbing like she was eager for questions. He walked over and dropped a quarter in the jar, leaned toward the bars to meet the owl's face, her eyes perfect black orbs ringed in glowing yellow. "Should I write back?" he asked.

The Oracle clawed the air with one foot, then suddenly froze, like a taxidermy version of herself. Excel reread the sign by the cage. "If she hoots, it's a YES. If not, it's a NO."

Several seconds passed, a full minute. The Oracle said nothing, and Excel had his answer.

THAT NIGHT, HE USED THE PROPANE STOVE FOR THE FIRST TIME, made two bowls of instant ramen with boiled egg. He cut an apple into thin slices, arranged them like a fan on a saucer, then set everything on the two-person table. It was the first meal he'd cooked in Hello City, and he felt pleased with himself, the whole routine of it—working all day, then coming home to make dinner for his girlfriend, who'd be on her way home soon. But Sab arrived later—and more tired—than expected. "Fifteen hours a week, maybe twenty," Sab said, opening a bottle of Cerulean Spark. "That was Lucia's offer when I said I'd come. But she wants to work nonstop, like she's creating a goddamn soap empire." She leaned back in her chair. "She's great in a lot of ways. We're just very . . . different. Like, she always wants to high-five. What's that about?"

Excel covered the bowls of ramen with saucers. "I thought you were her favorite cousin."

"I'm her *only* cousin." She took a sip of beer. "Oh well. It's not like I have anything else lined up. How was your day?"

"My day?" He considered the question, though he was fixed on the dinner on the table, suddenly anxious that it would go uneaten.

He told her about the hours cutting up newspapers and magazines, how odd that kind of work was; even odder that he'd actually been paid for it. "I guess that's what it's like, to work for an artist," he said. He didn't mention Maxima's e-mail, or that he'd asked the Oracle if he should reply or not.

"Dinner looks nice," Sab said. "I like the apple."

"I saw it on a cooking show once." He sat. "Let's eat?"

Sab picked up her spoon, stirred it in the soup, folded the ramen noodles into themselves. "I'm not really hungry," she said. "I'm going to sit outside for a while, try to relax. Is that okay?" She got up before he could answer.

"Sure," he said.

She kissed the top of his head, then stepped out of the bus and walked toward the helipad, the night so dark she seemed to fade into it; from inside the bus, he couldn't see her at all. He ate his ramen, the boiled egg, left the apple for Sab.

14

Where she was the night before, Maxima doesn't say and Excel doesn't ask. But he watches: how hard she punches The Bod and how long she lasts, how deeply she prays into her morning orasyon and what she looks like when she opens her eyes. There are no bruises or marks on her face. No anger or sadness. She's the same.

Later, she enters the living room in her robe, towel turbaned on her head and face green as a Martian. "Avocado, coconut oil, Splenda, and lemon," she says. "Cleans the skin, makes it smooth. I want to look good for tonight."

"Tonight?"

"The showing of my movie. You forgot?"

He did. "Of course not."

"Well, if you have plans, don't worry about it." She sits on the couch and turns on the TV. "I know you have your 'important discoveries.'"

He wonders how long she'll use those words against him, how long he'll let her believe that he really was out there somewhere, excavating. Maybe it's better that she thinks the world holds more opportunities for him than either of them thought. Maybe it'll make it easier for her, the next time he leaves.

"No plans. Just the movie," he says. "Can't wait."

"Good. I can't wait too."

All day, Maxima stays in her robe on the couch in front of the TV. She watches bits of random shows—a young Puerto Rican couple argues over which Brooklyn condo to buy; a pair of middle-aged white guys tries not to perish in the Alaskan wilderness; harnessed fashion models, shrieking and weeping, dangle from a crane over a canyon. But whatever she watches, she says nothing and doesn't react, her face calm to the point of blank. She isn't so much lounging and relaxing as she's keeping still, as though exerting as little energy as possible, saving it all for the night ahead.

F.O.F.F.F., THE FULL-ON FILIPINO FILM FESTIVAL, IS SHOWING *ANG Puso Ko VS. Ang Baril Mo* at seven o'clock at Sightline Community College. It's fifteen minutes away on the freeway, but Roxy picks them up at five, the school like a ghost town when they arrive. "Why are we here so early?" Excel says.

"This is once in lifetime," Maxima says. "I want the best seats."

They walk around campus, go building to building, each one like a gigantic rectangular concrete block. Nothing is scenic or lovely, but Maxima makes Roxy take her picture by anything she assumes is a campus landmark—a small terra-cotta fountain, an oak tree covered with pink ribbons, an outdoor sculpture shaped like a giant kidney bean. In each picture, Maxima poses with her hands clasped over her hip, eyes off to the side. She's not wearing an evening gown, but her new dress—knee length and black, sleeves speckled with silver, and purchased for $54.99 at T.J. Maxx (she's kept the tags, plans to return it for a full refund tomorrow)—gives her a real-life glamour Excel hasn't seen before. With all the posing, she seems to know it, too. "New pictures for my online profile," she says, "good for business."

Still too early, they kill time with another loop around campus ("I didn't know college was so ugly," Maxima says), then sit on a bench to eat the sandwiches Roxy packed in her purse (canned corned beef, mayonnaise). "Opening night for *Ang Puso Ko* was the best," Maxima says. "Red carpet, fans, reporters, after-party at Studio 53—ours was first, believe me. My gown looked like real gold, and the eye patch–wearing son of a bitch brought fake cocaine, just to look cool. We even got our picture in *PSSSSST!* magazine, swear to god." She continues reminiscing, and if the story is even partly true, Excel knows Maxima is bound for disappointment: later, approaching the Math and Sciences auditorium where the film is being shown, he can see there are less than fifteen people gathered beneath F.O.F.F.F.'s sagging banner (it says, FILM EVENT), and the bored-looking girl sitting behind a folding table makes only a half-hearted effort to sell more tickets. "It's still early," Roxy says, squeezing Maxima's shoulder, "let's get the best seats." Before they enter, Maxima puts on dark glasses and a baseball cap. She doesn't want to run the risk of being recognized, of word leaking out that an ex-Philippines action star is a TNT in America.

Inside, just outside the auditorium doors, a mounted poster of *Ang Puso Ko VS. Ang Baril Mo* sits on an easel. Like the poster for *Malakas Strike Force 3: Panalo Ako, Talaga!* in the kitchen, this one is an illustrated collage of big action moments, lifelike in detail, garish in color. "It's you!" Roxy says, pointing at the top, where Maxima, in character, stands atop a pile of rubble, feet wide apart and arms up and out, a pistol in each hand, her whole body like an X.

Maxima stands next to the poster. "One more picture," she says.

"For your profile?" Roxy asks.

Maxima removes the hat, the dark glasses. "For me."

By 6:50 p.m., people have stopped trickling into the auditorium. At best, the movie will get half an audience. But Maxima, glasses off but hat still on, can't stop smiling, her hands clasping and unclasping on her lap.

Excel thinks they have the row to themselves, until a girl with a McDonald's bag sits a few seats down from him. "Hey," she says, leaning over, "was there a sign-in sheet somewhere?"

He shakes his head, unsure what she means. "Sign-in sheet?"

"For Asian American Studies 26, with Quirante? It's for extra credit."

"I don't go to this school."

"Where do you go?"

He's unsure how to answer, if he even should. "Nowhere," he says.

"Oh," she says, "that's too bad," then takes out what looks like an entire value meal from her McDonald's bag.

Excel turns toward the screen. The last time he saw a movie was in Hello City, when they were showing *Cool Hand Luke* and *The Hustler* for Paul Newman night at the Square (an annual thing, though no one knew why). He wasn't into either film, but it was one of his favorite nights—sitting on a tarp holding Sab, the two of them wrapped in heavy wool blankets, whole galaxies bright in the sky.

The F.O.F.F.F. organizer, a film studies student named Jun-Jun, steps onto the stage. He welcomes the audience, holds up a DVD copy of *Ang Puso Ko VS. Ang Baril Mo*, and gives a brief introduction, reminds the audience to stick around for a postscreening Q&A with a panel of film studies faculty. "They're eager to share their thoughts," he says.

Lights go dark, screen lights up. The film opens with a panoramic sweep of Manila—smoggy skyline and clogged traffic, luxury high-rises and tin-roof shanties—then zooms to a small girl, barefoot and dressed in pink, bouncing a green ball against a cinder block wall. A jeep pulls up, and out steps a woman in a blond wig, red heels, black trench coat. The woman speaks, and subtitles flash on-screen.

—Little girl. Where is your mother?

—My mother is dead, ma'am.

—Who cares for you?

—My father, ma'am. But he is a drunk who patronizes the whores!

—What is your name, little girl?

—My name is Mercy, ma'am.

—Mercy. Take this cash. Buy yourself some shoes.

—Thank you, ma'am. But ma'am, who are you?

—Could it be you do not know? I am your sister, of course!

The woman climbs back into the jeep and, in slow motion, removes her wig. She holds it for a moment, almost pets it, then flings it out onto the street. The jeep speeds off, and the girl snatches it and runs home, goes to the bathroom and looks in the cracked mirror, puts the wig on. "Sister?" she says. The moment freezes, fades out, then fades in to the present day, where the girl, now a young woman played by Maxima, stares into the same mirror, her reflection broken up by the cracks in the glass.

Excel has seen her on-screen before, always on their small TV. But on the big screen, it's perfectly clear how little she's changed; Maxima will always look like Maxima.

The title flashes in bright and blocky letters, followed by the opening cast credits, all the actors' names fading in and out against a backdrop of slow-motion explosions.

Fidencio Manalo Diaz as . . . Rico!

Petra DelMundo as . . . Girlie!

> Joey "Bing-Bong" Cacha as . . . JakeBoy!
> Valentina Cruz as . . . A Nun!
> and Maxima Maxino as . . . Mercy!

Maxima clenches her fists, presses them against her heart. "Okay everybody," she whispers, "here we go."

WHEN THE LIGHTS GO UP, MAXIMA IS ON HER FEET CLAPPING; SHE makes Roxy and Excel do the same. He scans the audience, sees fewer people than when the film began, most of them here, Excel assumes, for extra credit. Their applause is just enough to be polite, which makes their three-person standing ovation even more embarrassing.

They sit down and Jun-Jun steps back onstage, along with two film studies professors—one white woman, one Filipino man. Standing behind a podium, they discuss the film's significance, how it could be read as a post-Marcos, post-Aquino social document, a critique of the coexistence of grotesque wealth and abject poverty within the common spaces of Manila, even a third-wave feminist manifesto. Maxima nods with every point they make, as though her work is finally being understood.

"But we should also consider," Jun-Jun says, "that the film is—how to say this—bad. It's *bad*."

The girl next to Excel dips a cold fry in ketchup and laughs.

"The dialogue, the narrative logic, or illogic, I should say, and never mind the acting," Jun-Jun says. The lecturers nod, smiling, and admit that the film isn't exactly aware of its awfulness, that it does possess an earnest, if not misguided, commitment to its own implausible material. Their conversation is loaded with terms Excel doesn't know—*metanarratorial*, *social Darwinism*, *post-post colonialist*, *Ed Wood–esque*—but when he looks over at Maxima, she seems to understand them perfectly.

She removes her hat and stands.

Jun-Jun points to her. "Question?"

"It's a good movie," she says.

Jun-Jun nods slowly. "Given context, it has merits."

"Ano ba, ang *context*? It has a heartbreaking story, top-quality stunt work, a cathedral explosion"—she's counting the list on her fingers—"it's drama, it's action, it's *life*." She stays standing, waiting for a response, but no one onstage speaks, and the audience just stares at her, like she's someone who came only to disrupt. "Maxima," Roxy whispers, taking her wrist, "bahala na."

She sits, puts the hat back on, the dark glasses, too. But there's no need to wear them. Though everyone saw her taking down a group of machine gun–wielding cocaine dealers, rescuing Catholic schoolkids from a sinking canoe, and running through a collapsing church on fire, nobody knows who Maxima is.

AFTER, THEY GO TO THE F.O.F.F.F. RECEPTION IN THE FOYER. It's typical Filipino party fare—lumpia, pancit, banana-cue, several liters of soda. "They're serving Pepsi?" Roxy says. "Tacky."

"Why is that tacky?" Excel asks.

"Don't you know? Pepsi Riots of 1992. The Number Fever Contest? A million pesos for one winning bottle cap number, and Pepsi printed eight hundred thousand of them. They refused to pay up, thousands of dirt-poor Pinoys rioted. I lost an uncle in that riot. Pepsi kills, believe me."

"Never heard of it." He pours himself a cup, which Roxy dumps on the ground and refills with orange Fanta. "Know your history," she says, a line Excel remembers from the eighth grade, when his history teacher gave him a D+ on a multiple-choice Civil War test. "Know your history," she wrote in red, underlining *your* twice. Even then, Excel thought, *It's not my history*, one of the perks of being born neither in America nor the Philippines. The only history he needed to know was his own.

Roxy asks Maxima if she remembers the Pepsi Riots, and Maxima says, "Yeah, sure, of course," but she's agitated, scratching the back of her neck as she scans the small crowd. "I have to pee," she says, then walks off.

"Does she know about the baby yet?" Roxy whispers.

Excel shakes his head.

"Ano ba? It's still a secret? You have to tell her, Excel."

"I will. At some point. Before the baby comes, obviously. Sab and I just need to figure out a plan."

"*Plan?* She gives birth, you have a baby. There's your plan, di ba?" She shakes her head. "Bahala na, you know best. But take this, if it helps." She puts a twenty-dollar bill in his hand. This time, he doesn't even try to refuse.

Roxy steps away to make a call. Excel fills a paper plate with five lumpia, walks outside to eat on a bench. Had he known the showing would be held at Sightline, he might not have come. He'd skipped senior-year field trips to local colleges, shrugged off the idea of meeting with the college counselor—why bother with a future that would never be yours? But he feels more at ease than he thought, and the students around him—most of whom, because of the F.O.F.F.F. event, are Filipino—don't look so special, just people minding their own business, going about their day. Though Maxima had slammed a fighting stick on The Bod's head when he told her he wasn't even considering college, her anger faded fast, and he suspected that she was secretly relieved; now she wouldn't have to worry about Excel being found out by new college friends or overly concerned professors. But if he'd actually enrolled at a school like this one, maybe college might've worked. He doubts he would've thrived, but what if he'd done the absolute minimum, accomplished just enough to pass? What better way to hide than to be perfectly, invisibly average?

Excel hears Maxima shout his name.

He looks up, sees her coming, fast as a speed-walker. "Let's go, let's go," she says, "Roxy's waiting in the car." She knocks the plate of lumpia from his lap, pulls him up, says, "Move! Move! Move!" Now she's running and he doesn't know why, but he imagines police or Immigration or, for some reason, the paramedics who took Joker away, coming for them. "What's happening?" he calls after her, and someone passes him from behind. It's Jun-Jun, chasing after Maxima. "She took my movie!" he says, gaining on her. Now Excel starts running—he doesn't know what else to do—and just as Roxy's car pulls up in front of the campus, Maxima stops, spins, and grabs Jun-Jun by the shoulders, twists her leg around his, sends him to the ground. A bystanding student shrieks, a few others just stand and watch, perplexed. Jun-Jun gets to his feet, looks at Maxima. "Bitch," he says, and Excel remembers the move used against him nine months before, the morning he tried to leave forever: he kicks Jun-Jun in the back of the knee, uses all his weight, the full strength of himself, to bring him down.

SAFE ON THE FREEWAY, MAXIMA TURNS BACK TO EXCEL AND RAISES her hand for a high five. He doesn't give her one. "What were you thinking?" he says. "What if he calls the police?"

She turns back to face front. "It's fine."

"What about me?"

"What about you?"

"I could get in trouble too. I assaulted that guy."

"And you did a good job! I just wanted you to run, but instead you took down the enemy. Joker would be proud."

"It's true," Roxy says, smiling in the rearview mirror.

Maxima takes out the DVD from her purse. "And now I have this back. Do you know how long I've been searching for this? 'Metacolonialist Ed Wood.' Bullshit. Those sons of bitches don't deserve my movie." She holds the disc up to the light, so that from the backseat

Excel can see himself reflected in it. "How'd you learn to do that, by the way?"

"Do what," Excel says.

"That move. What you used against Jun-Jun."

"You know how," he says. "It's the Maximattack. I learned it from you."

She nods, satisfied. "I just wanted to hear you say it," she says.

THAT NIGHT, EXCEL WATCHES THE NEWS, SCARED THEY'LL REPORT the incident with Jun-Jun. He can barely remember the moment itself, but he imagines grainy footage caught on surveillance video or a bystander's camera—blurry versions of Maxima running and Jun-Jun in pursuit, Excel suddenly entering the shot, his takedown of Jun-Jun klutzier than he remembers, so that instead of skilled fighters, he and Maxima look like buffoons. He imagines the clip going viral, airing on a show like *America's Dumbest Criminals*, that Immigration or the police will see it and track them down.

"You think anybody cares?" Maxima says. "You think we're enough to make a story?" She takes the remote, mutes the TV because she needs the apartment quiet. "I'm working tonight," she says, then goes to her room.

But no matter what Maxima says, Excel can't shake the fear of getting caught, the paranoia of having been seen. Between the near-accidental shoplifting from Target, stealing from and assaulting Jun-Jun, even the awkward three-person standing ovation from Maxima, Roxy, and himself, he has never been so recklessly public, so utterly the opposite of who and what he's supposed to be.

Maxima, meanwhile, watches herself nonstop. She's borrowed Roxy's DVD player, and now *Ang Puso Ko VS. Ang Baril Mo* plays all day, and at night (on the couch, dinner plate on her lap) she watches again, rewinding favorite scenes over and over, sometimes so often that she never gets to the end. When Excel comes home late from The Pie, he'll sit through fifteen or twenty minutes, just to be polite, then go to his room and often to the roof, until he's tired enough to finally sleep.

Tonight, Excel returns home to find Maxima asleep on the couch, the movie on the screen, paused at a moment set in a street market—a long row of vendors on both sides of a narrow road, and tables piled high with skewered meat, fried fish, endless vegetables and fruits. He doesn't remember this moment from the F.O.F.F.F. viewing—it seems incidental, full of extras instead of real actors, maybe a transition to a more pivotal scene. But moving closer to the screen, he finds Maxima in the crowd, standing next to a vendor selling sandals. In the movie, she is Mercy, assassin and avenger, but she doesn't look ready to attack or defend, or burdened with a mission for revenge. She just watches the street, as though she didn't hear the director call "Action" and was, for a moment, out of character, simply herself.

He reaches for the remote, hits Mute, hits Play. The scene resumes, and Maxima steps into the road and walks a quick, straight line down the middle, the crowds ahead parting to clear a path. The camera zooms in on her hand, and she reaches into her purse and pulls out a knife, twirls it between her fingers, ready for the next scene's takedown.

Maxima snores on the couch, then gasps, says, "Ano ba? Ano?" Excel turns around, finds that she's just talking in her sleep. It's so strange to see her this way, curled up in her flannel robe and pink sweats, just beneath pictures of herself on the wall above—the eight by ten of Maxima in a gold gown, rocket launcher in hand; the other, in which she wields swords as she flies through the air.

She shivers. A throw blanket hangs over the arm of the couch, but Maxima is the lightest sleeper; no matter how carefully Excel lays the blanket over her, she'll flinch and shoot up, instantaneously wide awake. The best thing to do is let her be a little cold, let her sleep until morning.

15

Excel wakes and thinks of money.

It's been nine days since his return. He arrived in Colma with around $270 and now has $120 from Roxy, and with the fifty-two hours he's worked at The Pie so far (if Gunter will be a halfway decent human being, he'll pay Excel eleven dollars an hour, same as before), that should put him, after payday, at around $962. If he can maintain this rate, in ten or eleven (*maybe* fifteen weeks at most, given expenses?), he'll have $10,000, plus enough for a Greyhound ticket back to Hello City, with enough left over, he hopes, to buy snacks for the long ride south.

He tells himself: *The future is closer today than yesterday.*

He gets out of bed, showers, and changes. He goes to the living room and Maxima rises, still on the couch. "I fell asleep," she says.

"You were there when I got in last night," he says. "I didn't want to wake you."

She rubs her eyes and clears her throat, stands up, and walks groggily to The Bod. She scrunches her face like she's in pain.

"Everything okay?" Excel asks.

"My back." She digs her fists into her hips, bends to the side. "How did you sleep on that couch, all those years?"

"Guess I got used to it."

Breathing slowly, she reaches for the ceiling then arches backward, like she's about to do a backflip kick from one of her movies. Her ponytail, straggly and loose, sways back and forth, grazes the rug. "You should've had a real bed. I should've gotten you one." She straightens up. "I'm sorry."

"It was fine." More comfortable, he realizes, than the bed he sleeps in now. "I slept fine."

She steps back and takes firm hold of The Bod's shoulders, but instead of kneeing him in the gut she remains perfectly still, like she needs him to keep her balance. "I'm off to work," he says. He bends down to tie his shoes, and when he looks up, Maxima is still the same, motionless, just staring at The Bod's blank blue face. "I'm leaving," he says, and she barely nods.

Excel walks out, shuts the door behind him. But he doesn't leave, not until he hears it again, finally: Maxima strikes to start the day.

ONCE OUTSIDE THE LA VILLA AURELIA GATE, HE CALLS SAB. JUST one ring and she picks up, a gesture (intended or not) that makes Excel the happiest since he's been back, but he warns himself: *Don't read into it.*

"Hey," he says, "did I wake you?"

"Can't wake me if I haven't slept."

"Is something wrong?" His first thought is morning sickness, though he doesn't exactly know what morning sickness is. "Should you go to a doctor?"

"Don't worry. It's just really hot. One hundred and two degrees yesterday. I was awake the whole night."

"You need to keep cool. For your health." *And for the baby*, he wants to say, but holds back.

"I'm at Lucia's, blasting the AC. So instead of sweating to death, now I'm freezing."

Fancy as it is, Lucia's Airstream is full of what she calls "Helsinki-inspired Danish modern midcentury" furniture, every chair too small, too firm. He pictures Sab sitting upright, body tensed and shivering. "I'm sorry," he says. "I should be there with you."

"No, you shouldn't."

"I shouldn't?"

"I didn't mean it like that. I'm just saying . . ." She goes quiet, the blank of her voice filled in by the low background hum of Lucia's AC unit, like white noise meant to lull someone to sleep. "I'm just saying you need time to figure stuff out. Hello City isn't the right place for you to be right now."

"Hello City is the right place for anybody. That's why it's there."

"Excel. You burned down the Square."

She doesn't say it accusingly (there's no accusing when it's simply a fact), but there's judgment in her tone, he can hear it. "I know what I did," he says. "But it was an accident, and I'm going to pay them back. Ten thousand dollars. More, if that's what they want. Gunter is giving me good hours. I can probably borrow money from Roxy. And that's how Hello City works, right? You screw up, you fix it. And if nobody wants to forgive me even then, I can live with that. I just want us to be together, back at home."

"*Home?* Home is about a thousand degrees right now. Home is a bus with a busted fridge."

"The fridge broke?"

"Don't worry about it."

"We'll get it replaced. I'll send money. Whatever helps."

"If you want to help, do me a favor."

"Name it."

"Don't call. For real this time, please. Just let me"—her breath seems to catch, and she clears her throat—"just let me be for a while."

"How long is a while?"

"Long enough to figure out what I want to do. And when I'm ready, I'll call you, okay? Please."

There's no choice but to abide, he gets that. But maybe it's worth a discussion, or even a fight, to persuade her otherwise, because an unforeseeable stretch of time without seeing her, without talking to her, is too much. Without Sab, what else is there? Excel takes a breath, ready to speak, to fight, if that's what it takes. But it's too late; Sab has ended the call.

GUNTER IS BEHIND THE CASH REGISTERS WHEN EXCEL ARRIVES AT The Pie, rearranging shifts on the work schedule clipboard, crossing out names, adding others.

"So here's the deal," Gunter says, without looking up. "We've lost Marta and Santos, so it's double shifts for everybody today, probably all week. I hope you'll make that work."

"Double shifts? I'll take whatever I can."

Gunter takes the pen from behind his other ear, crosses out "Marta" and writes in "Lydia." "By the way, you're in the dining room today. I need you on the floor."

The floor means tips, and a bit of good news for today. "That would be great. Thanks, Gunter."

"Glad you think so. Because today, you're the Sloth."

Excel keeps his face a neutral blank but wants nothing more than to take the clipboard and slam it down on Gunter's head. Being Sloth the Sleuth is even worse than ball pit duty, and gets zero tips. "I thought we retired the sloth, after the Svetlana incident?"

Gunter rolls his eyes, snorts. "Svetlana. Whole lotta drama for nothing. The girl didn't hydrate. You won't make that same mistake, right?"

Excel thinks of his budget calculations, his approximate timeline for getting back to Hello City. "Right," he says. "No mistakes."

In the break room, Excel lifts the lid of a large Styrofoam cooler and finds a face looking up. Like the animatronic version, Sloth the Sleuth's headpiece looks drugged up and high, the eyes a pair of droopy slits, the mouth a dopey grin. "Fuck you," Excel says, then takes it out.

The door opens and in walks Z, roll of paper towel in one hand, spray bottle of blue disinfectant in the other, which means Gunter has him on bathroom duty. "It's Saturday," Excel says, "you should be at home, relaxing."

Z looks at the headpiece, gives Excel a look of pity. "You too."

Excel pulls out the rest of the costume—a pair of black oven mitts, a papier-mâché magnifying glass the size of a pizza pan, a big bodysuit covered with matted silver-gray shag splotched with lime green, which, Gunter explained, is supposed to be algae ("That shit grows on sloths," he'd said). It's 10:45 a.m. Excel has fifteen minutes before he has to get into the costume and be on the floor.

"Z," he says, "if you were home, in Serbia, what would you be doing right now?"

"If I'm in Serbia"—Z takes a breath and sits, contemplating the possibilities—"I sit in the park. With my daughter."

"You have a daughter?"

"Yeah, yeah. My youngest. Next month, fifty years old."

Excel could imagine Z coming to California to join a child. But it's another thing, he thinks, to leave one. "You'll go back," he says, "you'll find a way." He forces a smile, trying to feel positive, to amp himself up for the long shift ahead. He unzips and steps into the bodysuit, the legs and sleeves already itchy, humid. He picks up the headpiece, takes a deep breath, becomes the sloth.

Ninety minutes in the costume and Excel's whole body is one big gush of sweat. The air inside the headpiece is a thick steam of disinfectant mixed with the collective perspiration of every person who's ever been Sloth the Sleuth. The slits-for-eyes make it hard to see, and kids ram into him from all sides as he staggers table to table through the dining room. He tells himself: Keep going, do your job, this day will end.

But Gunter isn't pleased with Excel's performance. "You're a *sloth*," he whispers when he passes Excel in the dining room, "do it right." Years before, at an employee training session, Gunter had demonstrated proper sloth movement by walking in extreme slow motion, shoulders leading and knees half-bent, holding the papier-mâché magnifying glass at eye level as he turned his head slowly from side to side. Two guys in the back snickered, whispering in Spanish, and one of them raised his hand and asked if Gunter could demonstrate a few more times. Gunter obliged, but when he finally understood he was being mocked, he threatened everyone in the room. "One phone call, you sons of dicks," he said, "one phone call and you're all back in the mother country."

Excel turns to Gunter and nods, walks and waves in slow motion to no one in particular.

The Pie is even more packed by three p.m. Parents demand Sloth the Sleuth photos with their kids, but most are terrorized and cry in his lap. One kid—he looks like a six-foot-tall twelve-year old—just scowls and punches him in the chest. But Excel doesn't *break character* (Gunter's term, learned from an improv class), just holds up the papier-mâché magnifying glass, pretends to search the kid's face for clues. "Spies don't use magnifying glasses," the kid says, and Excel gives a slow-motion shrug of the shoulders. "One more picture," the kid's mom says, and when Excel turns, he sees a baby—an *infant*—coming his way. "Be good, baby boy," she says, then gently places him in the cradle of Excel's arms. She steps back, tells them to smile. Excel sits, head bowed, trying to see the baby through the slits of the headpiece, but too much sweat washes down his forehead, blurring his vision.

He closes his eyes, tries to feel the faint weight of the baby in his arms. *One minute*, he thinks, *let me have one minute.* But the mom takes the picture, then takes the baby away.

Slowly, Excel waves good-bye.

He rises, still hot then chilly then suddenly both, like being inside an AC-frozen Airstream while the world outside bakes. Knees bent, he moves forward, giving lazy waves to the families he passes, then approaches the final booth, where an Indian boy with thick glasses sits, parents on one side, grandparents on the other. They've gone with The Pie Who Loved Me Birthday Caper—two large pizzas, a pitcher of Pepsi, a small cake with Sloth the Sleuth's face. But both parents are on their phones, the grandfather keeps dozing off, and the grandmother, swathed in a blue, gold-flecked sari, looks irritated and bored, like she knows she's too elegant for a place like this. All pressure to look festive is on the boy—he's the only one wearing a party hat—but he just stares back and forth between the animatronic band and empty space, elbows on the table and chin on his fists.

The father puts his phone down, lights the candles; the mother smooths the boy's hair, tells him to sit up straight. *I should sing for him,* Excel thinks, *make him feel he's not alone.* But the boy just looks down at the table, staring at his name on the cake—Ranjit—and when he looks up from blowing out the candles, Excel knows, with absolute certainty, who he is: the boy from the apartment upstairs, the one who saw Excel standing in the middle of the Sharmas' living room, the night he returned to Colma. "I know you," Excel says, the words ricocheting and echoing inside the headpiece. He feels simultaneously compelled to sit with Ranjit and run from him too, and his body seems to act on both compulsions, like he can be in two places at once. He takes one step to the side in sloth slow-motion speed, waves an equally slow good-bye, and then, faster than he knows, begins to fall.

16

Weeks after Excel cut up the headlines, Red e-mailed him again. Help me smash stuff? he wrote, and Excel replied, Sounds fun.

They spent the next day carefully removing screens from the televisions, then smashing—delicately—each one, saving the shards in plastic bins ("We can always use them for something," Red said). They replaced the screens with plastic sheeting, like Saran Wrap but stronger and thicker, a slight gray film on its surface. The day after that, they began stacking the televisions on top of each other, experimenting with different arrangements; each time, Red would take five steps back and study the configuration, rub the end of his beard between his fingers, then do the same thing again from another vantage point.

They removed wires from the TVs, then added new ones, connected them with what seemed like miles of extension cords. When the work day was done, a few other artists from Infinity Inc. dropped by to check on Red's progress, and brought along a case of Pabst Blue Ribbon. They were strangers to Excel, and he turned to leave, but one of them offered him a beer and Red, who didn't drink and opened a bottle of something called kombucha, insisted that Excel stay, to toast to a day's good work.

EVEN IN THE DARK AND DESPITE ALL HE DRANK, EXCEL FOUND HIS way to the bus. Sab was drying dishes when he entered, had already eaten dinner. "There's spaghetti," she said, "but I ate all the sauce." He said he wasn't hungry and kissed her on the cheek, told her about his day and the artists he'd met, how he wondered if he should try making art too. "Maybe a collage or some kind of sculpture," he said, "something where I take junk and make it cool. How was your day?"

"Just more thrills at Pink Bubble," she said, "but now I have this." She lifted her sleeve, showed a red welt on the side of her arm, just above her wrist. "I accidentally touched the edge of a boiling pot. So much for Lucia's stirring technique. I hope it doesn't scar."

He kissed her again, said he was sorry, asked what he could do. "Nothing," she said. "But if you want to do something artistic, you could paint the bus. It's so gray in here, it's depressing. And by the way, I still don't have the picture of my mom. I called my aunt last week and she keeps forgetting to send it." She walked to the front of the bus, leaned against the steering wheel. "What if we went back for it? Just a quick trip."

It was late October. Almost two months since they'd arrived, too soon to even think of returning, especially since that was never the plan. "That's a long way to go for a picture," he said.

"It's my *mom's* picture."

"I know that. All I meant is that we're just settling in, and if we take a trip now, that's hours lost that we could be working—"

"Working? I'm the one working full-time."

"If I could find regular work, I'd take it."

"Then *look outside* Hello City. Go to Whyling. Try El Centro. Maybe—"

"I can't drive. You know that."

She pulled the pins from her hair, let the loose bun fall, the purple streaks still there. "You can't drive. Right."

Until now, his lack of a driver's license hadn't been an issue. He'd always meant to get one, he said when they'd first met, just never gotten around to it. When the subject came up again, on the drive down to Hello City, he admitted that he hadn't been completely honest with her the first time, and explained that a car accident from childhood ("My uncle died in it," he'd lied) was the reason he couldn't be behind the wheel. Sab said she was sorry about his uncle, promised him that she didn't mind all the driving. "I like being the one who can take you places," she'd said. But seeing her now, leaning against the steering wheel, arms folded and eyes to the floor—he wondered if this was the moment to tell her the truth—*If I drive, I might get caught*—and to see what more he might confess. But she looked frustrated, even lonely, without her mother's picture. There would be a better time to tell her.

"I'll learn to drive," he said, "soon. I promise." He apologized if he seemed insensitive about her mother's picture, and said they could send Sab's aunt the postage in advance, so that she'd have no excuse not to mail it off. "We'll get the picture," he said, "and the bus will feel like home."

She stayed staring at the floor. Excel couldn't tell if she believed him or not, and he wondered if a secret was just another kind of lie. "My arm hurts," she said. She opened the minifridge, took out a Cerulean Spark and pressed the cold glass bottle against the burn. Excel thought of lifting his shirtsleeve to show the scar just below his shoulder, as proof that injuries heal and that hers would too, but the scar was a story he didn't want to tell.

RED MADE THE ANNOUNCEMENT AT THE NEXT TOWN COUNCIL MEET-ing. "I don't know if I'm done," he said, "but there's nothing more I can do." He would show his newest work the following Saturday. Everyone was invited.

The night of the opening (as Red called it), Lucia made dinner for Sab and Excel, a shiitake mushroom and caramelized onion flatbread ("'Flatbread,' not pizza," she made clear). After, Lucia offered a joint (Sab accepted, Excel said no thanks), and the three walked to Infinity Inc. The gate was wide open, music blasted from all directions—bumping techno, electric guitar, bongos—and candles lodged into empty beer cans lit several paths into the commune. Dozens of people, more than a hundred, were already gathered, and most were not from Hello City. "They think we're all kooks," Lucia said, "but they know we have the best parties." Then she waved to some friends, ran to join them.

Excel and Sab wandered off to explore. Despite working for Red, Excel had seen little of Infinity Inc. and didn't know what to make of what he saw—a twenty-foot-high arch made out of toilets, a small grove of trees with mannequin arms for branches, a row of flashlights planted into the ground, shining beams up into the night sky ("Waste of batteries," Sab said). There was nothing in Colma like this. Just cemeteries, Targets, and The Pie, those come-and-go planes at SFO, all those flights he'd never take.

They gathered at Red's helipad at midnight. He looked as he al-ways did—ratty T-shirt and ratty jeans—but he wore a bright green bow at the bottom of his beard. Behind him, the stacked televisions looked like giant blocks, configured into a silhouette of a squat city skyline. He thanked everyone for coming and his fellow Infinity Inc. artists for their camaraderie. "And special thanks"—he searched the crowd—"to Excel for all the help. Where are you, Excel? Raise your hand." Excel didn't expect acknowledgment, and though he was embarrassed he waved quickly to the crowd, which drew a few claps.

Red cleared his throat. "This is *Unaired Television Pilot*," he said. He stepped behind the wall of television sets, plugged several cords into a generator. The whole thing lit up, the screens emanating a gray and ghostly light, and in the middle of each one were different words and phrases. They were the headlines Excel had cut up, and though most were rearranged by Red—"I am Not the Invasion," "POTUS Crowned Miss America," "We Are Not the Friend"—Excel recognized one of his own: "End of an Era Still to Come," glowing on a flat screen in the middle of the top tier of TVs. He led Sab through the crowd for a closer look.

Red approached, patted Excel on the back. "Don't worry," he said, "you'll get credit for that one." Excel said there was no need, that payment for his work was enough, but he couldn't help but feel proud, to see something he'd done, out in the world, glowing.

He pointed at the screen, looked at Sab. "I did that," he said.

DAYS WENT BY, AND A CROSS-EYED JACK-O'-LANTERN IN THE FRONT window of Lucia's Airstream made Excel realize it was Halloween, a big deal in Hello City: that night, a banner that read HELLO-WEEN CITY hung in the Square, and Rosie and her band played country versions of "Monster Mash," "Thriller," and the theme song from *Ghostbusters*, over and over. People came in costume: Heddy and Ned, the couple who did the headstands, were dressed in business suits streaked with dirt ("We're dressed as corporate scum," Heddy said), and a group of Infinity Inc. artists wore capes, gloves, and boots, and called themselves the H-Men, Hello City's resident superhero mutants. Excel had actually trick-or-treated only once, his freshman year, with Renzo. They dressed up as Tomo and Kon, two characters from *You Don't*

Say, Junichi! In orange-and-green striped T-shirts and blue shorts, they found that nobody knew what they were supposed to be.

By November, Sab had taken more responsibility for Pink Bubble, was in charge of boxing and shipping, driving to Whyling and El Centro for pickups and deliveries. And though she still hadn't received it, she'd stopped mentioning her mother's picture, a sign, Excel thought, that they were finally and truly settled. Excel worked on and off for Red—they made papier-mâché scarecrows resembling the last five US presidents, used the TV screen shards to make a mosaic on the side of Red's trailer, and made a miniature sculpture garden out of old bathroom fixtures, toilets, bathtubs, and sinks half-buried in the ground at obscure angles. In between, Excel would pick up odd jobs here and there—cleaning people's RVs, working shifts at the B&Q, sometimes washing dishes for Hot Food. Once, he helped an ex–tech guy pack all his belongings into a U-Haul; after a decade in Hello City, he was ready to rejoin the world. When he asked how long Excel planned to stay, Excel said, without hesitating, "Forever."

They celebrated Thanksgiving in Lucia's Airstream. Lucia roasted quail and fried up some brussels sprouts, then they ate sweet potato pie by the firepit outside. It had been a long, lazy day, and because he'd never celebrated Thanksgiving before, he didn't think of Maxima once, not at all. But the next morning, knowing Christmas was only a month away, he began feeling uneasy, a little anxious, knowing how much time had gone since he'd communicated with Maxima. They were never extravagant or overcelebratory, had done a Christmas tree only a handful of times, but Maxima and Joker had always made sure to give Excel a few presents, usually things he needed—underwear, a six-pack of socks, a new toothbrush. Excel did the same, gave each of them similar necessary things. But even the previous Christmas, their first without Joker, Maxima had done her best to make the holiday a little festive. She'd brought home a poinsettia (nabbed from the cemetery, Excel knew) and strung some lights, even put a Santa hat on The Bod and set him in front of the window. On Christmas Day, Maxima cooked pancit for lunch, and when they finished eating, she gave Excel two presents—a pack of white undershirts and, for reasons he couldn't understand, a gold fountain pen, solid and heavy, the kind with a tip that looked like he should write in calligraphy. "For when you sign important things," she said. "But it's not from me. It's from Joker, okay?" She smiled, eyes filling, and Excel thought he might cry too. He clenched his jaw, dug his feet into the rug, and the feeling passed.

This year would be different. He wouldn't call Maxima—he didn't want to talk, not yet—but he told himself he would send her a Christmas card, in which he'd write a message saying he was fine, that he hoped she was too, and they would see each other again, one day soon.

17

"Always. Fucking. Hydrate." Gunter slams a fist against the wall, so hard the whole break room thumps. "What are the kids supposed to think, watching Sloth the Sleuth go down like that? That he died? And what about the parents? They'll sue my ass for giving that Indian kid emotional trauma. What if some asshole called 911, like with the Svetlana incident? I'd be in deep shit, and you, Mr. No-Papers, would be in deeper shit." Excel almost flinches at the profanity, not for himself but for Z, who stays quiet at the break table, reading through his dictionary while giving Excel quick, concerned looks, like a bystander who wants to help but can't.

"I'm sorry," Excel says. He takes a sip of flat Sprite, his body still damp inside the costume. "I was drinking water at first, but I lost track."

"*Lost track?* Your 'lost track' could mean *lost business* for me. But you know what's worse? You broke *the dream*. These idiot kids think they're in a world of real goddamn animal spies, and you go fainting on them. You think they'll give me repeat business? Fat fucking chance." But the Sharma family hadn't seemed traumatized or offended. The father helped Excel off the floor, the mother carefully removed the headpiece, the grandfather fanned him with a menu. Even the grandmother poured him a glass of water. Excel kept his head down as he collected himself, worried Ranjit would recognize him from the night he entered their apartment. But when they did make eye contact, Ranjit just blinked a few times, then looked away. He didn't know who Excel was at all.

"The family is fine," Excel says, standing up slowly. "I'll go check on them."

"Uh-uh, no way," Gunter says. "You're done for the day. Go home. And if you think I'm paying you for today, you've got donkey balls for brains."

It's almost six p.m. Excel has been here since ten, and the shift was meant to be time and a half, almost a hundred dollars. "You're not paying me?"

"Nope."

Excel smiles, briefly, at the ridiculousness of it all. "You have to pay me."

Gunter shrugs with open palms, like there's nothing he, or anyone in the world, can do.

Excel stands up, moves toward Gunter. "You have to pay me."

"Step back," Gunter says.

Excel doesn't.

"*Step back*, shit-wipe."

Z sits up. "No shit-wipe, Gunter. You pay X. Please."

"You stay out of this," he says to Z, who slips into Serbian, gesturing toward Excel with shaky clasped hands. Gunter answers back, shouting and moving toward Z, his finger in his face. "Leave him alone,"

Excel says, stepping between them. Gunter shoves him aside but Excel steps back in, pushes Gunter back once, twice, telling him to back off, then to fuck off, and Excel thinks *Maximattack*—kick to the knee, bring the body down. But it's Excel who falls, the force of Gunter's fist on his face so hard his head slams against the employee lockers, metal clanging. Numb at first, the pain settles in, then courses like electricity through his skull, and when he finally catches his breath, he swallows blood.

Z steps toward him. "I'm fine," Excel says, hands up like he's surrendered. He gets to his feet slowly, cautiously, regains balance. Without a word, he changes out of the costume, back into his normal clothes. "I'm fine," he says again, to no one in particular, and on his way out he catches a glimpse of next week's schedule above the watercooler. He'll be back, he knows.

Planet-stricken, Excel thinks, *I feel planet-stricken*, then walks out the door and goes home.

THE APARTMENT IS DARK BUT MAXIMA IS IN HER ROOM, WORKING. "No, I don't believe it!" she says, and whoever is on the screen says, "It's true! It's true!" and the two of them laugh.

Excel goes to the kitchen and opens the freezer, the light so bright it hurts his face. He fills a plastic bag with ice and sits on the couch, carefully presses it over his eyes and the bridge of his nose. He'd felt hopeful when he woke this morning, was almost positive that he'd figured out a timeline and plan for returning to Hello City, for earning what he needed to pay for what he'd done, and to start again with Sab and, maybe, a baby.

He looks down, realizes there's blood on his shirt.

He picks up the remote and turns on the TV, sees that the DVD player is already running. *Ang Puso Ko VS. Ang Baril Mo* is on the screen (of course), but he's too tired to search for anything else. He lets it play.

A scene of Manila traffic switches to a high-class hotel lobby, everything marble and edged with gold, a fountain with twin life-size mermaids in the middle. Maxima, in a worn leather jacket, cutoff shorts, and boots, enters, approaches the front desk. The hotel clerk—sharp cheekbones, bloodred lips—eyes her suspiciously. "Itong babae," Maxima says, showing a picture of her sister, the same one who gave her money at the start of the film. "Nasaan siya? Nandito ba?" The clerk shrugs, says she hasn't seen her, demands that she leave. Maxima turns, and the camera zooms in on the photo and on her sister's heart-shaped earrings, then zooms in on the hotel clerk, who wears the exact same pair. "Ang earrings mo!" Maxima says. She reaches for them but the clerk steps back, presses a red button under the counter. A man and a woman in black T-shirts and black tights emerge from an elevator and charge toward Maxima, who takes her purse and twirls it like a bola, smacking both in the face. She gives a karate chop to the man's throat and a kick to the side of his head, then grabs a broom—out of nowhere, it seems—and thwacks the back of the woman's legs so hard she flips backward in the air, head crashing onto the marble floor, knocking her out cold. The hotel clerk leaps over the counter, a dagger in each hand, but Maxima wraps the long strap of her purse around her neck, pulls her close then judo flips her, then yanks the heart-shaped earrings right off her earlobes, blood gushing as the hotel clerk screams. "Nasaan ang sister ko!" Maxima demands. "Mga hayop kayo!" Above them, a crystal chandelier starts swaying, and an earthquake suddenly hits. "Lindol!" someone screams. "Lindol!" The ceiling comes crashing down, everything now dust and debris. But from a pile of rubble, a hand appears, then the arm, then Maxima, who slowly, desperately, digs her way out.

She looks to the heavens and screams. "Hindi ako puwedeng patayin!"

Excel hears Maxima down the hall. He mutes the TV, plays the English subtitles.

—Who is there to help me? Nobody? Then so be it!

She pulls herself out, gets to her feet.

—I cannot give up.

—It's true, by God! I will find my sister!

Covered in dust, legs scratched up and bloodied, she raises her fist to the sky, slowly reveals the earrings, gold and shining, still in her hand. She puts them on, staggers away from the ruins of the hotel lobby.

—I won't be defeated. I won't be killed. It's not possible!

—I will defeat animal men who stand in my way!

From her bedroom, Maxima laughs.

—Wait for me. I will find you.

—Do you hear me, God? Do you hear me, life?

—Nobody can defeat me!

From her bedroom, Maxima weeps.

Excel leans back, head resting against the wall. He dozes off, the movie still playing, and sometime later wakes to a blank blue screen. The bag of ice is water now and his face throbs—he hurts even more than before. Maxima's bedroom door opens, and she comes down the hallway, flips on the living room light, almost gasps at the sight of Excel's face.

"I need your help," he says, and Maxima, moving closer and without hesitation, says, "Of course."

18

Excel tells Maxima part of the truth, the only part that matters. "I owe money."

The job in the desert, he says, did not go as planned. He worked twice as many hours than he was being paid for, the pay itself far less than promised, which led to frequent fights with the archaeology professor who'd hired him. "I tried standing up for myself," he says, "but it wasn't enough." Then one night, after an especially heated argument just outside the professor's research tent, Excel smoked a cigarette to calm himself down ("I quit!" he promises Maxima), flicked it into the air when he was finished. But it wasn't out, and the still-burning butt landed at the bottom edge of the tent, in what must have been a tiny puddle of oil or fuel. "The whole thing went up in flames. His research, his equipment. Worth almost ten thousand dollars." That professor, he explains, has government contacts, is connected to high-powered law professors at his university. "If I don't pay him back, and if he takes me to court—"

"Then they'll know about you," she says.

He nods, explains he's back in Colma because The Pie is the best work he can find. But the pay isn't enough, and the professor wants his money, sooner than later.

"Ten thousand dollars?" Maxima says, then mutters something in Tagalog Excel can't quite hear and doesn't understand. "I don't have that kind of money."

The men, Excel wants to say, *ask the men.*

"Give me time," she says, "and I'll find a way."

His shoulders literally slump—he thought for sure Maxima had a large amount of cash stashed away somewhere. "Whatever you can do, would be a big help."

She gets up from the table, her eyes on Excel. She looks like she believes his whole story. "But your face," she says. "What happened?"

"This," he says, putting the sandwich bag of melted ice back over his nose, "this was just me being stupid."

She believes that, too.

EXCEL IS OFF THE NEXT DAY, STAYS IN BED PAST NOON. HIS WHOLE head throbs. His neck aches. Blinking hurts. He gets up only to pee, and when he looks in the mirror, half his face is swollen, blotched bluish-purple with shades of yellow. And yet there's a part of him unfazed by what he sees, as if the reflection before him was somehow inevitable. *Sooner or later*, he thinks, *someone was going to punch me in the face.*

He takes four aspirin and goes back to bed.

The following morning he's still bruised and hurt, but he's scheduled for a shift and can't afford to give it up. He goes to work, straight to the break room, finds Z already there, his dictionary closed on the table. "Your face," he says, shaking his head.

Excel puts on his uniform. "I'm okay. Are you okay?"

"Yeah, yeah. Gunter yells at me," he says, "but only yells."

The shift schedule says "Lydia/FD," which means Excel is working the front door, greeting customers all day as Peter the Greeter, Sloth the Sleuth's chameleon sidekick. He goes to the front of the restaurant, sees Reynaldo, the assistant manager, loading tape into the cash register. "You can only take a twenty for lunch today, Gunter's orders," he says, then whispers, "but I'll let you take thirty, it's cool." Excel says thanks, but knows the shift is another punishment. Peter the Greeter never gets tips, and while it's nowhere as torturous as being the sloth, it's more publicly humiliating. He puts on the trench coat ("Collar up," Reynaldo reminds him), then the hat with giant chameleon eyes and horn in between, and ten minutes later welcomes the first customers, young twentysomething parents and their two screaming kids, one boy, one girl. "Welcome to The Pie Who Loved Me," he says. "Should you choose to accept this mission of delicious pizzas, beverages, and desserts, please follow me and I'll be happy to seat you." The family follows him to the dining room and he hands out menus, wishes them luck on their mission, and as he walks away he hears the mother say to her husband, "His face. *Nasty.*"

The rest of the shift is no better, nor is the next day, or the day after. But he gets through them. Besides Maxima, the only person he talks to is Z, who's back to learning and testing out words whenever Excel is on a break. *Sentiment*, *perimeter*, and *unquestionable* are the newest additions to his vocabulary, and though he uses each of them in a sentence correctly, the dictionary on the table looks heavy as a brick, its thousands of words a reminder that even if Z learns every one, he'll never really be able to speak.

AT THE END OF THE WEEK, ON FRIDAY AFTERNOON, JUST AS HE'S about to leave work and head home, Excel looks at the break room calendar and counts ten days since he and Sab have spoken. On one hand, he's proud of himself: he's lonely and missing her voice, but he's proving he can honor her need for time and space. On the other, he fears not calling Sab sends the message that he's fine without her, that life in Hello City was a fluke, that whatever future they might have together is hypothetical, always has been.

On the way home he stops at the other Target (in Serramonte, the one where he didn't almost shoplift). He grabs a basket and searches the dollar bins, picks up two packs of Kit Kats and two packs of gummy bears, some AA batteries, always useful in Hello City. He agreed not to call Sab, but neither of them had said a thing about letters or care packages, so what does he have to lose? He picks up a set of ballpoint pens for $2.49, two pairs of women's wool socks for $3 each; it's warm now, but they'll help in the Hello City winter. He wanders the store, and the sight of an old Vietnamese man comparing prices between a bottle of Tide detergent with the Target brand reminds him so much of Joker that he has to stop and shut his eyes tight, keep it together until the feeling passes. When it does, he finds himself wandering toward the baby section, where he sees the Nirvana onesie hanging at the end of a rack. He finds the same size—0–3 months—lays it flat on his palms, stunned again by its smallness, and the fact that a person could, at some point in life, take up so little space in the world.

STANDING IN LINE AT THE POST OFFICE, EXCEL THINKS THAT THE care package to Sab is like a mini-version of a balikbayan box. Like many Filipinos, Joker would send one every Christmas to the two siblings he still had in the Philippines, filling a television-size box with cans of corned beef and Spam, dish towels, toothpaste, cheap San Francisco T-shirts purchased at flea markets, five for ten bucks. The post office lines were horrifically long, and Excel would whine, ask Maxima why Joker couldn't just send a card with a McDonald's gift certificate. "Knock it off," she'd say, twisting his ear, "or I'll put you in a balikbayan box and send you back too," which, Excel realizes as he approaches the counter, was a shitty thing to say to a kid TNT.

The clerk takes the box, sets it on the scale, asks if there are liquids or flammable materials. "No," Excel says, "just candy, snacks, and some socks." He doesn't mention the onesie, and isn't sure what sending it actually means. It's not pressure, he tells himself, just a nudge maybe, a way to help Sab see the possibilities.

"Five to seven business days," the clerk says, then drops the package on the long metal table behind her. Excel pays and, just before exiting the post office, takes another look at the box, knows it's officially en route to Sab. He feels desperate; he feels hopeful. Like a castaway firing a last flare, or flinging his one bottle into the ocean, tiny SOS rolled up inside.

RESTLESS TONIGHT, SAD IN WAYS HE CAN'T QUITE PINPOINT, EXCEL sits on the roof, watching Colma. It's Friday, and both Target parking lots are full, even after store hours have ended. Though the cemeteries have gone black, more than a few cars keep looping through them, like they're desperate to visit graves they can't find. He imagines all the flower-chomping deer stunned by their sweeping headlights, then darting off to hide.

Past midnight, planes still take off from SFO.

Finally tired, Excel climbs down the fire escape, pauses at the Sharmas' living room window. It's open again, lights on inside. He wonders if Ranjit will appear; he seems like the kind of kid who might stay awake after everyone else falls asleep. Excel has no intention of going in or saying hello, but after he collapsed at the Sharmas' table at The Pie, he wants to make sure Ranjit is okay.

Ranjit never shows.

Excel goes back down the fire escape. Just as he's about to climb through his bedroom window, Maxima appears in her own. "I found a way," she says.

19

Despite a New Year's Eve party at the Square that involved bottle rockets, a roasted pig, two kegs, and a bottle of absinthe (Sab took a sip, Excel spit his out), the new year already felt like the old—cold desert air, endless cheese sandwiches and instant ramen, evenings spent on lawn chairs on the helipad, staring at the sky. Sab's days were especially monotonous; Pink Bubble orders were high in demand and only increasing ("I *want* that Whole Foods account," Lucia would say, half-joking), so Sab worked well over forty hours a week, sometimes Saturdays, too. "I thought nine-to-five workdays were illegal in Hello City," she said one night, so exhausted she nearly dozed off at the table. But they needed the money. Odd jobs for Excel became less frequent, and he tried killing time by cleaning the bus and finding cheap ways to eat (when Sab couldn't take ramen anymore, he learned a box of couscous and a can of black beans, which he'd first had at the Hot Food cart, could last two, sometimes three meals). There were days when he'd sleep until noon, and spend afternoon to evening at Beans!, flipping through their stack of old newspapers and magazines. One day, sitting at a computer, he did a Google news search and typed "Colma" to see what, if anything, was happening back there. Not much, of course, though he saw a story about a new Japanese discount grocery store opening near the good Target, that the official grand opening was scheduled soon, an event he could imagine Maxima attending. She'd stroll through the aisles, accept any offers of free samples, wait ten minutes, then ask for more. If there was entertainment, like a singer on a stool strumming a guitar, or teenagers performing some kind of cultural dance, she'd find a spot in the shade and watch, applaud politely, then scan through the crowd in a way that looked like she was actually searching for someone, a thing she always did, though Excel never understood why.

He finally wrote her in March. He'd never responded to her e-mail from the first weeks in Hello City, but she'd sent another in January. He searched his inbox, opened it. Happy New Year, Excel, it read, I hope you stood up, a reminder that you were supposed to be standing when midnight struck, that it would bring good luck in the new year to come. It was a Filipino superstition, one he'd done all his life (he couldn't count the number of years Joker yanked him awake from the couch, forcing him to his feet), but this time, in all the noise and chaos of the Square's New Year's Eve party, he'd forgotten to stand, and was seated on a crowded bench, wedged between Sab and a Hello City person he didn't know or even speak to.

He typed his message to Maxima:

Hi. Yes, I stood right when the year changed. Hope you did too. Things are fine here. Lots of work, very busy. I hope you are doing good. I'll tell more soon.

He reread it several times, tried to hear his voice in the words; like Maxima's e-mail, they were just text on the screen. But he found himself cutting and rearranging the phrases and words, like the headlines he'd found in Red's newspapers and magazines.

> Here I stood right
> soon more home
> when changed you are doing good

He looked up from the screen, noticed the sun had set, but that the evening wasn't cold anymore, not at all. Spring, he thought. He reread the e-mail a final time, clicked Send.

THE FOLLOWING WEEK, RED ASKED FOR HELP AGAIN, AND EXCEL said yes.

The Hello City Town Council had asked if *Unaired Television Pilot* could be moved to the back of the stage in the Square. They'd been looking for ways to rejuvenate the space; having Red's piece there would be a first step. Red was reluctant at first, concerned that his art might be seen as merely decorative, like a painting loaned back and forth. He agreed to donate it to the Square on the stipulation that the piece become more interactive, that anyone in Hello City be allowed to make words and phrases to be projected on the plastic screens, which would be changed each month. "That way, it becomes an evolving, living thing," Red said, "and that's what art is all about, am I right?"

Excel said yes, absolutely, though he was secretly disappointed by the idea that the phrase he'd come up with—*End of an Era Still to Come*—would be gone, his one contribution no longer on display.

They dismantled the wall of TVs, one row at a time, loaded twenty sets onto the truck, drove them to the Square. They unloaded, and returning to the truck, Red tossed Excel the keys. "You drive," he said.

Excel felt his face warm up, more from embarrassment than all the lifting. "I don't know how," he said.

"Then you'll learn," Red said, getting into the passenger's seat.

Excel opened the driver's-side door. Far as he knew, there were never police in Hello City, but still. "We have work to do," Red said, "c'mon."

Excel sat in the driver's seat. The truck was an automatic, which Red said made driving a no-brainer. He pointed out the accelerator, the brakes, the gear shifts. Excel turned on the ignition, looked out the windshield and both side windows, but the strange logic of the rearview mirrors threw him; it made no sense to look behind you in order to move forward.

"Excel," Red said, almost sternly, "*go*."

He released his foot from the brake then stepped gently on the gas and took off. Hello City had no roads or lanes, just dirt, so there was nothing to swerve around or dodge. Still, he couldn't believe how little strength, the near-zero effort, was required to move an object as big as the truck.

"Faster," Red said.

"I can't," Excel said, eyes fixed straight ahead.

"Go"—he slammed both hands on the dashboard—"*now!*" and Excel flinched and pressed hard on the gas, sending them down the dirt faster than he'd ever imagined he could move.

Red had Excel drive the rest of that day, and when they returned to Infinity Inc.—Red always parked the truck just outside the front gate—he told Excel he could use it whenever he needed it. All he had to do was ask.

"I don't have a license," Excel said.

"It's HC," Red said. "Nobody cares."

Excel walked back home, buzzing from the high of driving for the first time in his life. He hadn't gone far, drove what was essentially a straight-shot, back-and-forth route, and few, if anyone, had actually seen him. But should Sab know he'd driven? If so, she'd ask him to apply for a driver's license, so that he could drive himself to possible jobs outside Hello City. Or she'd insist on returning to Colma to get her mother's picture, the two of them taking shifts on the long drive up. She might plan road trips, destinations that crossed straight lines.

He wouldn't tell her, not yet, though she clearly suspected something was off. "Excel," she said, as soon as he entered the bus, "why are you smiling like that?"

EXCEL AND RED REBUILT *UNAIRED TELEVISION PILOT* THE NEXT DAY; at the town council meeting the following week, Red plugged the entire wall of TVs in again, this time showing new phrases and messages on each individual screen, put together by the people of Hello City.

I Am Afraid

SCOTUS Votes to Storm the World

Takedown and Stay

There were dozens more, too many to read. Rosie, still in charge of running meetings, asked the audience to vote either for or against keeping the wall of TVs as a temporary backdrop for the stage. She called for those in favor and everyone, including Excel, who had never voted on anything before (and had always assumed he never would) raised his hand. It was a unanimous decision, but Excel still felt he'd made a difference.

After the meeting, Rosie and her band took the stage; with all the TV screens behind them, they really did look like they were performing in a new venue altogether, backlit by the glowing words and phrases. The TVs cast a cool and eerie light on the Oracle, which made her look even more mythical, like she truly possessed an otherworldly knowledge, and all her answers were unquestionably right. Volunteers went beyond overboard with decorations, stringing up even more lights, connecting everything with rainbow-colored streamers, paper flowers, even piñatas of the letter *H*. The Square was like a birthday party with no end in sight.

20

NAME:	Jerry Borger
AGE:	55
WEBSITE:	Fil-Am Catholic Hearts Connections
LOCATION:	Concord, New Hampshire
OCCUPATION:	Civil Engineer
EDUCATION:	College (plus MASTER'S!!)
STATUS:	Single
CHILDREN:	None
FAVORITE MOVIE:	Forrest Gump
FAVORITE TV SHOW:	Gilligan's Island, CNN
FAVORITE SONG:	You Needed Me by Anne Murray (learn Anne Murray!)
FAVORITE FOOD:	Tex-Mex, American
HAPPIEST MEMORY:	sailing with parents
HOBBIES:	Computer chess, Ship in a bottle, living life to the fullest

GREATEST FEAR:	Not living life to the fullest, trapped in small spaces, snakes
LIFE GOAL:	Living life to the fullest, visit all 7 continents
MOTTO:	Every day is another day to make the most out of life

Read it again," Maxima says.

Excel yawns, rubs his eyes. It's past midnight and they're in Maxima's room—he's sitting at her desk, she's installing a pull-up bar in her doorway—and Excel is reviewing the file of Jerry Borger, the man Maxima thinks could give them the ten thousand dollars. On the first read, everything on the sheet seemed so vital, like the personal information on a driver's license or passport, or any document guaranteeing your identity—things Excel doubts he'll ever have. But on the third read, the facts of Jerry Borger's life seem like a jumble of trivia. On paper, he's just another of Maxima's men.

"All right," he says, and tucks the sheet back into the manila folder, "done."

Maxima jumps up, catches the bar. "You'll want to review it again," she says. "It's good to memorize it in advance."

"In advance of what?"

She does a pull-up, then another. "Of meeting him."

"Meeting him?"

"Ano ba? I'm supposed to do this on my own? You're part of this too." Children, she says, are a hardship. You have to clothe and feed them, take them to the doctor, pay for their school; all those things are a justification to ask for money. And men who are open to the possibility of stepchildren are sometimes willing to give even more. Jerry Borger, she thinks, is that kind of man. "We talked twice, and he knows about you. And if things go right, he'll want to meet." Excel looks at Maxima's computer, tries picturing himself talking to this

Jerry Borger guy on the screen. Instead, he imagines talking to Sab as she sits at a Beans! computer terminal in Hello City, a baby wearing the Nirvana onesie bouncing on her lap.

But maybe it's a trick, talking to people through screens. A way to make you feel closer to someone than you really are, a denial of the actual distance between. Phone calls and text messages, even voice mails—those things are honest and real, remind you that you're not together at all.

"So when I meet this guy," Excel says, "what am I supposed to say?"

"Say hello," she says, "and see what happens."

She does five more pull-ups then drops to the floor, does ten push-ups without breaking a sweat. She gets up and stands behind Excel, reaches over him, and flips on the webcam. "You need to *acclimate*," she says, "learn to see yourself." She grabs his head, positions it in view of the camera. For the first time, he sees himself on-screen. He'd imagined it was like looking in a mirror, but when Maxima shifts his face left and right, there's the slightest second of a delay. The same thing happens when he waves, smiles, even blinks; it's like the Excel on-screen is from a parallel timeline just one moment behind his own. And when he looks at himself, the Excel on-screen can't look back; his eyes are slightly downcast, like he means to type something on the keyboard. Despite all this technology, you still can't look yourself in the eye.

"I get it," he says. "Please let go of my head."

She steps back, sits on the edge of her bed. "Now, a few more things. First, work on your Filipino accent. But not too thick, okay? Americans don't like it."

"Accent. Got it."

"And wear nice clothes. But not too nice. We don't want to look too poor, but we don't want to look like we have money. So when you meet, don't wear that ugly drunk face shirt. Wear the Target one."

"I will."

"And don't look too American."

No one has ever told him that before. "I don't know what that means."

"It means . . ." She looks at him, tilts her head like she's slightly perplexed by his face. "It means this." She slouches one shoulder, hunches over a little, lets her head hang to the side. "You look so casual, so lazy. Like everything is so easy. Stand up straight! Be tall! Look slender! Like you're ready and willing to work hard! Tingan mo ako." She straightens up and stretches her neck, smiles an almost disturbingly pleasant smile. "See? Like a good Filipino boy. Understand?"

"A good Filipino boy. Got it."

She doesn't look convinced, but there's time to get it right.

For now, the plan is to talk to Jerry a few more times before he and Excel meet. Excel's job, in the meantime, is to practice. "And one last thing," she says, "your name is Perfecto."

"*Perfecto?*"

"Perfecto. P-E-R-F-E-C-T-O. Jerry thinks my name is Perfecta and that my son is Perfecto. We never use real names, don't you know?"

Perfecta. Perfecto. Excel thinks of amateur magicians or lion tamers. Maybe a washed-up pop duo from the Philippines. "Those names are ridiculous," he says.

Maxima looks offended, even hurt. Her great-great uncle on her father's side was named Perfecto, and her family, she explains, had a long tradition of giving children names that suggested good fortunes to come. She lists names of far-off distant relatives (some living, most dead), people Excel has never heard of and will never meet: Royce, Princessa, Guggenheim, Beethoven, even a pair of third cousins, twin brothers named Harvard and MIT, who run an import-export business in Guam. "It's always been like this," she says, "since the beginning. It's why I named you Excel, di ba?"

THIS WON'T BE THE FIRST TIME EXCEL WAS SOMEONE ELSE.

Years before, tenth grade. On a rainy spring afternoon during World Cultures and History class, the teacher, Mr. Funston, an ex–pro surfer who wore ripped jeans and skinny ties, stood at the dry-erase board and wrote "PERSPECTIVAL AUTOBIOGRAPHY," then looked back at the class. "Who can tell me what this means?" he asked. Nobody answered. "What this means," he said, "is, 'Who are you? What are you? Why are you?' In other words, 'Why do you think the way you think?'" The questions were meant to inspire, to rouse the students into believing there was something revolutionary in looking inward, in exploring your identity, but everybody knew they were Mr. Funston's lame attempt at introducing the tenth-grade self-reflection assignment required by the school district.

"I want to understand how you came to be," Mr. Funston said. "Why do you see the world the way you do?" He used himself as an example, explained that both his father and grandfather were champion surfers, and his own relationship to the ocean—"the swells, the waves, the calm"—helped him understand his place in the universe. "I'm a teacher who surfs and a surfer who teaches," he said. "That's who I am. Now, who are you?" He asked the question over and over, pointing to a different student each time.

"Who are you?"

"A Vietnamese American."

"Who are you?"

"Native Californian."

"Who are you?"

"A big sister."

"Who are you?"

"An extremely bored student in your class."

"Who are you?"

"Libertarian. Like my dad."

Mr. Funston pointed to the back corner of the room, at Excel. Excel had barely spoken all year, in any of his classes. With Renzo gone, he didn't really talk to anyone.

"Who are you?" Mr. Funston asked.

Excel shrugged.

Mr. Funston shook his head. "You're gonna have to do better than that, my friend."

Part one of the assignment was a worksheet, a fill-in-the-blank family tree that stretched back five generations. Part two was taking that information and writing a mini–family history, and explaining how your ancestry, along with other outside influences, helped you become the person you believed you were. If he filled it out honestly, Excel's worksheet would have two names only: his own and Maxima's. Excel never knew his grandparents' or great-grandparents' names, and whatever stories Maxima told about her own upbringing rarely included them. Sometimes, his entire family history seemed nonexistent, a blank that spanned generations. As if history began only with Maxima.

Lying would be easier. Two weeks later, the night before the assignment was due, he filled in the family tree blanks with names as ridiculous as his own. His grandfather was named Maximilliano, who was the son of Xerxes and Fortuna; he named his grandmother Galaxina, who became the daughter of Novacento and Castleanna. By the time he finished, the sheet looked as though he'd descended from a line of wizards and sorceresses.

Part two of the assignment would be a more involved lie, but he knew how it would go; he'd simply follow everybody else's Filipino American story. There were plenty of Filipino kids at his school, their origins nearly identical: their fathers or grandfathers enlisted in the

US Navy back when its bases were active in the Philippines, served on ships for years and years, married, then finally had their requests for transfer to America granted. There were a few whose parents were scholars or professionals—they had gone to university in the States and found ways to stay, or came as nurses and doctors, secured permanent jobs here. Excel took these details, plugged them into a rough outline, but when he finished, he felt a pang of jealousy and resentment at how easy and familiar that story was. Nothing like his own.

Who are you?

He wrote, "TNT." Then he wrote, "TNT American."

Who are you?

He wrote, "Dynamite," then, "Dynamite American." It sounded like a new identity beyond ethnicity or nationality, and he liked the sound of it, the image it conjured up: an American flag with fifty tiny sticks of dynamite, no stars.

He started the paper over.

It was past midnight now, the paper was due the next day; he had to work fast. He couldn't get online—they didn't have Internet hookup back then—so Excel went through Joker's 1977 edition of the *World Book Encyclopedia,* looked up "dynamite," learned it was invented in 1867 by a Swedish guy named Alfred Nobel. He went to the family tree worksheet, went four generations back before his name, erased "Felixiano" and wrote "Alfred Nobel" in his place. He read a quick summary of how Nobel invented dynamite: alone in his laboratory, tinkering with nitroglycerin, he discovered that the way to contain a substance so explosive was to encase it in some kind of absorbent material; Nobel used clay. For his essay, Excel invented a Filipina woman and named her Maria (he liked the simplicity of it, how normal it sounded), made her Nobel's live-in maid (he thought of his auntie Queenie, how the world was full of Filipina maids, so why not?). When Nobel toils in his lab from morning to night, it's Maria who brings him his meals, a mix of Filipino and Swedish delicacies ("lumpia and Swedish meatballs," he wrote). Maria is loyal and duti-ful, possesses a genius of her own, but given her station in life, she isn't allowed to tap into it.

One day, Nobel asks Maria to take a walk with him, to keep him company as he thinks through his experiments out loud. How to contain and stabilize such an explosive substance? Maybe it's impos-sible? Walking along the edge of the river, Maria notices a pretty blue stone, bends down to pick it up. That's when she notices the peculiar texture of the almost claylike dirt coating her fingers. "What about this?" she says. "Could something like this work for your invention?" Nobel dismisses the suggestion at first, but, out of options, he collects a sample and brings it to his lab. For several days they test its reaction with the nitroglycerin, holding dangerous test explosions in a nearby cornfield, and one day, after forming the clay into a stick that he soaks in nitroglycerin and rigs with a fuse, it goes exactly as planned: Nobel strikes a match and lights the stick, throws it across the river, and *BOOM*—dynamite is born!

That night, they celebrate with a feast—more lumpia and meat-balls, too much wine. It's not long before a kiss; not much longer before sex (in the actual essay, Excel wrote, "they got drunk and made forbid-den love"). But their affair is short lived; trouble back in the Philippines requires Maria to return. Their breakup is painful, but Nobel knows he must see his invention through. Had he known Maria was carrying his child—Excel's great-great-great grandfather—he would have aban-doned his work, sacrificed his place in history to be with his true love.

The story played out vividly in his mind, but the version in the essay was one long summary. In the final paragraph, he tried to make it real. He wrote:

There are letters documenting this. Unfortunately, they've gone missing. But I have seen them. My ancestor, Alfred Nobel, my great-great-great-great grandfather, is the person who influences me. His invention of dynamite, a.k.a. TNT, is the reason I exist today, and is an important part of my heritage, of who I am, and who I will one day become. The end.

Mr. Funston returned the essays the following week; as he handed them back, Excel could see all the crossed-out lines, the margin notes in red ink, and he hoped for at least a C, though prepared himself for worse. He received his paper last, no grade indicated, just two red words near the bottom of the last page: "SEE ME."

The bell rang and the class emptied out; Excel stayed in his seat, the essay on the desk. Mr. Funston brought a chair over, turned it around and sat backward on it, as if trying to assume the coolest, most chill sitting position possible, which made Excel 100 percent positive that Mr. Funston knew his essay was four pages of pure bullshit.

"Now, your essay has some issues," Mr. Funston started, then with red pen in hand, pointed out run-on sentences, misspellings, tense shifts. "But your actual *story*"—he leaned in—"is tight. Off the charts. Incredible." He called the essay a remarkable autobiographical sketch, a perfect example of why he was a history major in college. "The past is always changing, it's *alive*," he said. "Just when you think the facts have presented themselves, along comes a *new truth*."

Mr. Funston picked up the paper, drew big red circles around the Nobel sections. He leaned in closer. "Listen," he said, his voice suspiciously low, "I know it's a personal story, but have you ever thought of going public? I don't always talk about it, but I'm actually a writer, and I could write an article on this . . ." He said he'd written short journalism pieces in the past, dabbled in nonfiction, and was confident he had the chops to turn Excel's story into something truly special. "I'd need to verify sources, of course, interview your mother, your grandparents too . . ." Excel imagined Mr. Funston rewriting the story, releasing it to the world; reporters would come knocking, historians would call to verify, challenge, and finally dismantle an entire family history, then demand to know the real one. He pictured Maxima at home, organizing her bottles of nail polish by color and shade at the kitchen table (she was selling makeup door-to-door back then) when someone would come knocking—the police, Immigration, border patrol, Mr. Funston himself.

He wondered if Mr. Funston was testing him, egging him on to admit he'd made the whole thing up.

"No thank you," Excel said.

Mr. Funston blinked.

"The story is a secret," Excel said. "I was never actually supposed to tell anyone. But the assignment inspired me. Thanks for giving me the chance to let it all out. To express myself."

Mr. Funston gave a slow nod, like he was in disbelief that a student, who sat in anonymity in the corner every day for nearly a year, would pass up such an opportunity. "Well," he sighed, "it's your story, I guess."

Excel thanked him again, got up from his desk, stuffed his things into his backpack. Then he asked, "What did I get?"

Mr. Funston looked confused.

"On the paper. What grade did I get?"

"Your grade. Right." Mr. Funston skimmed the pages quickly, giving it one more read. He uncapped his pen, wrote a clear and red C– next to Excel's name, underlined it twice, reminding Excel of the grammatical and mechanical errors ("Edit, edit, edit!" he said). "The larger issue is some of the content. No verifiable sources, obviously, and there's a glaring factual error. TNT and dynamite aren't the same thing." TNT, he explained, was a chemical compound, explosive when mixed with other substances, but not nearly as powerful as dynamite itself. "Get your facts straight," Mr. Funston said.

He wished Excel a good weekend then got up, started wiping the dry-erase board, and on his seat was Mr. Funston's wallet, which had a tendency to slip through the ripped back pocket of his jeans. Excel reached down and took the cash from the wallet, set it back on the chair, walked out of the classroom, and counted $97. Mr. Funston made no mention about the stolen cash the following Monday, or the day after, or ever, but Excel became hyperaware of occasional glances from his teacher, and tried interpreting them: maybe Mr. Funston was just in frustrated awe that one of his very own students was a descendant of Alfred Nobel and yet couldn't tell anyone about it. Or, more likely, he understood that the whole essay was a lie, that Excel had no real life to write about, and so out of pity, let the lie slip by with a below-average but still-passing grade.

With Jerry, Excel will get the story right.

21

To Jerry Borger, Maxima is Perfecta Santos and Excel is Perfecto Santos, a single mother and her fourteen-year-old son living in Olongapo City, just outside the former US naval base, in a simple but clean one-room apartment with an outdoor kitchen and bathroom shared by an entire floor. Perfecta is a widow—her husband took two bullets in the chest in a karaoke incident ("Trust me," Maxima said, "it happens"), only months after Perfecto was born. It's been just the two of them ever since, and she has raised Perfecto to be a responsible and respectful boy, hardworking and studious, who always earns high marks in school. Though they are poor—Perfecta's job selling plastic sandals at the market doesn't earn much; neither do Perfecto's constant part-time jobs—they are happy, and Perfecta still allows herself to dream that one day she'll meet a good and honest man, someone who will love her as well as her son and, most important, allow himself to be loved.

Maxima's movies, Excel thinks, are much more realistic.

Over the next two days, she talks online to Jerry three times. Everything goes well, so well, in fact, that Jerry is willing, even eager, to meet Perfecto the next time he and Maxima talk.

"Tomorrow," Maxima tells Excel, "we begin."

He's anxious that night, anxious when he wakes the next morning. *Perfecto*, he reminds himself, *I'm Perfecto*, and he imagines the life Maxima created for Perfecto and Perfecta, tries thinking of it as a memory, not just a story to memorize. At work, he's Peter the Greeter again, but so distracted that he sometimes forgets to greet customers properly, just hands them menus and shows them to their table. "The *mission*," Gunter says, after catching Excel's mistake. "You didn't ask if they choose to accept this mission of delicious pizzas, beverages, and desserts. This ain't Pizza Hut, genius. Get it right." Excel nods and makes deliberate eye contact with him, holds his stare for a moment. If everything works out with Jerry, if he can do as Maxima says and not screw this up, the time will come soon when he'll never have to look at Gunter's face again.

He's back home by early evening. When he enters the apartment, he finds Maxima at the kitchen table, head bowed and hands clasped, whispering an orasyon. He's not sure she knows he's there, so he stands motionless in the kitchen doorway, waits until she lifts her head and opens her eyes. "You're here," she says.

"Everything okay?"

"I asked Joker for help," she says, "to watch over us when we talk to Jerry."

"Are you worried?"

She shakes her head. "It's just a little different this time. You've never met the men. You've never seen me work."

"I've watched your movies." He tries to sound reassuring. "I've seen you act."

"Not like this." She gets up from the table, leaves the room. "This is a different thing."

TIME, MAXIMA WARNS EXCEL, GETS MESSY WHEN TALKING TO THE men. "They think I'm in the Philippines, fifteen hours ahead of California. If they think they're talking to us at eight p.m. Philippines time, we need to talk to them at five a.m. our time. And Jerry, who's in New Hampshire, will be talking at eight a.m. *his* time. Understand?"

Excel looks at the alarm clock next to Maxima's bed, repeats the logistics in his head. It all sounds like nonsensical time travel, a loopy sci-fi paradox. "So Jerry will be thinking we're twelve hours ahead of him," Excel says, "but really, we're three hours behind?"

"Exactly."

Maxima will start the conversation at five a.m., but Excel is ready at four. He hasn't slept, has spent most of the night reviewing Jerry's file, practicing a Filipino accent based on a classmate from seventh grade, a newly arrived Filipino kid who overenunciated every word. Now, in the last minutes before meeting Jerry, he's staring at himself in the bathroom mirror, doing what he can to make himself look fourteen years old, the age of Perfecto. The Target shirt helps—a men's small is still too big on Excel, which makes him look even younger. But his face. It's still bruised around the eyes and nose from Gunter's fist, and he worries that the time in Hello City has aged him. He shuts his eyes and massages, squeezes, and pinches his forehead, cheeks, and chin (what this does, he has no idea), then takes a step back and opens them.

Fourteen, he thinks. *Easily.*

He hears Maxima get up from her chair. She opens her door and motions for Excel to enter, brings him in front of the computer. "Jerry," she says, "my son, Perfecto."

Excel sets a chair next to Maxima, sits. They squeeze together, fitting themselves within the camera's view. Jerry's head fills most of

Maxima's screen, and though Excel saw a picture ahead of time—in it, he's wearing a baseball cap and a Hawaiian shirt—he looks different from what he'd expected. He has a pale and squarish face, graying hair with little left on top, small eyes with slightly droopy brows. Excel can imagine him behind a bank teller's window, delivering mail, or on a real estate agent's flyer—a face familiar and entirely forgettable.

"Sir Jerry," Excel says. "Hello!" He says it more emphatically than he'd meant to, brings it down a notch. "Hello, sir."

"Hello, Perfecto." Jerry gives a big wave on-screen. "How are you?"

"I am very fine, sir. And yourself, sir?"

"Can't complain, can't complain. Always a good day when I get to see your mother's pretty face."

Excel doesn't have a follow-up line; moments pass awkwardly, and Maxima pinches him in the middle of his back. "Oh yes, sir. She is very pretty, sir." He smiles, tries not to look at himself in the tiny window at the bottom corner of the screen.

"You know," Jerry says, "we don't have to be so formal. No need to call me sir. Jerry is just fine. You can even call me JJ. That's what they called me back in school."

"I will call you 'Jerry.' Thank you, sir."

Excel asks Jerry what kind of work he does ("Civil engineer, a builder of bridges," Jerry says); Jerry asks about Excel's classes (at fourteen, Excel might be studying geometry, so he mentions how he has trouble remembering the point-slope formula). They share their favorite foods, books, and music, and Excel thinks back to Jerry's fact sheet, then says his favorite film is *Forrest Gump* ("Mine too!" Jerry says). When Jerry says he has a passion for building ships in a bottle, Excel tells him that he's always wanted to learn how to build one.

"Well, how fortuitous," Jerry says, big smile on his face.

"Talaga," Maxima says, "fortuitous."

Maxima tells Jerry it's getting late, that Perfecto must return to his chores and then his studies. Excel says good-bye, then fakes a coughing fit, not so extreme that he looks like he's in pain, but just enough to make clear that he's not feeling well—a sign for Jerry that, despite their names, their lives are far from perfect.

EXCEL WAITS IN THE KITCHEN FOR MAXIMA TO FINISH. WHEN SHE finally enters, it's almost daylight.

"Did I do okay?" Excel asks.

"You did fine. A little nervous at first, but that's understandable."

"I got caught up in remembering his file, then the accent, the time difference. It's a lot to keep track of." Hearing himself, he's suddenly impressed with how Maxima manages to keep everything straight.

"Next time, you'll be more relaxed."

"*Next time?* I thought I just had to say hello, that was all. And then we could, you know, ask for money."

"You think it's that easy, that you get what you need"—she snaps her fingers twice—"just like that? Once you start, you keep going."

He has no choice but to follow her plan. "Okay. Just tell me when we talk again." He goes to the freezer to get ice for his face—it always hurts in the morning—drops a few cubes into a plastic bag. "It's strange," he says, "the whole time we talked, Jerry never asked about my face."

"Actually, he did. After you left, he asked what happened." She goes to the sink, fills a glass with water. "I told him you had a job with a bastard boss who hit you."

"I didn't think we were supposed to tell the truth," he says.

"If we can use the truth, why not?" She grabs Excel's bag of ice, takes two melting cubes and drops it into her glass, returns to her room. Outside the kitchen window, the day in Colma begins.

THEY MEET AGAIN TWO DAYS LATER, FIVE A.M. MAXIMA TALKS FOR twenty minutes, then invites Excel to say hello. The plan is for Excel

to be brief—it's too soon for a meaningful conversation—but to make
a strong connection, too. The day before, Excel found an article online
about a blind man in Australia who builds ships in a bottle, and it's
the first thing he mentions to Jerry. "It's quite interesting, sir," he says.
"He does it all from memory and a sensitivity to touch."

"Fascinating," Jerry says, taking notes as Excel talks. Then he tells
Excel about a terrific ship in a bottle article in *Popular Mechanics*. "His-
torically comprehensive, but written in a really hip tone. Give me your
e-mail address and I'll send a PDF."

"My e-mail address?" He pauses for a moment, remembers the fake
e-mail account Maxima created for him, in case Jerry wanted to cor-
respond with Excel directly. "Yes, sir. I will say it slowly so that you may
write it down. Perfecto. Is. A. Good. Boy. At. Hotmail. Dot. Com."

"'Perfecto is a good boy.' I like that," Jerry says. "Maybe I should
create a new address. Jerry. The. Average. White. Guy. At. AOL. Dot.
Com." He laughs, and Excel knows to laugh along with him, then
Maxima laughs, too. Jerry makes up more gag e-mail addresses for
the next five minutes ("ThisIsJerry'sEmailAddress@aol.com" is Jerry's
favorite), then Excel excuses himself to finish his homework, fakes a
brief coughing fit (Maxima had left a tiny Post-it note on the keyboard
with the word *COUGH!* written on it), and says he looks forward to
receiving Jerry's e-mail soon.

Later that day, Excel gets on Maxima's computer and checks the e-
mail account. His inbox is already receiving junk mail—someone named
Irina, apparently, is waiting to be "SPECIAL XXX FRIENDS"—but
at the top he sees a message with the subject heading "From Jerry." He
opens the e-mail.

Dear Perfecto:
Thank you again for telling me about the blind Australian
fellow who builds ships. It's amazing what the human spirit can
accomplish. I feel inspired!

Also, I hope I'm not out of line for saying this, but your mother
let me know about the abusive situation at your job gutting
fish at the local market. I know the income is important,
but remember you have rights as well, and shouldn't have
to tolerate that kind of abuse. Does the market have an HR
("Human Resources") office? Or a higher-ranking supervisor
of some sort? If not, I hope you'll find other work, or if at all
possible, try to focus on your studies. One of my mottoes has
always been "Education is the key!" and as I know you are a
bright young man, school will be the key to your success, too. It
saddens me (and your mother) to think you may be suffering at
a job that only detracts from your studies.
If you'd like to talk about it more, I hope you'll let me know.

Yours,
Jerry

PS. Per our conversation, I'm attaching the article I mentioned.
Enjoy!

Unlike the e-mails he'd received from Maxima in Hello City,
Excel can actually hear Jerry's voice when he reads the message, like
a true voice-over from the movies—clear and calm, a little too cheerful. If this had been sent by one of Maxima's other men, he might
almost laugh at its earnestness (who says "fellow"?), delete the e-mail
and the attachments with it. But this is important business; he and
Maxima have worked hard to get to this point, and he knows there's
more ahead.

He clicks Reply and types.

Dear Sir Jerry,
Salamat ("thank you" in Tagalog) for your e-mail and for sharing
your wise motto. I agree that "education is the key!" so I will
follow your advice and quit my job gutting fish at the market.

I will do my best not to find more part-time jobs, so that I can
focus on my studies. If I can do that, then I know I can SUCCEED
and EXCEL in life, just like you.
I hope we may talk again soon, Sir Jerry.

Respectfully,
Perfecto

PS. Salamat for the article. I will read it after I study.

Looking over the e-mail, Excel can't hear his voice, but he's starting to hear Perfecto's. Still, he's pleased with himself, how he managed
to slip his real name into the message. A bit of truth to use, just like
Maxima said.

He clicks Send.

22

In Hello City, Excel forgot how old he was.

He was sitting at Beans!, killing time until Sab was off work. Heddy and Ned, in matching tracksuits again, were sitting nearby, reading a copy of the *Los Angeles Times*, when Excel noticed the date on the front page, May 17. His birthday. "Is that today's paper?" he asked.

Heddy looked at him and laughed. "It's old news, sweetie," she said. "Today's the twenty-seventh."

Excel had turned nineteen ten days before.

Birthdays didn't mean much to Excel, not since his tenth, when Maxima told him everything at Pier 39. In recent years, they had barely celebrated, which was fine by him. But now, he was fixated on this idea that, for ten days, he'd believed he was younger than he actually was. Maxima, he knew, didn't know her exact birthday; her parents had drowned when she was a child, left no documents behind. She could be younger than she believed, too, with more life ahead than she'd imagined.

That evening, drinking beer on their lawn chairs outside the bus, he told Sab that his birthday had passed ten days before. He shrugged, tried sounding casual about it. "Birthdays aren't really my thing," he said.

She rubbed her eyes, tired from the day. "Oh geez. Sorry about that."

"No big deal." He reached over, put his hand on hers. "I forget birthdays all the time."

"I didn't forget. I actually don't know when your birthday is."

Excel noticed Sab was staring at his hand on top of hers, couldn't tell if she wanted it there or not. He gave it one more squeeze and let go. "No big deal," he repeated.

"We should celebrate. What if we drive to El Centro, look for a Mexican restaurant or something. We'll splurge on extra guacamole, my treat."

He hadn't been to El Centro since picking up the television sets with Red. It seemed even farther now, and the thought of being on the freeway, after they'd each had a beer, seemed reckless. He imagined Sab accidentally speeding, just a few miles over the limit, and the glow of red and blue police lights in the side mirror, moving closer.

"Let's just go to the Square," he said.

"*The Square?* For your birthday?"

"Why not? We shouldn't waste money or gas driving so far. Besides, it's curry night at Hot Food."

"If that's what you want," she said with a shrug, "sure."

They sat, silent, looked out into the field. Above, the sky was darkening, turning into a sky almost similar to one they'd seen long before, the night they arrived in Hello City.

SAB'S LAST-MINUTE GIFT TO EXCEL WAS A DOLLAR'S WORTH OF QUES-tions for the Oracle. "I'll get you something else, too," she said, pinching his rear, "promise." She gave him four quarters and a kiss on the cheek, then went to stand in the Hot Food line.

Excel walked up to the Oracle, bent down to say hello. The owl was motionless, perched at the end of the branch, right against the side of the cage.

He dropped a quarter into the jar and asked his first question. "Will this be a good year?" He leaned in, heard a low, guttural chirp, took that as a yes.

He dropped another quarter. "Will I find a steady job?" The owl stayed silent. Excel reminded himself to post another flyer, looking for work.

He wanted to ask about Sab. She'd been working long days, was always tired, and sometimes seemed frustrated and bored, weighted down with a low-energy restlessness. He feared he was the cause, or at least part of it. Though he'd told her that his birthday meant nothing, he'd hoped she might be a little happier tonight.

He dropped the quarter into the jar, unsure what to ask, how to formulate the right yes or no question to help him understand what might be troubling her.

But he asked a different question. "Will I always be TNT?" he whispered.

If she hoots, it's a YES. If not, it's a NO.

A minute passed, then another. The Oracle remained perfectly still, bright yellow eyes frozen, completely silent.

"Thank you," he said.

He walked to Sab, who sat on a bench near the stage. "Did you get good answers?" she asked.

Excel nodded.

"What were your questions?"

He shook his head. "They're like birthday wishes," he said, dipping a spoon into the lentil curry. "A secret."

A Hello City Town Council meeting was about to start, and Lucia arrived with bottles of beer in a metal pail. "Cerulean Spark!" she said. Excel and Sab each took a beer, decided to stay. Rosie stepped onstage and began with a list of announcements—Hot Food was still taking canned goods donations, the supplies store in Whyling would be closed for a week while the owners were on their Key West vacation, and there still was no decision about the stop sign controversy, though people, as always, were welcome to share their concerns. Rosie continued, and Excel looked at Sab, and thought, *Now*. If he told her he was TNT, he would, in essence, no longer be one, at least not to her. Maybe that was his first step to no longer hiding, to proving the Oracle right.

He would tell Sab tonight. In the bus. Or maybe on the helipad as they looked at the stars.

Then Rosie said, "Where's Excel?"

He looked up. Rosie picked up her fiddle, played the first notes of "Happy Birthday."

"You told them," Excel said to Sab.

She shrugged. "Why not?"

Rosie played and everyone—around thirty people—sang. Excel knew most of the crowd, if not by name, then by face, which likely meant that they all knew him, too. He hadn't lied to Sab; this kind of attention really did make him self-conscious. But tonight, if he didn't exactly welcome it, he was grateful, and their singing made up for what he suddenly realized was missing—a birthday message from Maxima. She hadn't sent an e-mail, had made no attempt to call. Not that he blamed her. He was the one out of touch, the one who was gone. And all she would've done for his birthday was recount the story of it, which she'd done every year since he turned ten. That story was nineteen years old now, too.

MAXIMA WOULD TELL THE STORY LIKE THIS:

She's eight months pregnant when she boards a Philippine Airlines flight bound from Manila to San Francisco. It's her first time on a plane, in a window seat, no less.

Takeoff makes her nervous, but once the plane is steady in the sky she relaxes, thinks she might even enjoy the feeling of being in the air. She won't pay for headphones, but she watches *Moonstruck* (she likes Cher's movies, not her music) on the video screen up front, manages to follow the plot even if she can't hear the characters speak. The in-flight dinner is so-so—chop suey, salad, a buttered roll—but what she loves is eating them out of small trays with their own compartments. In America, she thinks, she'll eat all her meals like this.

It's a seventeen-hour flight; by the fifth hour, she can feel how pregnant she really is. Her seat is like a fist squeezing her body, her back aches and feet swell, and the passenger to her left, a nun who looks like she's fifteen, hogs the entire armrest. But America is the only choice, Maxima tells herself, her only hope. What's left for her back home? She has no job, no income, no family. The movies don't want her anymore. She's finally rid of the eye patch–wearing son of a bitch (better to raise her baby on her own anyway), and her sister Queenie, her only real family, is trapped in Saudi Arabia forever; she'll be a live-in maid until the day she dies.

Thank god for Joker. Still loyal, after all these years. He's promised her a good place to live, will help arrange whatever paperwork she and the baby need to stay in California. Had she known it would be this easy, maybe she would have come a long time ago.

But then the plane shakes, hard as an earthquake, despite no solid ground beneath. The captain requests all passengers take their seats and fasten their seat belts, but Maxima feels too miserably pregnant to buckle up, so she just grips her armrest (the one against the wall, since the nun still won't share) and whispers an orasyon to herself and her baby: "Let us fly through the air safely, let us land on the ground, softly."

The plane suddenly dips—Maxima lets out a muffled shriek—

then rises again, and the turbulence continues, though most of the passengers are accustomed to it by now, as though all are expert travelers. But the side-to-side shaking, Maxima fears, will somehow hurt the baby, and she wonders if leaving home is her all-time number one mistake, if the smartest thing a person can do is to stay in the place where you were born.

The turbulence ends; the plane cruises again. Maxima closes her eyes just to rest them, then falls into a sleep so deep she dreams she's already in America, lying in a clean, comfortable bed with a view of the Golden Gate Bridge, until the room tilts one way, then the other, then forward and back, and the dream becomes an earthquake, one so real she's jolted awake, but instead of the plane's violent shaking or sudden plunge, her body seems to pop. She inhales sharply, feels a warmth gushing over her seat, down her thighs and legs, then everywhere.

Maxima has been punched, kicked, judo flipped, has even rolled out of a moving jeep. But her body was trained; she always knew how to get back up. Now, squeezed in her window seat, she's helpless against the pain. She looks at the snoring nun beside her, taps her shoulder several times. "Excuse me, sister," she says. "Excuse me." But the nun just sleeps so Maxima pounds her fist like a hammer on the nun's thigh, and the nun shrieks awake. "Help me," Maxima says.

In minutes, three flight attendants walk Maxima to the front of the plane, where they've cleared the final two rows in first class. With great luck, the plane is full of nurses, Filipinos hoping for work in US hospitals, and four of them tend to Maxima. They give her water, dab her face and neck with cold towels, time her contractions. They come and go in shifts except for one, a male nurse named Rocky, who has been close by from the beginning and will be there to the end. "Huwag kang mag-alala," he says, "don't worry honey, you're in good hands." He fans her with what Maxima realizes is her own plane ticket, so that she sees, flitting back and forth just above her face, her name and confirmation number—XL0426. "XL," she whispers to herself, "XL, XL, XL," the rhythm of the letters like an incantation, a one-word *orasyon*. Rocky leans closer, not quite hearing her. "Excel," she says. "So whenever I say my baby's name, it also means, 'be good, be the best.'" She takes a deep breath, nods to herself. "*Excel. Di ba?*"

More turbulence, a jolt, and Excel is born, his arrival the end of Maxima's story.

THEY FINISHED SINGING "HAPPY BIRTHDAY" AND EVERYBODY clapped. For the first time since arriving in Hello City, Excel thought he missed home just enough that he could imagine tearing up. "You okay?" Sab asked.

"Sure. I'm fine. It's just really nice of everybody to sing for me." He looked up at the crowd, gave a wave of thanks.

Rosie took the stage again and went through final announcements. There was the possibility of a community chicken coop, so people needed to prepare their pros and cons for the next meeting. The Hello City Kite Club's bake sale was canceled, and there was a reminder for people not to leave food out, in case of coyotes. Finally, Rosie let everyone know that she'd gotten word that the border patrol would be doing a sweep of Hello City, likely tomorrow, given that there were illegals—her word—in the area, setting up camp. That last bit of news received mostly silence, but someone—several people actually—applauded, loud enough for Excel to hear.

Without realizing it, he stood up, tried to find the ones who'd clapped. Everyone looked at him, all their faces blank. It could have been any one of them.

23

Eight days after Excel mailed off the care package, Sab calls and says, "I can't believe you."

He doesn't speak, doesn't say hello.

"Baby clothes?" she says. "Are you kidding me?"

Excel is at Meadow of Life Memorial, on his way to Joker's grave. He doesn't remember rain earlier in the day or the day before, but the grass is damp, muddy splotches everywhere.

"Why would you send this, Excel?"

He shuts his eyes, tries to think. "It matched my shirt. The one I bought at the Square. I have the adult version, thought I'd pick up the baby version."

"*Baby?* I told you I haven't decided, and that I didn't want to talk."

"Right. *Talk.* But you didn't say anything about a care package."

"Bullshit. It's manipulative. Why not just throw me a baby shower while you're at it?"

She sounds tired, frustrated, and he remembers how hot it is in Hello City. Here in Colma, the ground is so damp he can't sit.

But he wants to talk again; he has so much to tell. Like how he took down Jun-Jun after he called Maxima a bitch, that he tried (and failed) to fight Gunter, and now knows what it's like to be punched in the face. And that he is learning to be someone else, a fourteen-year-old kid named Perfecto. But did all this, and whatever came before and whatever might come after, happen because he's TNT? And if so, will Sab still want him?

"I held a baby," he says.

"What?"

"At The Pie. I was Sloth the Sleuth and a woman had me hold her baby then took a picture." He didn't actually touch the baby, not through the thick shaggy costume and the oven mitts, but he could feel his weight, the presence of his tiny body in his arms. "I held a baby and it was . . ."

"It was what?"

"It was right. I think it was right."

He looks down at Joker's tombstone, sees chewed stems of what might have been roses. Deer had come at night.

"You really want this," she says, "don't you."

"Do you?"

"I asked you first."

"Yeah," he finally says, "I do. I think a baby could be a good thing. For both of us."

"Would it help?"

"What do you mean?"

"I mean, would a baby help you? Would having a baby that was born here, in California, make it easier for you to stay?"

"I don't know what you're saying." But he thinks he does.

"I'm talking about you staying here legally. Is that why you want this baby?"

He doesn't know if it's anger or hurt that gets his heart racing, but he takes a breath, calming himself so that he can speak. "I can't believe you said that to me. I wouldn't have a baby for that reason. I'm talking about family. Making a home."

"Hello City"—she sighs, sounding exhausted, maybe even fed up—"is not a home."

"Tell that to Lucia. Or Rosie or Red."

"It's different for them. They're not hiding."

He almost asks her to repeat what she'd just said, but he heard her perfectly. "I wasn't hiding in Hello City."

"You said it yourself. That night we introduced ourselves. You said you'd come to Hello City to hide. I even asked you about it later, and you didn't answer." He thinks back to that night, nine months before. He was high, he remembers, so perhaps misspoke, paranoid from the pot and nervous from all those strangers' staring faces. But he's almost positive: Sab is wrong. He didn't move to Hello City to hide. It was the exact opposite.

He won't argue the point. They'll agree to disagree on that night. Maybe on all the nights after, too.

"Hello?" Sab says. "Are you there?"

"I'm back at the apartment now," he lies. "I gotta go. Is there anything else you want to say?"

"No," she says. "You?"

"No," he says. "I'm done."

"Me too."

They hang up, no good-bye.

Excel bends down, picks up the chewed stems from the tombstone. Looking for a trash can, he remembers his original plan: before they'd left for Hello City, he'd meant to tell Sab he was TNT right here, at Joker's grave. The place where they met. The one place he'd miss, after he was gone.

Maybe he would have been better off not telling her at all.

MAXIMA OPENS THE DOOR BEFORE EXCEL CAN EVEN TAKE OUT HIS keys, as though she's been waiting all day for his return.

"I have news," she says.

He steps inside and removes his shoes, the tips flecked with mud and grass from the cemetery. "Good or bad?"

"Very good," she says. "We got three hundred dollars."

"Three hundred dollars? From where?"

"From Jerry."

"Already? What'd you say to him?"

"Not me. *You.* It's what you said. He got your e-mail. He feels bad that you quit your job, so he sent money to help us get by."

Instinctively, he does the math: *10,000 − 300 = 9,700 dollars closer to Hello City.* After his call with Sab, he's not sure what these numbers mean. "Jerry believes us?"

"He believes you. I didn't even have to ask for the money."

Excel thinks back to his e-mail, *Perfecto's* e-mail, wonders what choice of words, what specific phrase, might've made so strong an impact so quickly. Maybe it was the story behind it, how pathetic Perfecto's life must seem.

"Why is your face like that?" she asks.

He's not in the mood to hear that he's looking like a snot-nosed, ungrateful kid, rolling his eyes. "Like *what?*"

"Like this." Her eyes shift downward. She clenches her jaw, tightens the line of her lips. Whatever face she means to mimic looks tired, beat down, sad. "You should be happy," she says.

"I'm happy. It's just weird, fooling Jerry like this. Three hundred dollars is a lot of money."

"So is ten thousand."

He nods.

"Well, you're going to have to get used to this," she says. "We'll work hard, work fast if we can. And we'll only take what we need. Understand?"

He says he does.

"Good. Now go wash your face and put on your good Target shirt," she says. "We're celebrating tonight."

Roxy picks them up and they drive to Mama Chix, a new Filipino point-point joint in Daly City. Barely seven p.m. and the place is packed, Filipino families filling almost every booth and table. They pick up trays and line up, and Maxima orders combo plates for each of them, pointing to the pinakbet, fried rice, paksiew, laing, lechon kawali. When they reach the cashier, the food barely fits on their trays.

A table frees up in the middle of the restaurant and Maxima nabs it. "Lucky timing!" she says, but as soon as he sits Excel feels surrounded, like all the families are staring at them, the way the audience did at the F.O.F.F.F. screening, when Maxima forced their standing ovation for a movie that everyone knew was laughable crap.

"Okay, okay," Roxy says, clapping twice, "tell me about Jerry. Three hundred bucks! Excel, what did you say?"

"Just 'hello sir, how are you sir,' that kind of stuff," he says. "Nothing special." He looks at the food heaped on his plate, not hungry at all.

"He was better than that," Maxima says, practically beaming. "And the key was memorizing those facts. He has one of those photograph memories, talaga. Like the spelling bee, when he's in grade six. He memorized over a hundred words, stayed up all night for a week. Almost fifty students, and he came in second."

"I still lost," he says.

"What word did you miss?" Roxy asks.

"'Coalesced,'" Maxima says. "Alam mo ang word yan? I don't. But that's the word they gave him. The kid who won—white girl, di ba?— they went so easy on her. What was her final word? 'Ball'? 'Cat'? 'Ice cream'? Something like that." She describes the moment: Excel and the girl (Tammy Lundell, Excel remembers now) side by side on the auditorium stage, Maxima and Joker in the third row, cheering their boy on. "Joker was nervous 100 percent, and my heart was like this"— she knocks on her chest with her knuckles, five times fast—"because nothing this big ever happened to us before. Joker is squeezing my hand, I'm saying an orasyon, and the whole room is true suspense, talaga. But it's okay. You did your best." She reaches over, gives Excel's shoulder a squeeze, begins to eat.

"I knew the word," Excel says.

She puts down her spoon.

"'Coalesced.' I knew how to spell it. C-o-a-l-e-s-c-e-d. It means 'coming together.' I knew the word."

"You knew the word," Maxima says.

He'd entered the spelling bee only for extra credit, which he needed to offset his C– average, but it wasn't until that moment, when the spelling bee was down to its final round, that he actually realized he could win. From the stage, he could tell that Maxima and Joker believed it too. But when all the students were eliminated and only Tammy and Excel were left, he remembered that the previous year's winner, Bonaventure Nguyen, was presented with a leather-bound dictionary and a hundred-dollar check from the City of Colma, and that his picture was taken for the *Colma Weekly*, his name, even the names of his parents, printed in the caption. For Excel to see his and Maxima's names in print, with an accompanying photo—that was the opposite of hiding. He could win the spelling bee, but lose everything else. When it was his turn, his last turn, he dropped the second *c* in *coalesced*. "I'm sorry," the spelling bee announcer said flatly, "that's incorrect." As he took his seat, he could see Joker trying to smile but Maxima made no effort, just folded her arms across her chest, teeth digging into her upper lip.

He looks at Maxima. "Why is your face like that?"

She doesn't answer.

He turns to Roxy. "All you got for winning was a stupid gift card and a book. No big deal."

"How can you say that?" Maxima says. "All those kids, and you could've beat all of them! That's a true victory!"

"It was a long time ago," he says. "Doesn't matter."

"It does matter. To Joker. To me. We cheered for you. I prayed for you. And you do this to us?" She shakes her head and stares at some faraway point beyond the restaurant windows, like she has never been more ashamed of him. "You had something good and you threw it away."

"I didn't," he says.

"You did. And that's a sin, Excel."

"A *sin*. You think throwing a stupid spelling bee is a sin. You know what a sin *really* is? A sin is pretending you don't know an old man when he's dying at Sizzler. A sin is acting like a stranger when they wheel him away into an ambulance while you just stand there. A sin is making your son do it too." His voice is rising now, he can hear it, is almost shaken by it, but he can't stop. "I would've gone with Joker in that ambulance. I would've been there when he died. And if they'd taken me away and handed me over to the police or Immigration or whoever the hell we're always *hiding and hiding* from, at least he wouldn't have been alone. 'We owe him everything,' that's what you always said, and look what we did to him."

Maxima has no expression on her face, none that Excel can understand.

He gets up, goes outside, and walks to the curb. He sees, across the street, in the Home Depot parking lot, a small girl pushing an orange cart with a potted lemon tree inside, her parents two steps behind her. The mom pops open the trunk and the dad sets the tree inside, ties the trunk down with rope. The girl is jumping up and down, so excited that she does two cartwheels, one away from her parents, then one right back.

Excel closes his eyes, puts his head on his knees.

Later, he feels a hand squeeze his shoulder, firm and strong. He lifts his head, wipes his face with the back of his hand. He looks up, expecting Maxima, but finds Roxy standing there instead. "Come on, hon," she says, "I'll take everybody home."

24

He could not get the applause from the Hello City Town Council meeting out of his head. It was two or three people, maybe four, but that small number only amplified the sound of their clapping, like the first drops of rain pelting the roof of the bus. Maybe it would've been better if everyone had clapped at the news of the border patrol sweep, so that the applause was less sharp in his memory, just white noise instead. And then he'd know to keep his distance from everyone, instead of always wondering who in the Hello City crowd could not be trusted.

It was the middle of May. The day of the sweep hit ninety-six degrees. Excel stayed inside the bus the entire day, most of it in bed. He'd never been to the Outerlands, but remembered the way Lucia described it when he'd first arrived—it was criminals, addicts, people who wanted nothing to do with other people. But all he imagined were men and women in the desert, children too, doing their best to stay cool. Sab worked all that day but had come by for lunch, then later to change into a cooler shirt, Excel in bed the whole time. "Are you okay?" she finally asked, sounding more annoyed than concerned. Excel said he was fine, just tired, that the heat was getting to him. "Yeah," Sab said, "tell me about it," then left and went back to work.

The sweep happened and no news followed. No announcements were made at the next town council meeting, no rumors circulated. Excel, as casually as he could, brought it up with Red and Lucia, even Heddy and Ned, asked if anything had become of the sweep. They all shrugged, said they had no idea. The days, for now, could go back to normal.

But not for Sab. She was exhausted, which was understandable— Pink Bubble orders seemed to increase every week—but there was a shifting distance between them that Excel couldn't track. One night, she had dinner with Excel on the bus, but took a sleeping bag and slept on the helipad right after. Two days later, she blew off work and stayed in bed, and asked Excel to do the same, but rolled away when he tried holding her, saying it was too hot inside the bus to be touched. May was ending and Excel realized it was almost a year since they'd met and nearly nine months since they'd arrived in Hello City; these days, he seemed to know less and less what she was thinking, what she felt.

One day, another without work for Excel, Lucia dropped by with a padded envelope. "Addressed to Sab, but care of Pink Bubble," she said. She handed it to Excel and left.

Sab was gone for the day, getting supplies, mailing off orders. It wasn't his place to open it, but he saw it had been sent by Sab's aunt, and he knew what was inside. Carefully, he opened the envelope, pulled out a small silver picture frame.

The photograph was black and white, a high school portrait, wrinkled and scratched in the middle with a corner torn off. Sab's mother wore what looked like a blouse with a sailor's collar and tie, her hair in pigtails, and held an unrolled diploma with Japanese characters written on it. "Cancer killed her when I was seven," Sab had said, but in the picture she looked confident and proud, a true smile on her face. Nothing, he knew, could brighten up the bus more.

He propped it on the dashboard, the first thing she'd see when she came back home.

SEVEN P.M., THEN EIGHT. SAB WORKED LATE SOMETIMES BUT NOT like this, and when he hadn't heard from her by nine thirty, he walked to Lucia's Airstream but she was gone too, out for the night. He'd already left a voicemail but left two more, checked his e-mail right before Beans! closed—nothing. He even considered calling the police (wherever they were—Whyling? El Centro?), unsure if this qualified as an emergency. What it took for a person to become missing, he had no idea, and he was, admittedly, scared for himself: to call the police, he'd undoubtedly have to explain his relationship to the person in question, then give them his name.

Sab was fine, he told himself. Just wait.

He stayed awake the entire night. In the morning, he took the picture frame off the dashboard to protect it from the sun, and just as he slipped it back inside the padded envelope, she texted him. I'm OK. Be back soon.

He stayed in all that day and finally went out at night, but only as far as the helipad, where Sab had left the sleeping bag. He picked it up and shook it out, brought it back inside.

The car pulled up just past eleven p.m. He was in bed but wide awake, and he heard Sab's slow footsteps into the bus. He turned on the light, sat up.

"I woke you," she said. She set her keys on the table.

"I've been awake," he said. "Since yesterday. Waiting."

"I should've called. I know."

"Where were you?"

"Out. In El Centro. At a hotel."

Excel had never stayed in a hotel in his life.

"A Best Western," she said. "Nothing fancy. I didn't mean to do it. But I drove past it, and next thing I know I'm making a U-turn, parking my car, and checking in."

"What for?"

She shrugged, leaned back, looked at the ceiling. "I wanted to take a bath. I wanted to watch cable in bed. I wanted to sleep in an actual room."

He got out of bed, joined her at the table. "I know the bus isn't perfect, but we can change it. We'll get better furniture, paint the walls a happier color. Yellow, blue, whatever. This is our home. We just have to invest, you know?" He put his hand on hers, but he could feel, from the stillness of her own, that she didn't want it there.

He went to the shelf, pulled out the padded envelope. "This came yesterday. I'm sorry I opened it."

She reached into the envelope, pulled out the framed photograph. "Mom," she said, thumbs pressing into the glass. She blinked back tears, set the frame on the table.

He crouched down in front of her. "See? It just takes time. We'll be all right."

"I don't know," she said.

"Of course we will. I know it." On his knees at her feet, looking up at her, he felt like he was pleading.

She put her hand on his shoulder, gestured for him to get up. He stood, sat back in his chair. "I need to tell you something," she said, and he immediately thought of Renzo, that night on the roof years before. How Renzo had told him the truth, how Excel refused to tell his. What he lost because of it.

"The reason I went to El Centro was to go to the CVS. I bought a pregnancy test. Two of them. I took the first test in the CVS bathroom, if you can believe it"—she shook her head—"and took the second one at the hotel. Positive. Both times."

"You're pregnant."

"Yeah," she said. She looked at her hands, rubbed her thumb over the spot on her wrist where she'd burned herself while making soap. The skin had healed.

"This is okay," he said. "We'll handle this."

She looked up at him. "What do you mean?" He wasn't sure what he meant, but found himself speaking on instinct, planning as the words came out. "We can make this work," he said. "We have somewhere to live that we can afford, you've got steady work with Lucia, and I can take over your job while you recover." He took her hand, didn't let go this time. "We're in a good place," he said, and the more he talked, the more he knew it was true. His own birth had been a catastrophe—born on a plane, whisked off to a hospital upon landing, accruing a bill so large that Joker had to beg his brother Bingo to pay it. But he and Sab were set and, in their own way, even lucky. They didn't have much, but they had enough, and in Hello City, enough was just that. They could raise a kid, be a family, live a life. Be at home.

"I don't know," Sab said. She looked around the bus like she meant to escape it, overwhelmed by everything Excel had said, the future he'd suddenly mapped out. "Maybe I should've waited to tell you. Tried to figure it out first."

"No," he said, "I'm glad you told me," and he was: life, he knew, was about to change; knowing this filled him with the unexpected need to change it more. "I have something to tell you, too." He leaned close, and told her as gently as Maxima tried telling him, nine years before, when they stood at the rail overlooking the water. "I'm not really here," he said.

25

On the freeway, Roxy sings along with Gloria Estefan on the radio, trying to keep things upbeat. But from the backseat, Excel can see Maxima's face in the rearview mirror, the crinkle between her brows and her rapid blinking. He doesn't know the damage done by all he said at Mama Chix, if it's irreparable, if he even cares.

Roxy pulls up to the gate of La Villa Aurelia. Maxima and Excel tell her good-bye and thanks, say nothing to each other as they walk through the complex and into the apartment. Once inside, they retreat to their rooms.

Excel is in bed by ten p.m., an early hour for him, but he hopes to get good sleep before their five a.m. call with Jerry. He doesn't get any, not one second.

Ten minutes before five, Excel and Maxima are side by side in front of the webcam. Neither speaks, not until Jerry's online call rings through. "Look happy," Maxima tells Excel, then clicks to begin the conversation.

"Good morning!" Jerry says.

"Hello, mahal!" Maxima says.

"Hello, Sir Jerry." Excel waves with both hands. "How are you, sir?"

"I'm great. But remember what we said about the 'sir' thing?"

"Sorry, sir! I mean, sorry, Jerry!"

"You'll get the hang of it," he says, laughing. Excel makes sure to laugh, too.

"Jerry, thank you so much for sending us the money," he says, "it's a big help. A big, big help." Though quitting his job gutting fish means a loss of steady wages, the three hundred dollars means he can buy books for school, and enough rice, canned meat, and bottled water to last them several weeks. "And if I can save some of it, I will buy new shoes for church."

"It's really nothing," Jerry says. He sounds sincere. Maybe three hundred dollars really is nothing to him.

Excel thanks him again, leaning into the camera to ensure his gratitude is visible and clear, because gratitude, Maxima had told him, is key to this kind of business. "These men," she'd said, "they like to be thanked. They like to know they can change your life, just like that."

Maxima nudges Excel to the side, centering herself in front of the webcam. "Jerry honey. By now, you know I am many, many things. I am a Catholic, a cook, a sandals seller, a woman with an infinite amount of love to give to others. But most of all, I am a mother." She puts her arm around Excel's shoulder, pulls him close. "And as a mother, I only want what is best for my son. But sometimes, I cannot always provide." She lets out a slow and quivering breath, dabs away a tear. "So thank you, Jerry. Maraming, maraming salamat." She kisses her finger and presses it against the screen.

Jerry says he should sign off, that his workday starts soon. "A bridge inspection and a retrofit," he says. "Oh boy!" and Excel can't tell if he's being serious or not. He thanks Jerry once more, then leaves to give him a few minutes with Maxima.

He goes to the kitchen and makes instant coffee, drinks it by the living room window. It's still dark outside, and down below, a few cars drive by slowly toward the front gate, early commuters off to work. He remembers that early morning, all those months before, when he and Sab were the ones leaving in the dark, bound for the freeway.

Maxima comes out of her room. Excel yawns, sips his coffee. "That went pretty good, right?" he says.

"Perfect," she says. She goes to the front door and puts on her shoes, slings her purse over her shoulder. She doesn't say where she's going, when she might be back. Maxima just leaves.

DESPITE OVER TWENTY-FOUR HOURS WITHOUT SLEEP, EXCEL IS WIDE awake. Talking online to Jerry, pretending to live in one time zone when he's really in another, has inverted his days and nights. He feels like two separate people living in two different times and places: if Excel is awake at four in the morning, Perfecto is studying at seven in the evening; if Excel is asleep by midnight, Perfecto's school day is coming to its end. Maybe this is what jet lag means—you fly into a time zone ahead or a time zone behind, but your body remains where it's always been, so that you've been split in two, separated from yourself somehow.

Excel's shift doesn't start until ten a.m., but he's out the door by eight. He walks down Junipero Serra Boulevard, past the Dodge dealership, where a morning cleaning crew is waxing and polishing all the floor models, their arms moving in fast, nonstop circles. Maxima worked on one of those crews once, and she'd tell him and Joker how she'd spend an entire shift on her knees, cleaning hubcaps. "That's it," she said, rubbing the ache in her wrists. "My arm in a circle. The whole day. That's my job."

Excel walks to Meadow of Life Memorial. Walking through to Joker's grave, he wonders if Maxima might be there, too—she was still gone when he left this morning—but there's nobody around when he arrives.

He crouches down and brushes away dead leaves and dried-up grass from Joker's tombstone, digs out a tiny pebble lodged into the engraved *J* in Joker's name. Then he shuts his eyes, not to pray, but to imagine apologizing, not for throwing the spelling bee and letting himself lose, but for the disappointment it caused after. And he thinks about what happened at Mama Chix. Had Joker been there, had he seen Excel speak to Maxima like that, he might've smacked him in the back of his head, not spoken to him for days. Excel apologizes for that, too.

He opens his eyes, gets up, and walks up and down the nearby rows of graves, checking for still-good flowers from dying bouquets that he might give to Joker. He finds nothing. But he has packets of pepper in his pocket, so he tears them open, sprinkles the pepper over the grass around Joker's tombstone, on the letters of his name—these things, at least, might be safe from deer. Excel checks the ground— it's dry enough—then sits with Joker until he has to leave for work, promises that no matter what, he will always return.

His shift at The Pie is split into different miseries. Bathrooms first, then greeting, then ball pit. No tips at all. At the end of the day, he finds an envelope of cash in his locker: $1,000 exactly, four weeks of shifts, minus the day he fainted. Even less than he thought. This, plus the $300 from Jerry and the $120 from Roxy means he's earned roughly $1,500 since coming back.

He steps out of the break room, hears Gunter yelling at someone in his office.

He imagines it's a kitchen guy on the receiving end, or a new hire Excel hasn't met and probably never will, not after today. The door flings open and Gunter storms out, walks past Excel like he's not even there. Excel waits until Gunter is back out on the floor then walks by the office to see who's inside.

He finds Z is on a metal folding chair, hunched forward, arms dropped at his side. Excel steps in, crouches down to meet his face. "What happened?"

He stares at the floor, doesn't speak.

"You can tell me," Excel says. "What happened?"

"I take money."

"What money?"

"The money. I need the money. So I take it."

"Take it? From where?"

Z points at the safe on the floor by Gunter's desk.

"You took money from Gunter?"

"Steal," he whispers. "I try to steal it." He blinks, like he's confused, unsure of what he's done. "But he sees me."

"You got caught." Excel pokes his head out the door to make sure Gunter is nearby, goes back to Z. "Why did you steal it?"

"Home," he says. "I like to go home. I *want* to go home." He clenches his jaw but it trembles, and he's on the verge of weeping. Excel puts his hands on Z's shoulders, rubs them gently—he doesn't know why, but it seems like the thing to do—and the motion tugs at the collar of Z's shirt, revealing the pale, loose skin of his neck and, just above his collarbone, a brush of bluish-purple with shades of yellow, the color Gunter's hands can leave behind.

Z says it again: "Home, home."

"You will," Excel says, "you will."

"How much can we make and how fast can we make it?"

Excel's question throws off Maxima, who's taking inventory of a small balikbayan box for Auntie Queenie. Inside the box are cans of corned beef, ham, and Spam, tubes of Bengay, rolls of bandages, a family-size bottle of Tylenol. "You screwed up my count," she says. "What did you say?"

Excel closes the door behind him, locks the knob and the dead bolt. "If I needed more than ten thousand, let's say fifteen, how long until we could get it?"

"There's not just one answer. It depends on the man, siempre. Sometimes, it's a little here, a little there. Sometimes, he might—"

"What about from Jerry?"

"Excel. What's going on?"

Walking home from The Pie, he'd thought of telling Maxima the truth—that Gunter is abusing Z, probably has been for some time, and that Z's safest option is a flight to Serbia, where he can live with his daughter until his dying day. *We need to help an old man get home*, he'd planned to say. But he knows how she'd respond. That it's none of their business. That they can barely take care of their own needs. Family first, always.

Instead, he tells Maxima what he'd rehearsed: the professor got hold of him (he had the nerve to call him at The Pie), letting him know that the damages from the fire exceeded ten thousand dollars, were closer to fifteen. And with his research now lagging, the lab needs repairs ASAP. "He even threatened me," Excel says, "he told me that he didn't want to get the university president involved, but I think he'll really do it." And that, he tells Maxima, could lead to lawyers, a trial, the police. "It's a huge mess," he says, "and it's my fault, I know."

She looks at him and shakes her head, like she's close to writing Excel off as a lost cause. "This is a lot of trouble," she says. She goes back through the box, tallying the price of each item, figuring out the box's total worth. She picks up a roll of packing tape, tears a strip off with her teeth, seals two flaps shut, then the other two, then all around. Nothing, not even air, could get in or out of it. She lifts the box, checking its heft and weight, then hands it to Excel. "First thing in the morning," she says, "go to the post office, mail this off. Run my errand. I'll clean up your mess."

26

The first Tagalog Excel taught Sab was "tago ng tago."

"TNT," she said. "'Hiding and hiding'?"

He nodded. "My whole life."

"When were you going to tell me?"

"I'd meant to, a couple times. Before we left, when we visited Joker. On my birthday. There might've been others."

Sab's mother's picture was still on the table between them. She laid it flat, photo side down, then took a shirt—Excel's—from a pile of laundry on the floor. She'd been working so much they hadn't had a chance to drive to the laundromat in Whyling; for days they'd been in dirty clothes. "Did you only tell me because I'm pregnant?"

"It's not like that. I was just waiting for the right time. And this was the time. And what does it matter anyway? I'm telling you now."

"It matters because it's June. *June.* I met you a year ago and this whole time you've said nothing. In case you haven't noticed, I don't have a lot of people in my life, so when the person I *do* have keeps something like this from me, I start wondering what else I don't know." Excel thought of other things he couldn't say—Maxima and all those online men, Joker dying alone while they sat in the apartment, waiting.

"There's nothing else to know," he said, "I swear." He joined her on the floor. "Our job is to focus on the future, on this baby. Right?"

She looked at him, confused, as though what he'd said made no sense. "I never said anything about a baby. I said I was pregnant. I haven't decided anything. I haven't even started *thinking* about deciding."

He sat back. *Baby. Pregnant.* In the moment, they'd meant the same thing to him, and the future—*life*—for once, almost seemed clear. "Right," he said. "I just—sorry. This is big news. I'm a little thrown off."

"Join the club," she said, folding the shirt. "I mean, let's say I do have the baby. What does that mean? Is it American? Would we get a lawyer? And what if you get caught, and end up deported? What happens to me and this baby?"

He took her wrist, held it tight. "Nothing's going to happen to you. Or to the baby."

"But what about *you*? Being tago tago, or whatever the phrase is, is that forever? And if I'm with you, does this mean we're always going to be watching our backs? How do we live like that? Where do we go?"

"Nowhere," he said. "We go nowhere. We're already in the place we need to be. The best place. And if we just keep doing what we're doing, then we'll be okay."

She pulled her wrist free.

He leaned closer. "Don't you want to be here?"

"Does it matter? Where else would I go." She picked up another shirt—hers—smoothed it against the floor. "No real family. No job. No college. Might as well live in a bus forever."

Her words stung. He wondered if he'd misread the past nine months in Hello City, if his version of their life matched hers. "We have a good thing here," he said.

"You do."

"What's that supposed to mean?"

"Nothing." She unfolded the shirt, started refolding it. "I don't know what I meant."

"I do. You're saying that because I'm TNT, I'm lucky to be here. But for you, Hello City isn't good enough. Isn't that what you meant?"

She looked at him, anger breaking, tears starting. "I never said that."

He got up, put on jeans and shoes, grabbed a flashlight.

"Where are you going?"

"Out."

"Where?"

He almost said *nowhere*, but that only confirmed what she thought of Hello City. "I'm gonna look at the stars," he said. "And those clothes, by the way, are still dirty, so you're wasting your time." Then he walked out of the bus without saying good-bye, which felt like the right way to leave.

HE LAY ON THE HELIPAD, RIGHT OVER THE H, THINKING OF WHAT it meant. *Helipad. Here. Home.*

An hour passed, another, still awake. He got up, saw the lights were off in the bus. At least Sab was able to sleep.

He made his way to the Square, found it completely empty. Sweeping through with the flashlight, the place looked as though a party had just ended or was about to begin—there were streamers all around, crisscrossing with the strings of lights above, swooping down and connecting with the food carts, Beans!, even the cage of the Oracle, who paced back and forth across her branch. Piñatas and bright paper flowers dangled everywhere, and on the stage, *Unaired Television Pilot* still had the giant red bow and ribbon hanging over it, Red's gift to Hello City. That party happened almost two weeks earlier, and no one had thought to throw the decorations away.

Standing in the dark, he remembered himself onstage that first night in the Square. He'd told the people who he was and why he'd come—*I'm Excel and I was hiding.* The truth, for once.

You owe us a gift, Rosie had said, but he'd botched the powdered nondairy creamer trick three times, barely gotten it right on the fourth, the flame so weak he could hardly see it himself.

The canister of nondairy creamer was on the Beans! counter, a book of matches on the arm of a lawn chair nearby. He grabbed them and stepped onstage, stood the flashlight on its end, its beam shining to the sky.

Timing was key and had been the problem before. That night, on his first three attempts, he'd waited for the powder to fall before flicking the match. He was faster the fourth time, but barely. Now, he knew to throw the match sooner.

He removed the lid from the canister, tossed powder into the air, threw a lit match.

Nothing.

He tried again. This time, fire.

Once more. Fire again, a long wave of flame.

He kept going, struck match after struck match, getting it right each time, the split-second burn of the air so bright it seemed to illuminate the Square. He was pleased with himself, even proud, that he was mastering the trick, and decided he'd perform it again at a future town council meeting. He finished the book of matches and was about to get another when he noticed that the Square stayed bright, flickering, and a flash of heat came from above. The streamers were burning, flames traveling the crisscrossing grid, igniting the strings of lights.

He jumped off the stage and stepped back. He ran to the food carts, thinking a fire extinguisher would be nearby but found nothing, no source of water either, and soon Red's wall of television sets was burning, the plastic sheet screens popping open, shrinking into flames. He cried out "Fire," he cried out "Help," over and over, so loudly he could feel the back of his throat sting from the strain. But there was no one nearby to hear.

Then the sound of something like a distant horn, a howl, flap of wings. The Oracle.

Rushing toward the cage, he saw the owl scurry back and forth across her branch, taking tiny hops meant for flight, crashing against the bars each time. Excel kept shouting for help, tried spreading his arms around the cage to lift it, but the entire thing was bolted down to the table, the tiny door padlocked shut. Shaking the cage did nothing, only frightened the owl even more, and there were no tools close by to pry the bars apart. But he saw cinder blocks stacked against the table and he picked one up, slammed it hard against the cage, again and again until two bars gave way, bending just enough that the owl could squeeze through, but she was panicked and jumpy, oblivious to the escape route before her.

The fire trailed closer, the air thick with smoke. Excel reached through the bars and pulled out the owl, her body squirming, her beak taking tiny stabs at his arms. He dropped her to the ground, shouted, "Go! Leave!" but the Oracle stayed where she was, as if she'd forgotten how to fly from all the years caged. Only when Excel stomped on the ground did the owl finally take flight, rising and fading into the dark sky.

The stage was all flames, the food carts were burning away, and the fire didn't stop; nothing of the Square would be saved. Excel ran back in the direction of the bus. He'd left his flashlight behind, but the fire was so bright, it lit the path back home.

By early morning everyone was at the Square, what was left of it. The charred frames of the food carts. The perimeter of the stage, its center a black hole. *Unaired Television Pilot* was a sunken wall, melted and burned, and Red searched through it, trying to find something worth saving. Excel had lifted so many of those TV sets, had helped find the words that glowed in their screens.

Everything else was rubble and ash, though a folding lawn chair had somehow stayed perfectly intact, bore no signs of fire.

Rosie surveyed the damage with members of the Hello City Town Council, then stood on a crate and addressed the crowd. "Well, as you can see, the Square is gone," she said. "Those of us who've been here long enough remember what it took to build it. All that sweat, all that hammering, and all that hooch, of course." She tried laughing, but her breath seemed to catch, and her face squeezed tight to hold back tears. She cleared her throat, then reported that damages were in the thousands, maybe ten if they were lucky. "May not seem like much to the outside," she said, "but for the folks in Hello City, it's a lot. So as a start"—she removed her cowboy hat, dropped a bill in it—"here's a buck. Let's see where we go from here." She wiped her eyes, passed the hat around, then picked up her fiddle and played. People donated what they could, mostly coins or a few dollars, though Lucia dropped in a fifty, which drew some applause. She passed the hat to Sab, who put in five dollars, and she passed it to Excel, who, it turned out, was the last to receive the hat. All eyes were on him now, and he stood dazed and numb from everything he and Sab had told each other, from everything he'd burned down after. But it was Rosie's music—a mournful, twangy tune—that almost made him break.

There were no good options. The thing to do was tell the people what he'd done, take responsibility for it, and, if they'd let him, find a way to make it right. But telling that truth, he knew, could spiral into telling more, and what if the fire department got involved? The police? Confessing to crimes, even accidental ones, required your name and information, the circumstances of your life.

He cut through the crowd, brought the hat back to Rosie. She looked at him and smiled, mistaking his tears of guilt for sympathy. She winked, mouthed "Thank you," and played on.

After, people scattered around, walked through the damage. Excel went off on his own, the previous night still bright in his mind. He'd fled the fire and made it back to the bus, but didn't go inside. He sat on the helipad instead, let the fire burn all it could until the end. Only in the morning, when Sab came out to tell him that Lucia had called, telling her a fire had broken out in Hello City, did he finally get up.

People started leaving. Sab and Lucia. Red. Excel stayed behind, sat on a still-intact bench near the stage, watched as Rosie and two other town council members examined the burned cage of the Oracle. The owl, at least, had been saved. Excel thought of that first night in the Square, when Red asked him to guess the owl's age. He'd guessed five or ten, but it was actually thirty-three, and he remembered what Red told him about the bird's life span, its possibilities. Fifty years in the cage, fifteen in the world.

SAB WAS LEANING AGAINST THE STEERING WHEEL OF THE BUS when Excel entered. "The whole night," she said, "you were out on that helipad?"

He walked past her, sat at the table. "I didn't want to be in here," he said. "And I thought you needed space."

She nodded. "I noticed this morning, when I went out there to tell you about the fire, you came back in and changed clothes." At her feet were his black T-shirt, his jeans. What he'd worn when the Square burned down.

She went to him, looked him in the eye. "Those clothes smell like smoke. *You* smell like smoke. And what happened to your arms? What are these marks?" Excel looked down, remembered the owl's stabbing beak as she tried to break free.

He looked at Sab, moved a strand of hair from her face, realized that the purple streaks were gone and that her hair color was, for the first time since knowing her, completely brown. She looked exhausted, beaten down by everything they were learning about each other and themselves.

"Tell me, Excel," she said, "and don't lie. Did you have something to do with the fire?"

"All of it," he said. "Everything."

They went to Lucia. They didn't know what else to do.

It was evening, just past dark. The Airstream's door was closed, the curtains drawn, and Lucia paced back and forth, rubbing the back of her neck with both hands. "This really isn't good," she said. "I mean, I'm basically the one who brought you here. How do you think that makes me look?" She considered the options: Should Excel confess? If so, to whom? Would the town council kick him out of Hello City? Could anyone even be kicked out? And would they tell the police? "This kind of thing has never happened before," she said, "not since I've been here. I mean, the only real law around here is 'do unto others,' you know?"

"Did I break it?" Excel asked quietly. He was sitting on the floor. Sab sat away from him, in one of Lucia's Helsinki-inspired design chairs, her back perfectly straight and rigid, her face deliberately neutral, no emotion at all.

"I don't know," Lucia said. "But there's a bigger problem. Rosie saw the Oracle's cage."

"What about it?" Sab asked. She looked at Excel, like he was guilty of even more.

"The bars were pried open. With a crowbar or a hammer or something. It doesn't take a forensics expert to know that someone let her out because of the fire. Was that you, Excel?"

He nodded.

"The Oracle is ancient. All she knows is living in a cage. You think she can survive out there?"

Excel's last glimpse of the Oracle was of her rising in the sky, receding into the dark. But she had been reluctant to leave, didn't know how, and Excel could imagine the owl pivoting, flying a route back toward the Square, perched somewhere just on the edge of Hello City. Here, but not really.

"She might survive," he said. "Hopefully."

Lucia closed her eyes and took two deep breaths, reached into her refrigerator, and poured herself a glass of cucumber water. "Here's the plan. Excel, I believe you're a good person, but you fucked up. Big time. And while the people in Hello City are good people, I'm not sure they'd forgive you. So none of us, *none of us*, will say anything. But you"—she pointed at Excel—"you owe Hello City. You have to pay them back."

"How is he supposed to do that," Sab said, "without them knowing?"

"Call it a donation. Say he inherited money or had a bunch of cash saved, I don't know. But whether it's tomorrow or a year from now, doesn't matter. Hello City is my home, and it needs to happen."

He didn't argue, agreed with everything Lucia was saying. "What do I do now?" he asked.

Lucia looked over at Sab, then back at Excel. "There's no work for you here, no way you can make that kind of money," Lucia said. "The best thing is for you to go back. And when you've got the money, you can return."

"When should I go?" He looked at Sab. The fire, he knew, wasn't the only reason he should leave.

"Sooner is better," Sab said softly. "If you wait too long . . ."

"I'll find a bus schedule," Excel said. "But if people ask why I'm gone, what'll you tell them?"

"People here mind their own business," Lucia said. "No one will ask about you."

Sab said they should get back to the bus, start packing, figure out a plan for getting Excel home. She walked past him and exited the Airstream. He was still on the floor, almost forty-eight hours with zero sleep. Standing up, just the thought of it, seemed impossible.

EXCEL DID NOT HAVE MUCH TO PACK. HIS CLOTHES FIT INTO HIS backpack and duffel bag, and the things he'd bought at the Square—a small brass lamp on the floor by the bed, the plastic bowls for their ramen—belonged in the bus.

Sab waited in the car, engine running. Before stepping out of the bus, he took Sab's mother's picture, propped it up on the dashboard, just to the right of the steering wheel.

They drove to the Greyhound station in El Centro, the ride so silent and smooth against the road that it lulled Excel into dozing off, long enough that he dreamed they were back where they started, driving down the freeway to Hello City, the map of California spread over his lap, his head resting on Sab's shoulder.

The tick of the turn signal, when Sab was taking the exit into El Centro, finally woke him up.

She pulled up in front of the Greyhound station, a rectangular building the size of a small post office. "I'm sad to see you go," she said. "You know that, right?"

He unbuckled his seat belt but held on to it, the strap still across his chest. "I know."

"But so much has happened. You have this whole life I never knew about, and with this"—she placed her palm on a spot at the bottom of her chest, just above her belly—"I don't know what I want to do. Let's take the time to figure it out."

"I already figured it out. I want to be with you."

She leaned back against her headrest. Excel could see the tiny lightning bolt tattoo behind her ear. He'd noticed it back in the movie theater parking garage, the first time they'd kissed. "I'm tired," she said. "I need to sleep."

"I'll go," he said.

They stepped out of the car. Excel grabbed his backpack from the backseat, and Sab walked around to his side. She took his hand, asked him for some time. "Don't call," she said, "not for a while."

He promised he wouldn't.

They didn't kiss. Sab just placed her hand on Excel's cheek, two fingers pressing, gently, into his temple. "Be safe," she said, then pulled away. She got in her car and drove off, the red taillights shrinking into the dark.

He entered the bus station and walked up to the man behind the ticket counter, told him he needed to get home and asked how to get there.

27

Maxima's plan, for now, is more of the same. She schedules more talks with Jerry, sometimes twice a day, and Excel constantly hears laughter behind her door, sometimes tears, even singing—yesterday she belted out the *Titanic* love song in a falsetto he never knew she possessed. Always, she makes sure that Excel makes an appearance, if only just to say hello.

Excel and Jerry exchange e-mails, and to keep Jerry's interest, Excel researches more articles on ships in a bottle and looks up facts about New Hampshire, where Jerry lives ("Your state has impressive granite!" he writes). They mostly stay on topic, though Jerry sometimes asks questions, or offers bits of life advice, which Excel thinks through carefully before he responds. When Jerry writes, "Are there any places in the world you'd like to visit?" does Excel reply as himself and tell him that he's always wanted to visit those hotels made of ice, like the ones he's seen on the Travel Channel? (He ends up writing

"Disneyland! It is my #1 dream.") Or when Jerry writes, "The key to success is hard work, belief in yourself, and finding good lifelong mentors," should Excel write the truth, that those people don't exist in his world, and even if they did, why would they mentor someone like him? No matter how he replies, he reminds himself to do it as the person Jerry sees on the screen: it's Perfecto who will get what Excel needs.

At work, Excel looks after Z as best he can, keeps an eye out for bruises, scratches, any sign of pain, and every so often, just to make sure, he asks, "Do you still want to go home?" and Z always answers twice. "Yes, yes," he says. One day, after an early shift, Excel goes to the public library, gets online to price one-way tickets from San Francisco to Serbia. Belgrade, he learns, is the city of destination, and the flights take fifteen hours, sometimes longer. He's never been on an airline website before, had always assumed that booking a flight was a circuitous process that required writing long statements about your destination, your reasons for going, your reasons for leaving. But mostly, it's just type and click, type and click, pay and hit Submit. That's all.

All those years—his whole life—of watching the blinking airplane lights shooting through the sky from San Francisco International Airport. If he'd only had those documents, he could've been up in the air too. But he knows that the first flight he took, the one on which he was born, was possibly his last.

He doesn't buy the ticket; once he understands the routes and times of possible flights, that's all the information he needs. But he plays around on the airline websites until the library closes, typing destination after destination, learning the different ways to get there, the stops along the way.

Things stay the same—calm, quiet—for several days. Maxima makes more progress, and on a late Friday night, while drinking a wine cooler at her desk, she reports that Jerry has sent another two hundred dollars, this time to fix leaks in the communal kitchen and bathroom that Perfecta and Perfecto share with fifty other tenants. "Maybe I'll keep half for myself?" she says. Excel, standing in her bedroom door-way, blinks, unsure what to say. "Joke lang, joke lang," she says. "Don't worry. We're doing this for you."

"Thanks," he says, though the right thing to do is insist on split-ting the money, give Maxima the larger share. But if Jerry does come through, Excel will need every dollar he can get.

Maxima sips her wine cooler, sets it on her desk by the keyboard. Next to that, Excel notices, is the rubber wound. "Where'd you get that thing, anyway?" he asks.

She picks up a pencil, pokes at it. "At that magic shop, the one by the good Target."

"*Kadabra's*? What were you doing at a magic shop?"

"Just looking, walking around. I did a lot of that when you were gone." She takes another sip. "The owner was nice. From someplace— Georgia? Jordan? I can't remember. I'd stop by sometimes, and we'd talk. It's too bad they closed."

"It's gone? What happened to the owner?"

"Hindi ko alam," she says, shrugging. "Maybe he went back."

"Why do you say that? He seemed happy."

"Did you know him?"

Excel has never told Maxima that he'd applied to work there, that he'd almost gotten the job. He's already confessed to throwing the spelling bee; no point in telling another story of coming close and los-ing in the end. "I'd gone in once."

"Well, he always said he was fine when I asked, but I could tell"—she takes the last gulp of her drink—"it wasn't true."

She looks at the clock. It's 10:52 p.m. "Early call with Jerry tomor-row," she says, "get some sleep."

"I will," Excel says, but knows he won't.

EXCEL IS SITTING ON THE FLOOR OUTSIDE MAXIMA'S OPEN DOOR AT five a.m. the next morning.

He stares at the mustard-brown carpet, fights to stay awake. Dingy and worn, it's older than he is, and he thinks about the thousands and thousands of footsteps it's had to bear. Eons from now, what evidence might be found in the carpet to show they were the ones who walked over it? He imagines a far-in-the-future archaeologist examining a scrap with gloved hands. *This is where a TNT walked, this is how a TNT lived.* It's the kind of scenario he imagined when he described the fake job in the desert to Maxima. Maybe one day, this carpet will be someone else's important discovery.

Maxima continues talking to Jerry, and Excel tracks the line of sadness running through their conversation. She was distant at first ("I'm just tired, don't worry, darling," she said at the start), seems utterly hopeless now. Despite the generous money Jerry has sent, Perfecta's life just gets harder—the kitchen is still flooded, which means they can't cook, their water has been shut off for days, and every night she fears the future so much she gets chest pains from her racing heart. But what's truly devastated them is the loss of work: the market where Perfecta sells plastic sandals was burned down by an arsonist and is permanently closed, and Perfecto, hard as he tries, can't find a job. There's no money for tuition, and without school, what hope does her son have now? "But I have a solution," she says, her voice on the edge of breaking. She tells Jerry that a second cousin named Maribel, who works as a live-in maid in Saudi Arabia, has offered to connect Perfecta to a similar job. The demand for Filipina maids is high in Saudi Arabia, and though she knows Filipinos, the women especially, aren't always treated so well by their employers, she'll make the sacrifice if it means paying for Perfecto's school. "But to leave him"—her voice finally breaks—"I won't see him for a long, long time. Maybe forever."

She weeps, and that's Excel's cue. He rushes to her, sits beside her in front of the camera. "Hello Sir Jerry," he says. "I'm sorry for this, sir." He tells Maxima, "Sshh, sshh, *waag iyak*, don't cry, don't cry," and pulls her close so that she can weep on his shoulder, a moment they'd planned carefully (to see a son be strong for his mother: How can Jerry not be moved?). Maxima keeps crying, slumped so low she buries her face in Excel's chest, but now she says things in Tagalog that they didn't rehearse, things Excel understands only in bits and pieces: *I want to be something, but I am nothing. There is a child. What can I do? Stay and be poor. Leave forever, fly away. I try, I try. It's not enough? Screw it. I go on. I grow old. But what is the life?*

"I don't understand," Jerry says, looking worried, even scared. "What's she saying, Perfecto? What's happening?"

Excel looks directly into the camera. "She says she can accept a hard life for herself, but not for me. So if she must leave me in order to find a job, to pay for my school, then it's okay, because it's for my future." Which is the plight Maxima finally chose for Perfecto; instead of a wound or an illness, Perfecto's tragedy is his future—no school, no job, no hope. That, she's betting, is the thing Jerry will want to save, the thing that will convince him to send, sooner than later, fifteen thousand dollars.

Maxima nods. "Talaga," she says, "it's true, it's true." She rests her head on Excel's shoulder, then reaches her arms around him, keeps him in a tight embrace, like she never wants to let him go. Excel sees the two of them together in the smaller window at the bottom corner of the screen, and it all looks so real.

AT SEVEN A.M., EXCEL FINALLY TELLS JERRY GOOD-BYE. MAXIMA AND Jerry continue talking.

He goes to his room, lies down. The conversation, he thinks, was perfect; they hit all the notes they'd meant to hit. Excel has never acted before, but if that was acting, he thinks he did a pretty good job; anyone watching would've been convinced. He thinks of the

Sharma family above, wonders if they could hear them through the floor, if they might have believed, too.

He closes his eyes, tries to rest.

The heartbeat sound of Maxima pummeling The Bod wakes him. It's almost three p.m. He gets out of bed, goes to the living room.

"How long was I asleep?" he asks.

"A long time," Maxima says.

"You talked to Jerry more? After I left?"

She nods.

He sits on the couch. "What did he say?"

"He said he's worried for us. That he wants to help. And that he doesn't like us to be apart."

"You and Jerry?"

"Perfecta and Perfecto." She throws one more punch, then tells Excel the rest: Jerry can spare the fifteen thousand, send it instantaneously, if he wished, but said they need to be honest with themselves. How well do they really know each other? He swears he cares for the both of them, but that this is becoming real emotional territory; at his age, he must protect his own heart, too. So before he sends the money, he wants to meet in person, in real life, and is willing to fly all the way to the Philippines within the next month. "He told me he's done crazy things before," Maxima says, "but never for love. So he wants to make sure that you and I are a good investment. *Investment*. Like we're real estate or stocks."

Excel takes a breath, tries to stay positive. "Okay. So what's our best option?"

"Option? There's no option. What do you think? We'll fly to Manila and meet him?" She sits on the coffee table, across from Excel. "Ka sayang," she says, "what a waste. Most times, I'm the one who's supposed to fly to the men, like going to Nebraska or Delaware is a ticket to paradise. But Jerry offered to come to me."

"So that's it? After all that work. We're done?"

"What else is there?" She says she can try to find someone else online, look for more odd jobs that pay in cash; maybe Excel should do the same.

But he's tired of plans falling through, of coming close to finishing things after a promising start, then abandoning them in the end. Waiting for someone or something better to come along is no way to live. "We know Jerry and Jerry knows us," he says, "and we're so close. I know we are. There has to be a way." He looks at Maxima; if there's someone in the world who can make this work, it's her. He believes it, 100 percent. "Think of something. Please."

Maxima looks at Excel, then goes back to The Bod and strikes.

Someone knocks on the door. Neither of them moves. Excel thinks it's Roxy—no one else visits—but then imagines that it's Jerry who, somehow, has found them out.

More knocking. "Who is it?" Excel asks. He gets up, opens the door, and it's Sab.

28

As soon as Sab steps onto the fire escape, Excel wonders if a pregnant woman is meant to be so high above the ground. This is her first time at the apartment, and when he found Sab at the door, he was so stunned to see her that when she said, "Hello," he could only state the obvious: "You're here."

"A couple more steps," he says as Sab climbs. "Just don't look down."

She makes it to the roof, Excel right behind. She turns in a slow circle, taking in the view—the 280 freeway and the Targets on each side, the row of car dealerships, the endless green spread of cemeteries and Old Hoy Sun Ning Yung, just down below. The wind is strong, billowing her pink and black-checkered flannel shirt, whipping around her hair so that he sees faint strands of blue, color he's never seen.

He takes the two lawn chairs leaned up against the satellite dish, unfolds and dusts them off. He faces the chairs toward SFO, where a plane, small as a bird, rises in the sky.

They sit.

"So that's what she looks like," Sab says of Maxima. "She's beautiful. Though I thought she'd be super tall for some reason."

"Nope," Excel says, "just normal."

"Maybe it's the way you'd described her. But she does throw a mean punch. I almost felt sorry for that blue dummy guy."

"He's used to it."

"Your apartment is cute," she says, "cozy. And those are some crazy action photos in the living room. I can't believe you never told me she was a movie star."

"She did a few films," he says, "before I came along."

"Well, it was nice of her to offer me a wine cooler. I hope she wasn't offended that I said no." Excel assures her that Maxima was fine with it, which seemed true: though she looked caught off guard by Sab's arrival, she was polite and hospitable, without going overboard. There was no sense that she was acting.

The wind picks up and Sab hugs herself, rubs her arms up and down. Excel unzips his hoodie, wraps it around her. "Thanks," she says. "It was one hundred and two degrees in Hello City. I should be grateful for this weather."

"I can grab a blanket, if you want."

"This is good. But now you're cold."

He shakes his head. "Not at all."

Moments pass, silent. Sitting side by side like this almost feels like being on the helipad.

"So," she says, "this is where you'd hang out when you were a kid?"

He nods. "When I found out I was TNT, it's the first place I went when I got home."

"Who else hangs out up here?"

"Just me."

"I wish I'd had a place like this," she says. "When I was a kid, if I wanted to get away, I'd just go to the garage and wedge myself between the busted washing machine and the wall."

He asks again if she wants a blanket, but what he really wants to ask is, *How are you?* Simple as that. He wants to know if she's nauseated, if her back aches or feet swell, if she really does find herself craving weird combinations of food. Since Sab told him she was pregnant, since he learned he could be a father, they've barely been together. He has no real sense of what her life has been like.

"Excel," she says, "you're staring at me."

"I am? Sorry. I'm just really glad you're here."

She takes his hand, the first they've touched since she left him at the Greyhound station in El Centro. "Me, too," she says.

"So, when did you get back?"

"Day before yesterday. The drive up was faster than the drive down, for some reason."

"Are you staying awhile?" He thinks: *Let's leave tonight.*

"I moved back in with my aunt. She kicked the tarantula-collecting boyfriend out, so there's room again. The rent's cheap, free parking. It's good enough for now."

"You're back? What does that mean?"

"It means what it means." She pauses, lets go of Excel's hand. "It means I'm done. With Hello City. With the bus. With—"

"Sab, I'm sorry," he says. "I'm sorry that our last call went badly, and I'm sorry for sending the baby shirt. It was wrong of me. You need time and space to figure things out, and I'll give them to you, I swear. As much as you need."

The wind speeds up. She wraps herself tighter in the hoodie. "I'm not pregnant, Excel," she says. "Not anymore. I went to a clinic."

Only the sounds register at first—sharp *c* at the beginning, sharp *c* at the end. "A clinic?"

"Nine days ago. In El Centro. Lucia took me."

He imagines Sab inside a small waiting room, windowless and gray, a low stack of *Time* magazines atop a near-empty watercooler, like the room he'd sat in years before, in that downtown San Francisco office where Maxima and Joker paid a lawyer seven hundred dollars to see what could be done about their situation, their future. He imagines Sab being led into a sterile white room, disappearing behind a door.

"You didn't call me," he says.

"I thought about it. I did. But I worried that, if we spoke, I'd back out."

"We could've just talked."

"I didn't need to talk. I made the decision and it was the right one for me."

He gets up from his chair, stands near the edge of the roof. Below, a line of cars moves slowly into the complex—tenants back from work, after a long day gone. A blue sedan pulls into a parking spot, all four doors opening at once, the family inside stepping out and dispersing, then coming together as they file up the stairs. The father holds white plastic bags stacked with boxes of takeout, the mother tucks a bottle of wine under her arm as she digs for house keys. The kids—they look seven or eight—drag behind, taking turns socking each other in the arm, laughing.

"I wasn't ready," Sab says. "My mom died when I was seven. My dad wasn't around. My grandmothers, they basically housed me, that's about it. I wasn't raised, Excel. How can I raise a baby?"

I wasn't raised. Maxima always said the same of herself. But for better or worse, she raised Excel.

"I can't have a baby," Sab says. "Not now. I need to be on my own."

"On your own?"

She looks at the ground, moves a foot side to side in the rooftop gravel. "Without anyone."

When he saw Sab at the door, he wondered if she'd come for him,

if she wanted him back in Hello City. He'd hoped she was there because she missed him, because she needed them to be together. He'd
even thought that they might leave tonight, that they'd be back in the
bus by morning.

Excel sits back down and leans over, knees on elbows, forehead
resting on clasped hands. He feels Sab's fingers on the back of his neck,
each one pressing into his skin. He wants to tell her to go, to let him be
alone, but knows they might never be this close again.

"You're sure?" he asks. "This is what you want?"

Sab, her hand still on his neck, says it is.

Eyes shut, he thinks of the bus now, empty of their belongings,
no evidence that they'd once called it home. But something always
remains, and he wonders what he and Sab may have left behind—a
balled-up ramen wrapper behind the trash can, a sample-size bar of
Pink Bubble soap, unused headline clippings left on the floor. Who
would discover them? Lucia? Or the weekend guests who rent out the
bus? Whatever was forgotten, it's lost to him now.

Excel sits up, remembers suddenly that he took no pictures from
his time in Hello City. Did Sab? He doesn't ask.

29

Six days later, on an early Friday afternoon, Roxy drops off Maxima and Excel at the curb of the international terminal at San Francisco International Airport.

Excel grabs their bags from the trunk, a black carry-on with wheels and a blue duffel bag (it says O, *the Oprah Magazine* on the side, a freebie with Roxy's subscription). Maxima pulls boarding passes and passports from her purse, double-checks their names and confirmation numbers. A strong wind hits (from all those airplanes, Excel thinks) and tiny rectangles of paper come scattering along the ground. He picks one up, sees that they're American Airlines luggage tags. "Do we need to fill these out?" He holds up the tag.

"Not necessary," Maxima says.

He puts it in his pocket, a souvenir.

"Picture-picture!" Roxy takes out a camera, scoots Maxima and Excel together. Maxima demands a minute to redo her ponytail and lipstick, then tugs and straightens Excel's polo shirt, wipes off lint from his new corduroy pants. They stand side by side and smile. "Perfect," Roxy says, then gives them each a hug.

She steps back and fans her face with her hands, suddenly teary. "It's just so much," she says, "to be here again. This is where we arrived, all three of us. Nineteen years ago. Look how far we've come. And now, you look like you're leaving . . ."

"Don't be tanga," Maxima says, and gives a soft flick to Roxy's temple. "We're not going anywhere."

Roxy dabs her eyes. "I know," she says, "but still," then switches to Tagalog. Excel catches bits, but can barely hear. The curb is too crazy with taxis, cars, shuttle buses, and all the people coming out of them, nonstop. The whole world, it seems, is leaving today.

THEY ENTER THE AIRPORT, TAKE IN ALL THE SHINY MONITORS AND their glowing blue screens, the abstract metal structures suspended from the ceiling, even a monorail track curving along the building's outer edge. "It's like the future," Excel says, but one without Sab, without the baby. The past days, he's been so down, so lonely, he almost asked Maxima to call everything off, to end all contact with Jerry. *Let's just all move on*, he'd thought. But there was Z to worry about, what Gunter did to him. And he remembered Rosie, how she thanked him when he gave her the hat full of cash, none of it from him.

Maxima finds the Arrivals-Departures monitor, confirms that Philippine Airlines flight 714, coming from Tampa, will land on time at 3:12 p.m. Jerry, whose flight from Manchester, New Hampshire, is scheduled to land at 4:30 p.m. in the domestic terminal, will meet them here, near door 5.

It's 2:45 p.m. now. "We're early," Excel says, "maybe we should go to him?"

Maxima shakes her head. "If we look for him and he looks for us then everybody just misses everybody. Stick to the plan."

They take seats near the long row of ticket counters. There's Air China, Air Mexico, Air Canada, Air France, and Air New Zealand ("Everybody's a copycat," Maxima says), each one with snaking lines that grow longer by the minute. Most travel solo or in pairs, though the line for Air India is packed with whole families, and the one at the front of the line is its own crowd of loud and jumpy kids, the mother arguing with the woman behind the ticket counter while the father fumbles through a stack of travel documents, and grandparents who stand side by side, perfectly still and impossibly patient.

He wonders if the Sharmas, the neighbors above their apartment, have ever stood in that line. He wonders if Ranjit has ever been on a plane.

A pair of TSA agents (*Transportation Security Administration*— Excel had to Google what "TSA" meant, learned they were the ones to avoid) walks by, their shirts bright blue and covered with badges.

"You're sure this is right?" Excel whispers to Maxima. "What about customs or security. Shouldn't we get our hands stamped?"

"This isn't a dance club," Maxima says. "Tama na, enough. You're making me nervous. Here"—she reaches into her purse for a roll of Mentos—"have one."

He takes two, chews them fast. The last time he was here, he'd just been born, and he'd always imagined that SFO would be a welcoming place. But as they wait for Jerry, the airport starts feeling packed and stuffy, TSA agents are everywhere, and the people who arrive look no different from the people who depart. He watches the endless, twisty lines of passengers waiting to pass through the security checkpoint, sees how they fan themselves with open passports, as if flaunting their ability to come and go as they please. But they have hours and hours of travel ahead, some even have days; for them, the airport is only the beginning. For once, Excel and Maxima are the lucky ones, already at their destination.

ALL OF THIS IS MAXIMA'S IDEA.

The day after Jerry proposed visiting them in the Philippines, Maxima said yes, and suggested they start planning his visit ASAP. But the very next day, she shared tragic ("but maybe *fortuitous?*" she'd said) news: her beloved Auntie Fritzie, who'd only recently moved from Manila to Tampa to be with her son, Jojo-Boy, had died of a sudden brain aneurism. Jojo-Boy, knowing how close Perfecta and Perfecto were to Auntie Fritzie, insisted they attend the funeral, and bought them two round-trip tickets. The visit would be quick, just three or four days, but their return flight included a long layover in San Francisco, not quite a full day, but long enough that they could meet, have a meal or two together, get to know each other better in real life. Maybe, if flights were affordable and the timing was right, Jerry could meet them? "To see if we're a worthy investment," she'd said.

Excel was crouched on the fire escape outside Maxima's window as she waited for an answer, the switchblade twirling in her hand.

"I'm so sorry about Auntie Fritzie," Jerry had said, his face bright on the screen, "but maybe you're right? Maybe this is the universe giving us a sign?" He sounded hesitant, almost nervous, but he said he would check his calendar, try to rearrange some meetings, see how many frequent flier miles he had. "I'll let you know," he said.

He booked his flight the next day.

They would need documents. Maxima's passport had expired long before; Excel never had one. But Roxy knew a guy in San Jose who could make passable passports for cheap, for whatever country you wished. "His work is *the best*," she said. Roxy drove them down, and within an afternoon Maxima and Excel each possessed a maroon-colored passport, one for Perfecta, one for Perfecto, the word *Pilipinas* in yellow letters at the top and *Pasaporte* at the bottom, the Philippines coat of arms in the middle. The passports only needed to look real enough to convince Jerry, should for some reason he ask to see them, but Maxima was genuinely impressed. Excel didn't know if they looked real or not, but he was surprised, a little bitter, that such a flimsy and near-weightless booklet could give you so much of the world.

THEY SEE HIM BEFORE HE SEES THEM.

"Jerry!" Maxima calls out. "Darling! Over here!"

He turns, walks toward them. Though his face in real life matches the face on-screen, he's taller than Excel imagined, six feet at least, and pretty fit for fifty-five. In his blazer–polo shirt combo and khaki pants, he reminds Excel of certain substitute teachers in high school. Semiprofessional and pleasant, competent enough to get through the day, never to be seen again.

Maxima and Excel get to their feet. "Perfecta, Perfecto," he says, a little out of breath. "We made it. We're all here."

Maxima takes the lead, kisses Jerry on the cheek, then gives him a long, tight hug, like old sweethearts finally reunited. Excel takes this as his cue, holds out his hand. "Hello Sir Jerry," he says, then catches himself, "I mean, *Jerry*!" The flub was planned to lighten the mood, and it works perfectly: Jerry laughs and pulls him into a hug.

"Jerry, if we may," Excel says, "we would like to give you a pasalubong." He unzips the *O Magazine* duffel bag and pulls out three packs of Oh Fresh! dried mango, two tins of Ding-Ding mixed nuts, and a white T-shirt that says THRILLA FROM MANILA: CUTE-CUTE! in red, blue, and yellow letters. "*Pasalubong*," Maxima says, "it means a souvenir from the place you're coming from. These are beloved snacks from the Philippines, and see these colors?"—she points to the T-shirt—"that's like our flag. We hope you enjoy."

Jerry examines each gift, smiling and nodding, but Excel worries that the stickers and tags from the Dollar Tree in Colma might still be attached. He thought the whole pasalubong thing was going overboard, and told Maxima that Jerry wouldn't care if they showed up empty handed, and weren't Perfecta and Perfecto supposed to be dirt poor anyway? "Of course they're *poor*," Maxima shot back, "but they're not tacky. Of course they'll bring pasalubong!" If he didn't like her plan, she told him, he was welcome to strike out on his own.

"Well, I think pasa"—Jerry pauses, tries again—"pasa-loo-bong is wonderful and generous, and these gifts are very, very dear. Thank you."

Jerry checks his watch, apologizes for his flight's twenty-five minute delay. They exit the terminal and get into a taxi, Jerry up front, Maxima and Excel in the back. "San Francisco Marriott, Fourth and Market," he tells the driver. "And fast as you can, please. Our time is precious"—he turns around, smiles, and winks—"di ba?"

Jerry booked two rooms at the Marriott, one for Excel and Maxima, one for himself. Jerry checks them in and gives them their room keys, and they take an elevator to the sixteenth floor. "Meet in the lobby in thirty minutes?" he says, stepping off, and Maxima says, "Perfect."

Maxima and Excel get off on the twenty-second floor, find room 2270 at the end of the hall. Excel fumbles with the key—it's like a credit card, not an actual *key*, which seems unnecessarily confusing—but finally figures it out, and the room inside is airy and clean. Against one wall are two queen-size beds with wall-mounted leather headboards ("It's like they're floating," Excel says) and against the other, a mahogany dresser and marble-top desk, with the sleekest office chair Excel has ever seen. He sits on it and spins, rolls himself to the window, tall and wide as a wall with a view of the city, the water, the sky. He leans his forehead against the glass. He's never been this high up, never seen so much at once.

He wishes Sab were here to see it.

He turns to Maxima. She's on the far bed, lying on top of the covers, staring at the ceiling. "So what do you think?" he asks.

"About?"

"Jerry."

"Jerry? Jerry's fine. Better looking than I thought. Nice body, too. But his cologne smells cheap. Old Spice, maybe."

"Do you think he believes us?"

"If he doesn't now," she says, turning to the wall, "he will by the end." Her answer sounds like something between a bet or a promise, maybe even a threat. None of them as reassuring as he'd hoped.

Maxima says no more talking. She needs sleep, ten minutes, maybe fifteen. Excel turns back to the window, still amazed by the view. Years from now, he wonders which view he'll remember more: the galaxies and stars above Hello City, or the thousands of people twenty-two floors below.

ON THEIR DESCENT TO THE LOBBY, MAXIMA AND EXCEL LOOK AT themselves in the elevator mirrors. She wears a pale yellow blouse and a long gray skirt, a wool wrap borrowed from Roxy, and a gold necklace with a silver crucifix. He's in his gray Target shirt—tucked in, sleeves cuffed—and his Converse high-tops, the ones Maxima gave him as a gift out of nowhere, when she first made money from the men online. He's cleaned them so well that no one would guess he wore them for nine months in the desert. "We look nice," he says.

Jerry is in the lobby, polo shirt switched out for a white shirt and blue tie. To keep things simple, they have dinner at The Peppercorn & The Caper, the restaurant right off the lobby, where the cheapest entrée, Excel notices, is a $24 burger. "Cheese is *extra?*" he says, his Perfecto accent almost slipping.

"It's so expensive, Jerry," Maxima says, "I will pay, okay?" but he says absolutely not, that this short trip is their welcome to America. "I want to be a good ambassador," he says. "Consider tonight my . . . pasa-loo-bong." Maxima laughs, kicks Excel under the table. He starts laughing, too.

Dinner is what Excel dreads the most; the possibility for awkward lulls in conversation, and the fear that, in an attempt to fill that silence, he'll screw up Perfecto's story. But as soon as their food and drinks arrive (Jerry and Maxima order steak, Excel gets the burger after all) Maxima takes the lead, telling Jerry about Auntie Fritzie's funeral, how devastated the family was, but how lovely and youthful she looked in the casket. "Gone too soon," Maxima says, voice quivering, "but her lifelong dream was to be buried in America. The home of her heart. It's what she always said, swear to God."

"She sounds like an amazing woman," Jerry says.

She nods emphatically. "And she's so lucky too, because her son was with her, right until the end. Mother and child"—she places her hand on the table and, just as they'd rehearsed, Excel squeezes it tight—"should be together." Maxima dabs tears with her pinky and Excel checks Jerry's face, hoping it registers a look of approval or sympathy, some sign to indicate that saving Perfecta from a life in Saudi Arabia, and keeping her together with Perfecto, is worthy of his investment.

"Know what?" Jerry says, raising his wineglass, "I think so, too. So let's toast. To mother and child." Excel raises his Coke and Maxima her frozen piña colada, and the three of them toast, almost aggressively, the clink of their glasses so loud it startles them all.

DINNER MOVES SMOOTHLY, LIKE ONE OF THEIR ONLINE CONVERSA-tions. Jerry follows up on Perfecto's report on the history of Mount Pinatubo, recommends a good book on volcanology that he'd be happy to send. Excel asks if Jerry's company won the bid to build that proposed elementary school; no word yet, he says, but he's cross-ing his fingers. Maxima stays cheerful (the piña colada helps) but remembers to bring up daily hardships—the flooded kitchen, the closed market, the reality that no jobs are in sight. "You'll be just fine," Jerry promises, "we'll get through it together," and Excel, for some reason, feels reassured, finds himself genuinely smiling, even laughing, throughout the meal (Jerry's Forrest Gump impression—his favorite movie—is dead on). Later, after the waiter clears their table, Excel catches their reflection in the adjacent mirrored wall, the three of them relaxing in their chairs, comfortable in their momentary silence, like people who easily belong together—a son, a mother, a father. Excel imagines himself a father too, kneeling on the floor of the bus, arms open as Sab helps guide the baby's first steps toward him. When he learned Sab was pregnant, this scenario kept playing out in his mind: maybe he'd seen it in a diaper commercial, or at someone's family picnic at the cemetery. Maybe it's a moment that just makes sense—a baby learning to walk a steady path, ready to be held at the end.

"Perfecto?" Jerry says. "You okay?"

Excel blinks, shakes his head quickly. "Sorry, Sir Jerry," he says, "I'm a little tired. From the travel."

"No worries, my friend," he says. "I get terrible jet lag when I travel. It's like you're here, but your body's in another time."

"Yes," Excel says. "Thank you for your understanding."

We'll only take what we need, Maxima had said. Maybe they've al-ready taken too much.

THEY END DINNER WITH A SHARED BROWNIE SUNDAE AND ESPRES-sos, and rack up a $200 bill. Jerry hands the waiter his credit card, but Maxima shakes her head. "You're too generous," she says.

"It's worth every penny," he says, then excuses himself to the bathroom. Once he's out of sight, Excel leans in to Maxima. "How are we doing?" he asks. "Is this going well?"

She nods. "It's going good." She picks up her espresso spoon, slowly stirs the piña colada dregs.

"He seems to like everything we say."

"He does."

"And he's actually kinda funny."

"Good sense of humor," she says, "yes." She stops stirring, leaves the spoon in the glass but stares straight at it. She leans back, arms dropped at her sides. "Excel, how long have we been here now?"

"Since check-in?"

"No. How long have we been *here*. In the States. How many years now? What did Roxy say, when she dropped us off. 'Look how far we've come.' Ano ba? How far?"

Excel doesn't know how to answer, if he should even try. "Don't drink any more tonight," he says. "It just messes with your head."

She blinks twice, shuts her eyes, then flashes them wide open. "Yes. Okay. You're right. There's still more to do." She shakes out her hair, pulls it back again into a ponytail, so tight that Excel sees what might be lines of gray or, possibly, just a catch of white light from the chandelier crystals above.

THEY WALK TO THE EMBARCADERO TO SEE THE BAY BRIDGE at night. Standing at the rail overlooking the water, Jerry points to the sections damaged in the earthquake of 1989, explains the repairs made, how they're meant to withstand any earthquake to come. "Talaga?" Maxima asks. "*Really?*" Excel worries she's on the edge of overdoing her interest face, but Jerry believes it, not because he's a fool, but because he's earnest, and lives a life of positive thinking. What was it he'd written, in one of his e-mails to Perfecto? *Every day is another day to make the most out of life.*

You don't know my life, Excel had wanted to reply. But after these hours with Jerry, he starts to see how that philosophy might work for a guy like him.

They head north along the water, pass restaurants, galleries, the numbered piers. Maxima and Jerry are holding hands now; Excel slows his pace to fall behind and give them privacy, but stays within earshot. Maxima tells Jerry that the village where she grew up had a pier and a bridge. "But made of bamboo!" she laughs. Jerry says he would still love to see the Philippines one day, and he'd love for her and Perfecto to see New Hampshire. "The spring is lovely," he says, "autumn even lovelier. And people complain about it, but I think winter is pretty great. Have you ever seen snow?"

"I would *love* to see snow," she tells Jerry, "on one condition. I don't shovel!" They both laugh, but Excel knows that Maxima has used that line before.

Up ahead, throngs of people move toward bright lights, loud music. "Let's go see," Jerry says. He and Maxima walk ahead but Excel stops, realizes they're approaching Pier 39. Last time he was there, the day had started well, better than all the birthdays before. But Maxima wrecked it; he'd left Pier 39 ten years old, a different person entirely.

"Perfecto!" Jerry waves him over. "Let's have a picture!" He and Maxima are standing against the rail, Pier 39 and the darkening water in the background. *Photoshop me in later*, he wants to say, but knows he should pose for the photo. He catches up to them, and a blond woman with a hugely overstuffed backpack—she sounds like a German tourist—offers to take their picture, and the three of them rearrange themselves—Maxima, Jerry, then Excel. With a three-two-one count-down, they link arms and smile. "One more!" the German woman says, then hands the camera back to Jerry. "Lovely family," she says, and Excel thinks this might be the strangest day of his life.

THEY HEAD BACK TO THE HOTEL JUST BEFORE TEN P.M. MAXIMA AND Jerry walk together, her arm in his, Excel a few steps behind.

They cross the lobby toward the elevators, but Jerry says he's going to have a nightcap before heading up. He looks at Excel, puts a hand on his shoulder. "What a great day this was, Perfecto," he says. "Thank you for letting us have this time together."

"Thank you, Sir Jerry," Excel says. "I'll always have good memories of this day."

"Me too. But guess what? We still have tomorrow morning. So sleep well, buddy." He looks at Maxima and nods, heads to the bar. Maxima and Excel step into an elevator, return to their room on the twenty-second floor.

Once inside, Excel removes his shoes and sits on the bed, leans back against the leather headboard, just breathes. *I could hide here for a week*, he thinks, *maybe two. A month, a year.* He imagines Sab in a room at the Best Western, and understands why she checked in.

Maxima goes to the mirror above the dresser, reapplies lipstick. "I'm meeting Jerry in the bar," she says. "You'll be okay up here, on your own?"

"Sure," he says. "Take your time."

"Just one drink. To say good night."

"Do you think you'll ask him?"

"About what?"

"The money."

"The money," she says, "yes. If the timing is right."

"What if you didn't?"

She turns from the mirror, looks at Excel. "Ano ba? What do you mean?"

"I mean, what if we just get through this visit, then tell him we figured things out on our own, let him think Perfecta and Perfecto will be okay after all. Maybe he'll believe it?"

"You have a debt to pay, Excel. And we've come this far already."

Jerry has been generous. More than that, he's been kind. But Excel thinks of the fire he started, of everything it burned down. He thinks of Z, the ticket he needs to get home. "What if Jerry says no?"

"If he says no?" Maxima puts her lipstick away, then stares at her reflection for several seconds, like she wants to remember who she is in this moment, long after it's gone. "If he says no"—she grabs her purse, heads to the door—"then we had a nice night in San Francisco."

30

They're in a taxi by ten the next morning, Excel in front, Maxima and Jerry, who's wearing the THRILLA FROM MANILA: CUTE-CUTE! T-shirt under his blazer, in the back. Maxima didn't return to the room until after 7:00 a.m.; Excel heard her shower and change while he pretended to sleep. He doesn't know if Jerry agreed to give them the money; he'll ask when Jerry leaves. Whatever else happened last night is Maxima's business.

Jerry tells the driver to take all three of them to the international terminal, though he should be departing from the domestic. "What about your flight?" Maxima says. "You'll be late, mahal." But Jerry's flight, it turns out, is delayed by ninety minutes. "Now I get to see you both off," he says.

Excel looks back at Maxima. This isn't part of the plan.

They pull up to the curb, gather their bags, enter the airport. "We're checked in," Maxima says, showing Jerry their boarding passes (fakes also purchased from Roxy's guy in San Jose), and they walk to the departures board, find their outbound flight, San Francisco to Manila. "Would it be all right," Jerry says, "to have a moment with Perfecto?" Maxima says of course, and he takes Excel aside.

"I'm going to be up front and to the point," Jerry says. "I'm very fond of the both of you, and I hope our time together was the first of many, many more to come."

"So do I," Excel says.

"Now forgive me if I'm overstepping, but I need to tell you something. You're a very bright young man, and I know your life is full of challenges. But you have to commit to *yourself*, do you understand?"

"I think so."

"You need to work hard, stay in school. Make the most of your talents for you *and* Perfecta. You are her investment, so you need to be your own investment, too. Never forget that."

"I won't," Excel says, "I promise."

"And one last thing." He puts his hands on Excel's shoulders, gives them a firm squeeze. "Be good to your mother. The best you can be."

Excel doesn't know why Jerry says this, what he and Maxima might have discussed the night before; still, he promises to follow his advice. He steps forward, the first one to hug this time, and before Jerry lets him go, Excel whispers into his ear, "I'm sorry," then pulls away.

"Don't be sorry," Jerry says. "Good-byes are sad, never easy."

Jerry returns to Maxima. Excel stays behind to give them privacy, but he watches them whisper in each other's ear, as if all their parting words are secrets. They kiss then embrace, slightly swaying and holding tight, like neither is ready for the other to fly away.

Excel rejoins them. Maxima lets go of Jerry and dabs away tears (are they real? Excel can't tell), then urges Jerry on his way, to make sure he doesn't miss his flight. "I've got plenty of time," he says, "I'll walk you to the security checkpoint."

Excel looks at Maxima. Maxima looks at the floor. The plan was for Jerry to go to the domestic terminal, then for Maxima and Excel to meet Roxy at the curb of the international. They were never meant to go anywhere near security. "Well, darling, mahal"—Maxima takes a few slow breaths like she's biding her time to find an escape—"if you don't mind, then thank you."

They walk slowly toward the security checkpoint. Maxima and Excel say good-bye once more to Jerry, then walk to the end of the line.

In their blue shirts and badges, the TSA agents look like cops. The first one they encounter is an older white lady who looks like she's just woken from a nap. Like the passengers ahead, Maxima shows her passport and boarding pass to the agent, who glances them over, nods and waves her through. The same thing happens for Excel.

"That wasn't so bad," he says.

"We're not done," Maxima says, and he sees what she sees: the long line twisting toward two TSA agents checking boarding passes, scanning passports.

The line moves slowly, but by the time they round the first bend, Jerry is still there, standing next to a recycling bin, watching. Maxima smiles and waves, motions for him to go. He doesn't.

The line pauses. Excel counts the number of passengers separating them from the security agents—seventeen. "What do we do?" he asks Maxima, but she doesn't answer, just wipes sweat from her forehead with the back of her hand. She's flustered, a little panicked. "Maybe we should step out of line," Excel whispers, "tell Jerry our flight's been delayed, or got canceled."

"Don't talk," she say, "just let me think."

The line moves again, only fourteen passengers ahead of them.

Excel turns around, sees Jerry in the same spot, arms folded and face perfectly calm, like he knows what's to come.

Maybe they're the ones being conned.

Ten passengers now and reality hits even harder: they are TNTs with fake passports, fake boarding passes, fake names, and mere feet away from TSA agents. "Next in line," one calls out, "next in line," and Excel wants to run, but Maxima has her head down, eyes closed and lips moving, just barely. If they stay in line, if they actually meet the agents face-to-face, what happens? Will they take them away together? Question them in separate rooms to see who's telling the truth? To see who's the better liar? Six people are ahead, time is running out, and Excel knows he's the reason this is happening.

Maxima raises her head. Whatever her orasyon was, it's done. "Just follow me," she says.

"Tickets out, passports ready," an agent shouts. Excel looks at his passport, at his picture; he looks the way he imagined he looked at the Greyhound station, when the attendant said he was too young to travel alone.

The line moves. Maxima and Excel are next. The security agent, a red-haired guy with a bushy mustache, calls Maxima over. She steps forward but accidentally drops her purse, her makeup, keys, and wallet spilling out. She bends down to gather the mess, looks up at the passenger behind Excel and says, "Please, go ahead of us."

She puts everything back in her purse, stands up straight. The other security agent waves her over. Before she steps away, she takes Excel's hand, her grip so tight it's as though she means to hurt him or simply never let go.

Maxima goes forward. The agent is an older Filipino man, slightly hunched with gray slicked-back hair. "Kumusta, po," she says, nodding respectfully. She hands him her documents, leans in close, says something at a level just above a whisper. At first, she looks like she's exchanging pleasantries, paying respects to an elder. But then the agent glances over at Excel, up and down like he's evaluating him, then looks back at Maxima, does the same. *It's over*, Excel thinks, *we're done*.

The agent looks at Maxima's documents. He scans her passport, the pages not quite touching the glass, then lets her through. He waves Excel forward, does the same.

Excel looks up at the old man. "Go on," the agent says, then calls over the next passenger in line.

Maxima and Excel do what everyone else does: they remove their shoes, wallets, and belts, set them in trays and load them onto the conveyer belt, followed by their bags. They go through the body scanners—Maxima first, then Excel—then retrieve their things on the other side. Excel looks back through the crowd, through the long, winding line of passengers, and there is Jerry, waving good-bye and smiling, knowing his investment is safe.

THEY WALK TO A BENCH AND PUT ON THEIR SHOES AND BELTS, TUCK their passports and boarding passes into their bags. Hunched over, hands on knees, Maxima looks out of breath, lines of hair pasted to her forehead with sweat, like she's just gone twelve rounds with The Bod.

"Did that just happen?" Excel says. Like in a movie, he feels as if he could laugh and cry at once. "What did you tell that guy?"

"I told him"—she shuts her eyes and thinks, like the moment happened years instead of only minutes before—"I told him we're just trying to get home. That's all."

"We got lucky."

"Not lucky. Joker was watching over us, believe me."

"Joker?"

"Who else? He took us in, and now he took us through. He's always with us, Excel, believe it. Next time we visit him, you tell him thank you."

Whether she's right or not, Excel promises he will.

MAXIMA CALLS ROXY AND EXPLAINS WHAT HAPPENED, ARRANGES to meet at the curb in an hour, same place as yesterday. For now, the safest thing to do is stay inside until Jerry's flight finally takes off. "I'm not taking any chances," Maxima says.

They walk around, go in and out of gift shops. "Key chains, magnets, coffee mugs, ugly T-shirts," she says. "What kind of pasalubong is that?"

Starving suddenly, they check out the food court, buy a ham sandwich and bag of Fritos to split. Every table is taken, so they decide to eat at their departing gate—94, according to the monitors—and walk farther into the terminal. They reach the gate, find all the seats occupied, the entire area overflowing with passengers, nearly all of them Filipino.

Maxima and Excel take two seats at gate 93, directly across. "I'm so close," she says. "What if I go over there? What if I try to get on that plane?" He thinks she means it playfully, the way a person does when entertaining impossible things. But when he looks at her, she seems both hopeful and hopeless at once, her eyes unblinking as she stares at the people waiting to depart.

"We've made it this far," he says. "Let's not push it."

"That flight I took, Manila to here, nineteen years ago"—she shakes her head, amazed at the thought—"that was my first flight. Maybe my last."

"You don't know that," Excel says.

A small girl with pigtails charges toward them like she means to leap into their laps. Maxima hunches over and waves. The girl stops, laughs, hurries back to her parents. "Lots of families," she points out, "lots of couples. It's nice, that they can fly together."

"It must have been tough," he says, "coming here alone."

"I wasn't alone." She looks over at him. "You were there, too."

He splits the sandwich, gives Maxima the bigger half.

"I talked with Jerry last night," she says. "He'll give us the money. For Perfecto's schooling. For Perfecta's sad life. For all their problems."

Excel doesn't feel victorious—he didn't expect to—but there's no relief either, no sense of accomplishment. They simply got work done. "So he sends the money. What happens next?"

She shrugs. "I disappear. You disappear. That's how it works."

"What if he tries to track us down? For that kind of money—"

"That kind of money's not much for him, believe me. He'll just think you and me were a big mistake, that we're not the best kind of people. And then he moves on."

He imagines Jerry boarding his own flight soon, looking back on the past day, already making plans for the next time they meet.

They finish the sandwich, the Fritos. Maxima crumples the cellophane and napkins into a ball, throws it at a trash can across the way, makes it in. "The good thing is, you can pay that professor back."

"For sure," he says, "right."

Maybe it's guilt, maybe it's just exhaustion. Maybe it's the fact that they somehow managed to achieve the impossible, and are sitting side by side in an actual airport terminal. Maybe the lie of the past day is finally too much, and he just needs to speak some truth. "There's no professor," he says. "I do owe money, a lot of it, but there's no professor." He tells her about a place in the desert where he lived for nine months (he doesn't name it), how he accidentally burned the most important part of it down. But he says nothing about Sab's pregnancy, or the remote possibility that he could have been a father, and Maxima a grandmother. For now, that's too much truth to tell.

"When I left," he says, "I told you it was a couple months. I lied. I wasn't planning to come back." He doesn't look her in the eye, but he can tell that she's not angry, not even fazed. She's just listening. "I meant to be gone. Forever."

"I knew you weren't coming back," she says. "You're angry at me. For lots of reasons."

Maxima has done so much—too much—for him already. It seems unfair, even cruel, to tell her more.

"Since Joker," he says. He stares straight ahead through the windows, at the airplanes just beyond. "I've been angry since then. I think, sometimes"—he wants the right words but none exist, so he simply speaks—"that you let him die. You could've called 911 when we were still at the apartment. I wanted to do it, but you were the adult. *You* should've been the one. And then you made us act like strangers while they took him away, and then he was gone." He turns to face Maxima, finally. "I'm saying a terrible thing, but it's what I think is true. You let him die to save yourself."

He has no idea how she'll respond. She could slap him; she could weep. She could get up and walk away. But she just reaches over and straightens his collar, moves a strand of hair away from his face. "Not to save me," she says. "To save you." Her voice is steady, almost peaceful. "I did it to save you. That was Joker's last request."

"What do you mean?"

"Protektahan ang bata. 'Protect the child.' His last words. He was scared they'd take you. Separate us. We owed him everything, and in the end, that's what he wanted. I couldn't deny him that. You're the future. You have to be saved."

"Saved? For what?"

"Not this." She looks away toward the other gates, at all the passengers waiting to fly. "I'm sorry it's not a better life. When we came, I thought it was the best I could give."

"Do you still think it is?"

She looks back at him, her face troubled and hopeful, mostly uncertain. "It could be."

A voice on the PA system announces that Philippine Airlines flight 72, service from San Francisco to Manila, will now begin boarding at gate 94.

The people rise. They double-check passports and boarding passes, some nervously cross themselves with pre-flight prayers, but everyone is excited and ready, talking all at once, their voices a chorus of background noise, atmospheric, almost unnoticeable. But when Excel really listens, two words come through, not quite familiar, but he thinks he understands: *umuwi* and *uuwi*, the people say. *Going home, coming home.* As though everyone has two places where they belong.

31

In three days, and as promised, Jerry wires Maxima the money. "Twenty thousand," Maxima says. "He was more generous than I thought."

"We only took what we need, right?" Excel asks.

"And some extra. But he was fine with it."

Everything with Jerry is in the past now. Maxima deleted Perfecta's profile from Fil-Am Catholic Hearts Connections, the website where they met, Perfecta's e-mail account, too. Excel has no doubt that Jerry will be fine—positive thinking will get him through anything—but he imagines Jerry searching for Perfecta and Perfecto online, Googling their names, looking for faces that match their own. He wonders when Jerry will call off the search, at what point he'll understand that they were no one, just two made-up people he'd known for a handful of weeks and met in person, just once, in San Francisco.

But a few times, Excel checks Perfecto's e-mail, just in case Jerry has written; he's always a little disappointed to see he hasn't. Once, he actually clicks the Compose button, and when the empty New Message box appears, he types, "Dear Sir Jerry," and pauses, thinking of the things Perfecto would mention: his studies, recent volcano eruptions, the kinds of ships in a bottle he's recently seen online and hopes to one day build. But the e-mail he composes in his head always begins with an apology for what they'd done, ends with a confession of who he really is.

He deletes the e-mail, then deletes Perfecto's account.

Z is Excel's priority now. Z has a passport, has been in contact with his daughter in Serbia, who's eager for his return. Getting Z home is a matter of timing, of making sure Gunter doesn't find out or get in the way. Excel considers asking Maxima for help; if trouble comes up, he knows, with 100 percent certainty, that she'll get him out of it. But she's helped him enough already. He can figure this out on his own.

The next day at The Pie, Excel sneaks away from his greeting post and meets Z outside the service door. He asks him again, in the simplest, most direct English: "Do you want to go home?"

"Yes," he says, "*unquestionable*," a new word used perfectly.

THEY WAIT UNTIL SATURDAY, THE BUSIEST DAY AT THE PIE. EXCEL isn't scheduled to work, but he shows up in a taxi just past noon, when nonstop birthday parties have Gunter running back and forth between the dining room and the kitchen. Excel has the driver pull around the back, where Z stands waiting, dressed in his Pie shirt, a brown sports coat slung over his arm, backpack at his feet.

Excel gets out, takes Z's backpack, opens the door for him. "Ready?" he asks, and Z says, "Let's go."

Before the airport, they stop by the Serbian cemetery in Colma, though the driver seems annoyed by the detour; pulling over to the curb, he says, "Meter's running, FYI," his tone gruff, mouth open as he chews his gum. "Give us fifteen minutes," Excel says, helping Z out the door, "or however long we need, okay?" Hearing himself, he thinks he sounds confident, maybe cocky, but after all that's happened these past few months, he might be tougher than he thinks.

He walks with Z to the end of a brick pathway. "I'll wait here," he says, "take your time." Z looks down the row, his son's grave at the very end. He takes a breath, straightens up and clenches his fists like he's summoning strength, however much he needs to tell his son good-bye.

THEY STEP OUT OF THE TAXI IN FRONT OF THE LUFTHANSA SIGN AND walk into the international terminal. *Twice in one week*, Excel thinks, *and I still go nowhere*. He's not bothered by it. For now, it's just a fact.

They approach the Lufthansa counter, and before they get in line, Excel makes sure Z has brought all he needs for the flight in his backpack—one change of clothes, some bananas and cashews for the plane, a toothbrush—few enough items so that Gunter wouldn't have been suspicious of what Z brought to The Pie that morning. Excel reaches into his own backpack, pulls out an envelope and gives it to Z. "Two thousand dollars," he says. "Enough for a ticket, and something to save." Maxima gave him the cash a few days before, in advance of Jerry's deposit. He felt a little guilty, telling her he needed it for a cashier's check, a first installment in paying back Hello City. But if there's ever a good reason to lie, this is it.

They get in line, quickly reach the counter. Z asks for a one-way ticket on the four p.m. flight to Belgrade, shows the agent his passport. After lots of clicking, typing, and entering data, the ticket costs $820, and Excel has no idea if that's reasonable or not. Either way, it's the price of going home.

In less than fifteen minutes, Z has his boarding pass, which he tucks between pages in his passport. Excel envies Z's ability to fly, to arrive somewhere new and, if that place ends up being a mistake, to turn around and go back. *One day*, he thinks, *maybe*.

Together, they walk to the security checkpoint and stop at the entrance. "I can't go any farther," Excel says to Z. "You'll be okay, the rest of the way?"

Z says he will.

"I wish things had worked out better for you," Excel says.

Z shrugs, but smiles, too. "America good, America bad," he says. "The life is like that."

Excel nods, says it's true.

"And I am sorry for my grandson. He is . . ." Z struggles for a word, says something in Serbian, then finally shakes his head and sighs. "But you quit soon. Get your pay, and you go." Then he puts up a finger, like there's one last thing to do, and reaches into his backpack for his dictionary, holds it out it to Excel.

"That's yours," Excel says, "I can't take that."

But Z insists. "I pick words for you," he says. "You learn." He hands over the book, and Excel sees dozens of pages marked with yellow Post-its.

"I'll learn them. I promise." He puts the dictionary into his backpack. "Thank you, Z."

"Thank you, X."

It's time to go. Z puts on his sports coat, then his backpack, and Excel fixes his collar. "Come," Z says, holding out his arms, and Excel, a little shy at first, holds out his own, gently pulls him in. How strange, almost miraculous, to hold someone so old, so closely—Excel missed his chance with Joker—and the fragility of the body startles him, like it could come apart at any moment. He holds Z a little while longer, to keep it together.

32

There comes a stretch of days when life seems okay.

Excel works steady shifts at The Pie. Nothing torturous (Sloth the Sleuth has been retired again), just monotonous. He's Peter the Greeter most days, sometimes the cashier—nothing that will earn him tips, but he'll tolerate that for now. Gunter remains an asshole to everyone, though one day he comes to work humbled, with thick rubbery knee braces on each leg and a black eye. "Two nights ago I'm closing up late," he tells the staff, "and in the parking lot, some crazy bitch with sticks jumps out like Michelle Yeoh, clubs me in the knees and left hooks my face. It's a sad, fucked-up world out there, believe it." The staff members eye each other, as though the assailant is among them, but when Excel gets home he asks Maxima point blank: "Did you beat up Gunter?"

"I don't know what you're talking about," she says, sitting on the couch and opening a key lime wine cooler. She takes a sip and grabs the remote, *Ang Puso Ko VS. Ang Baril Mo* playing again.

Gunter never mentions Z, doesn't ask if anyone has seen him; Excel has no idea if they've communicated or not. But Z sends occasional e-mails to Excel (his daughter taught him to use the Internet, a thing Gunter never did), the messages brief and to the point, like talking to Z in person. How is the life. Did you learn the words.

Excel doesn't hear Maxima at night. No flirty talk or lament of daily hardships, no laughing that changes split-second into weeping. Maybe all the men figured out who she really was, warned others to stay away. Maybe Maxima just sleeps.

Sometimes, if they're both home, they eat dinner together—Spam fried rice, Taco Bell from Roxy. Twice, Excel makes them instant ramen with boiled egg, his go-to dinner back in the bus, and Maxima says it's pretty good.

Excel has made no decisions about Hello City. With Sab gone, he doesn't really have anyone, and there's no one there who really misses him. He has the money to pay for the damages now, and he often thinks of what Rosie said, his first night at the Square. *We don't care where you come from, we're just happy you came.* But he remembers what Lucia said, too, that people aren't always so forgiving. It's not the bravest, most honorable thing, but he sends a cashier's check for ten thousand dollars to Lucia's Pink Bubble PO box, along with a note that says, "Please forward to the Town Council. Please don't say it's from me." Even if he never moves back to Hello City, he hopes one day to be one of those curious weekend visitors, if only to see the Square, when it's back up and thriving again.

LATE ONE NIGHT AND BACK FROM WORK, EXCEL REALIZES HE FORgot his keys. He climbs the low wall of Old Hoy Sun Ning Yung and crosses over the graves, squeezes through the tear in the wire fence, climbs the fire escape. His bedroom window is open, Maxima's is too. She's sitting at her computer, dressed in a sweatshirt and denim cutoffs, switchblade twirling in her hand. For a second Excel thinks she's online with a stranger (*Jerry?* he thinks), then sees that she's just staring at her screen saver, not of the galaxy but of the sea, waves rising and falling, folding into themselves in slow motion.

Maxima turns, not startled but surprised. "You're back," she says.

He crouches down, crawls through her window. "Forgot my keys again," he says. "Everything okay?"

She closes the switchblade, sets it next to her keyboard. "I want to talk to you." She gestures to the edge of her bed, tells him to take a seat.

He thinks he's in trouble, that he's done something wrong. He sits.

"A couple days ago," she says, "I talked to Auntie Queenie."

"How's she doing?"

"My sister is"—she pauses, brows crinkled like she's stressed—"not so good." Queenie had a second stroke, Maxima explains, one that left her right side completely paralyzed. "It's hard for her to get around, to feed herself. Even just to breathe."

"I'm really sorry to hear it. Can we send more money, maybe hire a full-time nurse?"

"We can try that," she says. "But I think, maybe, it's not enough."

"What do you mean?"

"I want to help her, take care of her," she says. "Be with her."

"In the Philippines?"

She nods.

"When?"

"I don't know. Sooner than later, maybe?"

"If you go"—he pauses—"how long would it be?"

"I don't think I get to decide that," she says, which, Excel realizes, might mean forever. If Maxima leaves, she may not be able to return.

For now it's just a plan, she says, but one that's been on her mind for some time, maybe longer than she realized. "Joker was gone. You were in the desert. I was alone. Once in a while, Queenie would call and say, 'Maxima! Maxima! Nandito na ako, umuwi ka na. I'm home, I'm home, you come back too!' And I'm thinking, 'Why not? What's my life here?'"

"You have a life," Excel says.

"Maybe I did, before. There was Joker. There was you. But on my own, there's too much time. Know what I mean? And for what? Cleaning houses and washing cars? Crying to men across America so they can send me money? So now I'm thinking, 'Go back. Be with your sister. Take care of her. She's getting old.' Like me, di ba?" She pulls back her hair, points to the gray, tries to laugh.

"When you were gone," she says, "sometimes the only people I talked to were the men online. And the best night I've had in so many years was with Jerry. And even then I had to be someone else. What's that about?"

He looks at the rug, remembers the glimpse of hardwood floor beneath, from that morning he left for Hello City. "Is this because I was gone? Or what I said about Joker? I didn't mean to—"

"It's not you."

"If you go," he says, unable to look at her, "how will I see you?"

"I'm not sure. But after what happened at the airport, with Joker watching over us like that, we'll find a way. I have faith. And besides, I'm not worried about you."

"You're not?"

"When you were gone, I was so pissed at you for leaving, talaga. But then I knew you were okay, that you could take care of yourself. You moved to the *desert*. Then you kicked that Jun-Jun asshole's butt. You convinced a man you were a fourteen-year-old boy who builds that shipping-a-bottle thing. You even tricked *me* with that stupid professor story and your 'important discoveries.' You can get by, Excel. You know how to survive."

He looks at Maxima. "I learned it from you."

"I hope so," she says. "But even if I go, I'll still help. I saved some money, and Jerry gave extra. Not a lot, but enough for a while."

"Okay," he says, "thanks." He speaks so softly he can barely hear himself.

She gets up from her chair, steps over to her dresser, then the door, then back to her desk, like she's restless but has no idea where exactly she should be. She finally sits on the floor with her back against the wall, face toward the window. Excel imagines himself out there again, crouched on the fire escape, watching her. "Anyway"—she takes a deep breath and sighs—"it's just a plan. All in my head. Who knows what will happen. 'Every day is another day to make the most out of life.' Just like Jerry says, di ba?"

Excel nods, notices that Maxima's Virgin Mary night-light is on, its fading light barely there. "I'm sorry," he says.

"Sorry?"

"I'm sorry life wasn't better. I'm sorry I didn't try to make it better."

"Ano ba?" She comes over, sits beside him. "You did make it better. Of course you did. You came back, didn't you?"

He looks at her. Nearly a year ago, he was the one who meant to leave forever; now, he imagines a world where Maxima is gone.

"What'll I do without you, Mom?" he asks.

"You'll be strong," she says, "you'll be good, be the best." She touches his face, wipes his tears before her own. "Excel."

It's almost midnight. Maxima gets to her feet, rubs her neck and stretches, like she's just finished a training session. "Gutom kaba?" she asks. "Roxy dropped off some KFC. I'll cook rice, too?" Excel isn't hungry but says he is, and on her way out her bedroom door, Maxima reaches for the pull-up bar but only taps it, just barely, with the tips of her fingers, then disappears down the hallway.

Excel looks at the screensaver, watches the slow-lapping waves of the sea. He pictures Maxima filling the screen, pictures himself in a small box at the bottom corner; if she leaves, maybe this is how they'll meet. He won't look her directly in the eye—her webcam can't do that—but at least he'll see her face.

The room feels warm; Excel needs air. He climbs out the window and up the fire escape, steps onto the roof. It's a cool night, the departing planes from SFO blink especially bright, and the graves of Old Hoy Sun Ning Yung almost glow from a near-full moon. Compared with those nights in Hello City, when he and Sab would stare up at stars from the helipad, this view isn't much, but it's something, and he thinks about writing an *H* in the rooftop gravel, drawing a circle around it. Could planes passing above see it? Would anyone understand what it means?

Excel hears footsteps, knows he's not alone. He turns and sees Ranjit, who waves and says hello.

ACKNOWLEDGMENTS

Thank you to Julie Barer for her faith in my novel, and to Megan Lynch for helping me to finish it. Thanks to Sara Birmingham, Zachary Wagman, Caitlin Mulrooney-Lyski, and the folks at Ecco and The Book Group, for sending this book into the world.

For the gifts of time and space to write, my thanks to the Blue Mountain Center, the Mesa Refuge, and the *Paris Review* Writer's Residency at the Standard East Village. I'm especially grateful to the MacDowell Colony and Yaddo, for years of generosity. *Grazie mille* to the Bogliasco Foundation for a residency (and an epiphany) that saved this book, and to the American Academy in Rome for a year in Italy (and for the amazing food, excellent company, and great bar).

Special thanks to the staff at all the places mentioned above, who work so hard to provide a welcoming and inspiring environment to write.

For the Joseph Brodsky Rome Prize, my gratitude to the American Academy of Arts and Letters.

Thanks to Saint Mary's College of California, especially to the department of English, the MFA program in creative writing, and the Faculty Development Committee.

Tara Runyan and Serena Crawford read early versions of this book, and Bing Magtoto helped with translations. Thank you all.

And Bruce, for every word and sentence, all the chapters (good and bad), always to the end.

In memory of my godfather, David Magsino, with thanks and admiration for his endurance and courage.

Finally, my gratitude and love to my family: my father, who still gives us so much; my nieces and nephews, who keep the family going; my brothers and sisters, who bring me home.

And to my mother, whose name was Estrella.